Praise for Cynthia Smith & the Emma Rhodes mysteries

"You'll enjoy every moment of international hobnobbing with this high society sleuth!"
—Nancy Martin, best-selling author of the Blackbird Sisters mysteries

"I have been charmed right out of my high-heeled sandals by Cynthia Smith's *Impolite Society* . . . a refreshing delight."
—*The Washington Times*

"Cool, sardonic, and unflappable Emma Rhodes sparkles diamond bright in Cynthia Smith's clever, twisty tales. This highly original series has panache. A winning hand from Busted Flush Press."
—Carolyn Hart, best-selling author of the "Death on Demand" and Henrie O mysteries

"Wonderful! By Dominick Dunne out of Flora Poste, with a healthy mixture of Jessica Fletcher, the effervescent Miss Rhodes resolves sticky situations without ever getting her Manolos muddy. Encore!"
—Kerry Greenwood, author of the Phryne Fisher novels

"Kiss Miss Marple and Jessica Fletcher good-bye . . . here's a woman sleuth who provides us with vicarious glamour, brains, and beauty on an international scale."
—Judith Crist, film critic

D1118495

By Cynthia Smith

The Emma Rhodes series

Noblesse Oblige (1996)
Impolite Society (1997)
Misleading Ladies (1997)
Silver and Guilt (1998)
Royals and Rogues (1998)

Impolite Society

by
Cynthia Smith

Busted Flush Press
Houston 2009

Impolite Society
Originally published in 1997
by Berkley Prime Crime.

This edition, Busted Flush Press, 2009

Copyright © Cynthia Smith, 2009
Cover design: Jimmy Jack Bottlestop

ISBN: 978-0-9792709-7-0
First Busted Flush Press paperback printing, April 2009

BUSTED FLUSH
PRESS

P.O. Box 540594
Houston, TX 77254-0594
www.bustedflushpress.com

This one's for Sarah.

Chapter One

"PARDON ME, BUT what's that you're drinking?"

"White port and tonic," I answered.

This wasn't just an idle question. I could see she wanted to engage me in conversation. It was unusual to come across Americans or any tourists in the Algarve at this time of year, and my curiosity is always piqued by the unexpected, so I decided to oblige.

"It's the daytime drink around here. Tasty but not too lethal. It was invented by the resident English who consider it perfectly proper to tipple in the afternoon but bad form to get bombed," I said with a smile.

She looked like she needed a smile and a drink—both she and the man seated next to her, who I assumed was her husband. I had observed them earlier and noted that they hadn't exchanged a word in the past half hour, which wasn't all that unusual. Many older married couples, once their children left home, found they had lost their sole basis for conversation and companionship. But this couple's eyes projected an anguish that went far beyond that of facing the bleak future of living with someone with whom you have no common interests. I tried to imagine what they were doing here in March. Vila do Mar, Portugal, was on tourist schedules in spring and summer, the months we regular residents steered clear of the area. The town was then jammed with Europeans who came to enjoy the incredibly perfect sunny climate, the wide white-sand beaches abutted by golden cliffs that formed enchanting grottoes, and the cheap prices. At this time of year, it's unusual to sit in the square in front of Sir Barry's bar and find anyone you don't know.

Sir Barry was not really a sir. He was English, but the closest he ever came to a knight was the judge who sentenced him for running off with his clients' escrow accounts. While Barry sat out his prescribed time in gaol, his dutiful wife, Iris, scouted alternate career possibilities for a disbarred solicitor and came up with this saloon in the center of what turned into the hottest resort town in the Algarve. Now Barry affected a dragoon mustache and a slightly contemptuous lordly mien, which brought him the status of a major town character and a very large bank account.

I HAD BEEN here in Vila do Mar for a week in my small jewel of a house overlooking the Atlantic. I came for some R & R after completing a particularly demanding case in Brussels. Not that all matters I handle don't require full dedication in order to straighten out the usually convoluted complications besetting my client's lives, but this one involved an added wrinkle that upped the intensity—my life was on the line. Escaping two murderous attempts may have sharpened my wits but it did get a bit wearing. I came here to chill out and rest my little gray cells, and there was no better place to do absolutely nothing than this glorious fishing village on the southern coast of Portugal. Because of its low cost of living, which seemed to get less low every year, plus the idyllic climate and aspect, people from all over the world made their permanent residences here, which furnished me with a marvelously varied pool of potential friends to choose from. I was waiting for one right now, but time had little meaning in Vila do Mar, so the fact that Graham was thirty minutes late didn't bother me a bit. In London or New York (where I also maintained residences) I would have been foaming at the mouth by now or probably gone. Here in the land of what-can't-wait-till-tomorrow-probably-wasn't-worth-doing-anyway, I had lots of time to observe the couple at the next table.

They were in their fifties, dressed right out of the Land's End catalog in chino slacks, cotton knit shirts (hers pink, his green), Reeboks, and beige cotton sweaters. They looked tanned and fit, well-to-do, and seriously miserable. This was not the vexation of a lousy golf score or unsatisfactory hotel accommodations—this was deep distress. These particular people being in this particular place at this particular time of year was out of sync, presenting just the kind of enigma that jangles my antennae.

They both expressed surprise at the existence of a white port wine, and I explained that not too much of it was shipped out of Portugal. Mixed with Schweppes and ice it made a deliciously refreshing drink created by the local Brits.

The English, with their years of experience in discovering areas that offer good living at bargain rates, had many years ago landed full force in the Algarve. Their pensions in pounds went a long way with the lowly escudo. And the presence of the longtime fascist dictator Salazar had kept the people poor and uneducated, which made for a steady supply of domestic help at prices that would make a West End matron green with envy. By the 1960s, the place was discovered by the Dutch, Scandinavians, Germans, and lastly, the Americans like me, though I came along later. But the real big growth of the area started when the Salazar bridge was built over the Tagus river, giving easy access to the south. This brought down the wealthy Portuguese of Lisbon and the north, and turned the Algarve coast of Portugal into the poorer man's Riviera. I fell in love with Vila do Mar on a visit in 1987 and bought my oceanfront house in ten minutes from a rich alcoholic German who could no longer manage the long stone staircase down to the beach. He signed the papers with his left hand because his right arm, leg, and shoulder were still in a cast from his most recent misstep.

I gave the couple this little history of the Algarve to see if a diversion would distract from whatever it was that troubled them. They listened politely and smiled with their mouths, but the tragedy in their eyes remained.

I knew they would tell me about it in time. People always tell me things. I don't know what it is exactly, but I seem to project a simpatica quality that makes people pour forth the most intimate details of their problems within minutes of meeting me. It usually starts as a passive exercise to merely unburden themselves as one might to a bartender or hairdresser. But I don't deal in passivity—my deep interest in human behavior (an upscale euphemism for what's known in Bronx neighborhoods as a *yente*) plus my 165 I.Q. send my brain into instant action to work out ways to resolve their sorry situations. If the problem piques my interest (my threshold of ennui is rather low) and the sufferer is willing and able to pay my fee (which is rather high) I will offer to resolve their problems. My terms are very simple: I accomplish the task within two weeks or I'm out of there and they pay nothing, but when I succeed, they pay me twenty thousand dollars or the equivalent amount in whatever hard currency they wish. You may notice I didn't qualify it with "if" because success was always a foregone conclusion. My record was one hundred percent, which is the result of my intelligence and the fact that I only take on cases I know I can resolve (if that isn't proof of smarts I don't know what is).

I'm a P.R.—Private Resolver. Don't bother looking it up in the Yellow Pages; the business category is mine alone. I'm the sole practitioner of a unique profession that I founded, or rather found me. I was on a business trip in Denmark for the New York law firm that recruited me right out of law school and for whom I worked eighty-four hours a week to earn the large salary that I had no time to spend. On the hydrofoil to Malmö, Sweden, I met a high born Englishwoman who passed the entire voyage telling me between sobs the sordid intimate details of a sticky situation in which she was embroiled involving enough money, hate, and passion to make a Judith Krantz novel. It took me exactly ten minutes to figure a way out for her, but long ago

I learned the financial foolishness of giving clients quick results: (a) they don't trust the validity of solutions arrived at without days of deliberation and research; and (b) if it looks too easy, they're loathe to pay the big bucks. I offered to resolve the matter for her within two weeks and, being blessed with total self-confidence that some may regard as cocky smugness but I see simply as a realistic evaluation of my abilities, I demanded no upfront monies or expenses, just thirty-three thousand pounds payable only upon success. Two weeks later she sent me her check along with a glowing note of thanks and began recommending me to her friends. You can't imagine the lust, cupidity, and stupidity rampant in the upper classes, and I soon realized I had a new profession that was far easier and more lucrative than lawyering and a helluva lot more fun. My terms of employment are perfect for wealthy folks who love a bargain and adore a gamble. Unlike the other "helping professions" like lawyers and shrinks, who keep the meter ticking and charge for time but not necessarily results, I don't get a penny unless I perform. It's an offer you can't refuse, provided you have twenty thousand dollars to drop on the deal. Kinsey Milhone and any other fictional P.I.s battled injustice on the cheap, but I don't consider having a wardrobe of sweats and jeans, living out of ten-year-old VWs, and subsisting on a diet of take-out tacos and drive-in burgers either romantic, heroic, or necessary. Like them, I, too, get my kicks out of thwarting villains and righting wrongs, but I don't see why I have to live like an impoverished poet and dress like a bag lady while doing it. I developed a clientele that supports my very pleasant style of living, which includes a flat on the King's Road in London, an apartment on New York's Fifth Avenue, and my casita in Portugal, each equipped with closets filled with designer clothes. (If you could afford three homes, you shouldn't have to schlep garments from house to house.)

I was expecting Graham any minute so I decided to speed things along a bit. I have always found a direct question the best way to elicit information.

"What brings you to Vila do Mar at this time of year?" I asked.

They looked at each other and apparently made a decision. She was the spokesperson.

"Our son died here last week. He drowned. They said it was suicide."

"No way," said the father firmly. "Peter would never kill himself. Besides, the boy could swim like a fish—been in and around the water all his life." He shook his head emphatically. "No way."

"We came to bring his body back home—and to find out what really happened," said his wife. "We don't mean to sound chauvinistic, but somehow we felt that the local police are not, well, sophisticated enough to do a thorough job of investigation."

"That's why we had the American Consul step in and arrange to have Peter's body sent to Lisbon for analysis. That's where they discovered the presence of cocaine."

I remembered. It was quite a sensation in this little town. The body was found on the beach, his clothes folded neatly on the rocks, the classic suicide.

I told them I was familiar with the tragedy and expressed my sympathy. What I didn't say was that I knew it was always difficult for survivors to accept the suicide of a loved one. The guilt was overwhelming. *Why couldn't he come to me for help?* The sense of personal failure, unrealistic though it may be, could torture parents, as it was undoubtedly doing to these nice people.

"But what do you think you can accomplish here?" I asked. "The police considered it an open and shut case."

"The police are wrong," said the wife angrily.

"They do deal in evidence," I said gently.

"Yes, but they were missing one very crucial piece of evidence," she said.

"What's that?" I asked.

"They didn't know our son."

6

I should just nod my head and keep my mouth shut. But as anyone who knows me will tell you, silence and inactivity are two states I never enter.

"As I recall, there was a suicide note. And they, or the Lisbon medical examiner, found he had taken a large quantity of cocaine just before entering the ocean."

"No," she said firmly. "They said they found cocaine *in* him. No one has proven he had taken it."

The father reached into his pocket and took out a picture, which he handed to me. "This is our son, Peter, taken six months ago."

I looked at the picture and felt a frisson of shock. Around the neck of this very happy, open-faced young man was a clerical collar.

"He was a minister?"

"Yes," said his father. "One of the most popular young ministers in Westchester."

My home county. "What town?" I asked.

"You know Westchester?" she asked. Having spent the past ten years in London and Portugal, my speech has become an amalgam of accents so that no one country seems to want to claim me.

"I grew up in Rye," I said.

Their faces lit up. A neighbor—in this faraway strange place.

"We're from Larchmont. Peter's pastorate is—was—in Port Chester."

Port Chester was a depressed area, one of the fringe towns that seem to surround affluent areas. If Peter was a minister in Port Chester, his congregation was predominantly poor, black, and Hispanic.

"If you look closely at the picture," said the father, "it was an award ceremony for Peter's drug-free clinic that achieved the finest help record for youngsters in the entire state. Peter hated drugs. He didn't need them; life gave him all the high he needed. And he had seen what devastation drugs caused. If there was cocaine in his body, you can bet your life that someone else put it there."

"Why would he take his own life?" she asked.

"He came to Portugal on vacation. He was happy. He used to tell us that he was one of the luckiest men alive because he was able to really help people and contribute to this world. He had a mission—he felt fulfilled. You have to understand, Peter was dedicated to those kids. He knew he was their lifeline. He never would have deserted them."

People did strange things. And often had secret demons that could be invisible to those close to them, quiet agonies that drove them into deeds of desperation.

I looked at the sensitive face in the picture.

"Was he gay?" I asked.

"No," said his father. "Not that it would matter in our family. Our son Roger is gay and none of us has ever had a problem with it."

I had no more doubting questions. The police of Vila do Mar were hardly Scotland Yard, and their high rate of solved crimes came from the Claude Rains technique in *Casablanca*, which was to "round up the usual suspects." It was a resort town, and tragedy mixed poorly with suntan lotion, so the tendency was to look no further than the obvious and get the town fathers and hostelers off their backs by resolving unpleasantnesses rapidly.

"What are you planning to do here?" I asked. "By the way, my name is Emma Rhodes."

"We're Anne and Martin Belling," she said. "And actually, we don't have a clue what to do."

Martin took out some letters. "He wrote us about the people he met here. I thought we might start with some of them."

"But what will that do for us, Martin?" his wife asked. "We're strangers to them and you know how people hate to get involved. And what would we ask them? And how? We don't speak Portuguese."

But I do. Finding out what really happened to Peter Belling should be fairly simple for me since I know everybody in town—the people who are nominally in charge as well as the ones who really run the place.

"Perhaps I can help you," I said. "Actually, it's what I do for a living."

And I explained my unique profession to them. I could see they were startled and then slightly skeptical, the normal reactions to my rather unorthodox activities plus my looks. I'm a five-foot-six-inch, size eight, thirty-five-year old woman who nearly won the Miss Rye beauty contest that I entered as a lark while attending Sarah Lawrence College. I was disqualified for refusing to demean womanhood by submitting to the bathing suit parade. I have long brown hair, large brown eyes, and am generally classified as beautiful. Many consider beauty an enviable asset but it's often a working handicap because it gets in the way of being taken seriously.

"Look here," I said. "I've lived in Vila do Mar off and on for ten years. I speak Portuguese. I know everyone, and everyone knows me. I am on excellent terms with the local constabulary and the Establishment—I entertain them and their wives once a year in a large party to which they all look forward. I am one of the largest taxpayers in town. Everyone will talk to me, and if there's anything untoward about your son's death, I will know it within two weeks."

I told them my financial arrangements, and as I expected, the twenty-thousand-dollar figure caused nary a ripple.

"And if you come up empty we pay you nothing?" Martin asked.

"Exactly right."

They looked at each other, and with the wordless communion of all happily married couples, both turned to me and said, "You're on."

"One final thing before I start," I said. "Please do not introduce yourselves as Peter's parents around town. In fact, don't mention your relationship to anyone."

"Why ever not?" asked Martin.

"Because you'll get sympathy and then suspicion and everyone will clam up. If I start asking questions and they know you came here all the way from America, the locals

9

will spot a connection and no one will talk to me. They may not like the police, but they're their police, and the possibility that we do not respect the conclusions of their officials will only create antagonism and I'll hit a wall of silence."

They nodded their heads silently.

"I'd also like to point out that if Peter did not kill himself, someone else did. And any inquiries made indicating we're not satisfied with the police verdict alerts that person and makes him dangerous. Remember he—or she—killed once."

That shook them up and they promised to keep a low profile. I also advised them not to expect to hear from me for two weeks although they would certainly see me around since the town is small. I don't do progress reports; I find them time-wasting nuisances. Conventional investigators who charge hourly rates owe their clients periodic reports. Since clients don't buy my time, I owe them squat. Perhaps my fierce need for independence stemmed from those demeaning time sheets I had to deal with during my attorney days. There was a constant demand to turn in an outrageous number of billable hours so that the firm's partners could maintain their charge accounts at Barneys and Bouley's. I love my freedom and the fact that I don't have to account to anyone but me.

The Bellings were stunned. "You mean we won't know anything—you won't talk to us for two whole weeks?" asked Anne pleadingly.

One look at those two bereaved faces and I softened. What the hell; I made the rule so I guess I could break it.

"Look, I don't want anyone to know about our arrangement, but it would be perfectly natural for us to run into each other at Sir Barry's from time to time, just as we did now. You said you're staying at the Sol E Mar? I'll get in touch with you there—but only when I have something to ask or report."

Just then I saw Graham coming toward the square in no haste whatever even though he was now almost an hour late. According to Algarve time, he was within acceptable parameters, and because of Algarve time, I had a new case. That's what I enjoyed about my peculiar profession; its unpredictability appealed to me. I just lived and let things happen and they always did. I'm a strong believer in the "Emma Rhodes Conveyor Belt Theory of Life," which stipulates that numerous opportunities pass in front of every person during the course of a lifetime and the successful ones are those who had the insight, foresight, and guts to recognize and grab the right brass rings. I don't believe in luck. Being in the right place at the right time is a small part of it, but it's the ability to recognize the big chance and willingness to take the risk of acting upon it that separates the winners from the losers.

I'd been having a great time visiting with old friends and making some good new ones, but I didn't mind breaking into my vacation to take on a case that intrigued me. The only disquieting element was, if it turned out that Peter Belling was indeed murdered and I found the murderer, would it be one of those friends?

"Emma, you look great!"

I found myself pulled out of the chair and encased in a hearty hug. Graham Adams was my last year's lover. One of the endearing qualities about the Algarve expatriate group was that life was handled strictly one day at a time and one was never burdened with past obligations. The fact that we had a wild romance last year did not entitle either of us to expect an automatic resumption of intimacy. Graham was six feet tall, in his mid-forties, and enjoyed one of those maddening metabolisms that kept him trim no matter what, when, or where he ate. He had the typical long English face with the sort of prominent nose that the British accept only in themselves (i.e., Princess Di and Prince Charles) but term as Levantine when appearing on foreign faces. The only non-typical English feature was his straight marvelous white teeth, uncommon in the UK, where National Health pushes for fast, cheap extraction rather than long, costly treatment. The upper classes are the only ones who can afford proper dental care and thus have shining white teeth; it's the working and lower-middle classes who display dentures. I'm always shocked at screen closeups of British actors showing crooked, overlapping, often gray teeth, which is such a no-no in the U.S. Actually, Graham's smile could light up a screen as could his frequent infectious laugh. He still looked pretty good, but I hadn't checked out this year's crop yet.

I disengaged myself and turned to introduce him.

"Anne and Martin, this is my friend Graham, the man who knows everyone and everything about what's going on in Vila do Mar." I smiled and looked pointedly at Anne. She got the message and rose at once.

"Come on, Martin. If we want to get to Monchique for lunch, we'd better be off. It was nice meeting you, Graham."

Martin followed her with the usual bewildered look of husbands who are suddenly being pushed into an unexpected activity but have long ago learned not to question their wives' motivation until they are well out of earshot.

Graham sat down at the table and motioned to the waiter for *pao e mantega* (bread and butter) and *café branco* (coffee with milk, or white coffee).

Graham Adams was a young Englishman who had arrived in Vila do Mar with some money, minor local connections, and major chutzpah and within ten years had become a millionaire. He had that keen eye for opportunity and the gift of knowing how to work the system that characterize all big moneymakers. When most of the builders and consortiurns were busy constructing huge complexes for foreigners, Graham decided to tap the lucrative market of the Lisbon bourgeoisie. Backed with money from Lisbon banks, he built Clube Praia do Plata, an oceanfront development that offered apartments for sale to people who could use the places whenever they wished, and rent them out during the balance of the year.

The Clube managed the development and handled the rentals, collecting suitable fees, of course. This unique-at-the-time arrangement was an attractive lure for the Lisbonese, and Graham sold out within a month. He, too, was a person of multiple homes, with a flat in London, a house in Florida, and a casa in Vila do Mar. We never seemed to be in London at the same time but, like all Algarvian homeowners, were always sure to be here at this time of year.

I liked successful men. It wasn't that I had the depth of a bimbo; the fact was that I preferred my peers when it came to relationships. Long ago, I gave up pretending I had moderate means and intelligence in deference to the fragile egos of men who were threatened by achieving women. Graham and I had been a Vila do Mar item last year. There was still the possibility for this season. He was tall, fit, and smart and I always enjoyed our intercourse, both social and sexual.

I asked about everyone, caught up on the local gossip, and was looking for a way to lead into some casual inquiries about Peter Belling when he said, "Poor Leida; she's been a basket case since her boyfriend killed himself."

I'm a good actress; it's one of the major prerequisites for my profession. But this time I did not have to feign surprise; my jaw actually dropped. If ever there was an unlikely paramour for an idealistic minister, it was Leida Van Dolder, unless you believed that Somerset Maugham's Sadie Thompson relationships were possible.

"You couldn't mean that young American they found on the beach last week?"

"Absolutely," said Graham with the relish of a gossip-teller who has managed to shock his audience. "The poor bastard was totally smitten with our Leida, to the point of obsession, I'd say."

"Were they lovers?" I asked.

"Surely you jest. Leida probably thinks platonic is something bottled by Schweppes. She doesn't know how to talk to a man in an upright position."

"Did they have a relationship?" I asked.

"One might call it that on a sort of animalistic level. He was a minister, you know, and she had that fatherless child last year. He was out to tame her wild immorality with words but she was more into whips and chains so they met halfway—they just kicked."

Leida was the only child of Adriaan Van Dolder, the profligate padrone of Vila do Mar. Adriaan was a Dutchman who had arrived in the Algarve in the early 1960s and bought up miles of now priceless oceanfront land for something like three escudos an acre.

"How on earth did such an ill-matched pair meet?" I asked.

"In my house," said Graham. "I met Peter on my beach one morning. He seemed like a nice chap so I asked him up for a drink."

Graham and Adriaan had adjoining estates overlooking the ocean at the northern end of town. Since most tourists tended to congregate on the beaches closer to the village, both landowners regarded the usually unpopulated beach below as their private property.

"You can guess the rest. Leida just happened to drop in. It's uncanny. The girl can smell any open liquor bottle or eligible male within a radius of three miles," he said. "She's got the nose of a bloodhound as well as the morals."

"Well, who can blame her with that fine role model she has for a father?" I said.

"You know," he said, "we talk about Adriaan's immorality. Yet the man was supposed to have been a hero in Amsterdam during the war. Saved thousands of Jews from the Nazis at great risk of his own life. That's not the action of a decadent man."

"I've heard that, too. I even heard that his name is on one of the plaques along the Avenue of the Righteous in the Israeli Holocaust Museum at Yad Va Shem. There's a plaque under each tree commemorating a gentile who saved Jewish lives. But how do we know it's true?"

"Well, I grant you I never read it in the *New York Times*, but I did hear the facts directly from the great man himself."

I was silent for a moment. "Somehow I find it hard to reconcile a hero's image with the self-centered arrogant tyrant we all know and loathe."

Graham looked at his watch, a rare habit in the Algarve. "Good. Eleven o'clock, a perfectly reasonable time to have a brandy in my coffee." He signalled the waiter and looked at me. "You, too?" I shook my head. This was not just brandy—it was *aguardente medronho*, which required not only an acquired taste but an acquired immunity, and had caused many an unsuspecting tourist to become frozen to his barstool. It was a fiery brew made from the red berries of the arbutus shrub that grows wild in the Algarve and was commonly produced in homes in pot stills. Despite the constant urging of my Portuguese friends, I refused to drink the stuff. I was willing to try anything once, and I have, but if it burns your throat going down and plays havoc with your stomach when it gets there—what's the big bargain? I didn't understand the need to "develop a taste" for anything, which was why I never smoked. If something affected you unfavorably at the outset, why bother to repeat the experience? But then, I was never one to be persuaded into doing anything merely because it's cool.

I heard a loud shriek and Graham groaned. "Speaking of the devil, or the devil's daughter," he said as Leida Van Dolder swooped down upon us.

SWOOPED WAS EXACTLY the right word because Leida looked like an ungainly stork with red hair. Tall, willowy, and pretty, or as pretty as one can be with vacuous eyes, she had an awkward loping gait and drooping posture that made us question her claim of having been a model. But then, we all learned that pure truth was an incomprehensible abstraction to Leida. Perhaps it was because of her miserable childhood, which made her live in a wish-world where she found life easier when fantasy and fact overlapped.

As a byproduct of her parents' rancorous divorce, Leida lived only with strangers since the age of eight. She had the impassive soulless look one sees in ghetto children who have grown up without parental love or supervision. Knowing her pathetic background, we all accepted Leida's erratic behavior with empathy but not sympathy. She was a jarring note and a general nuisance we learned to live with much as we did the *formigas*, which are the ant scourge of the Algarve.

She threw her arms around me in her usual awkward, uncontrolled way and would have knocked me off my chair if Graham hadn't caught me in time. She then plunked herself down at our table, being careful to leave a spot for her dachshund, unimaginatively named Schotzie.

"I heard you were back in town," she said as she waved imperiously to the waiter. He nodded and returned shortly with a *café branco* that from the powerful aroma was liberally laced with *medronho*, obviously her regular order since no words had been exchanged.

"Where's Adriana?" I asked. She had named her daughter after guess who. Leida looked around and then, in the voice of a drill sergeant, yelled to a little blond girl who was roaming around the tables. *"Adriana!* Here! Sit!" Leida's dog was on a leash; I wondered why she hadn't done the same with her daughter since she obviously treated them both the same.

I felt a stab of pity as I saw the toddler approach her mother with none of the joy and animation that children usually display upon spotting their mothers. She sat down dutifully on the ground next to Schotzie and hugged him as he licked her, and I was glad the poor kid had some source of affection. But then how could Leida have had a clue about parenting? Adriana had the fair hair and skin and blue eyes that reminded me of the cover of my favorite childhood storybook, *Hans Brinker and the Silver Skates*. We had all heard conflicting versions from Leida about the identification of the baby's father. He was a Portuguese aristocrat who was mad with desire for Leida but whose family forbade the marriage. He was an Italian duke who was wildly in love with her but whom she considered too old for her to marry. He was the son of a sultan who would only marry her if she agreed to live in his desert emirate. But blue eyes are recessive, and the child's visage had no trace whatever of a Latin or Middle Eastern heritage. Tales of Leida's lovers seemed to come out of nowhere until I discovered a correlation with names mentioned in the latest copies of *Elle* and *Vogue*. Money was the only staple element in Leida's life; emotions were concepts that were beyond her ken, but money was a tangible she could understand. Even though her father was many times a millionaire and she his only heir, Leida handled every escudo as though it were her last. Like many aristocrats and superwealthy people who seem to develop some kind of misplaced sense of entitlement, she regarded reaching for a check as an exercise that was beneath her.

Vila do Mar was a small town, and Leida's reputation for mean and unlovable behavior spread quickly. The fact that she had a child out of wedlock didn't sit too well either in the very Catholic village. Since I liked to think of myself as a good and understanding human being, I tried to excuse her erratic and unpleasant conduct because of her sad childhood.

However, while a deprived background may have been an explanation, it was not an excuse for rudeness, stupidity, cupidity, and total lack of consideration. My high-minded tolerance evaporated the day she lied about stealing my favorite little house-guarding lion statue that stood on my terrace and had been carved for me by a marvelously talented old local stonecutter. She finally returned it only after I pointed out that her explanation of having recently commissioned one herself was flawed because the stonecutter had died three years ago. From that point on, disliking Leida was a luxury I allowed myself in totally good conscience.

Since my feelings matched those of everyone in town, her social life was entirely spent with visitors and vacationers who did not know her and were conceivably attracted by her looks and/or lineage. Like Peter Belling.

I needed to talk to her about Peter, but this wasn't the time and certainly not the place. "How's your father?" I asked.

"Daddy's fine," she answered, her face turning surly. Leida thought I had designs on Adriaan. He and I were fond of each other and enjoyed the stimulation of each other's company. But that was all. Since Leida only understood friendships based on sex, she assumed I had the hots for Daddy. She should have known that I was far too elderly for Adriaan; he was fifty-two and I was thirty-five, and the top cut-off age for his partners in prurience was fifteen. I'd never learned what the bottom cut-off age was and I preferred not to know. I had friends of all sexual persuasions and I viewed their bedroom behavior as totally irrelevant to our friendship.

"Is he home?" I asked. "I'd like to see him."

"He went to Morocco last week," she said with ill-concealed malicious glee. "I don't know when he's coming back." The poor thing was a case of simplistic emotions right out of Psych I. She knew and showed love, hate, jealousy, fear, happiness, and sadness and had never developed the sophistication of subterfuge. I used to be one of her favorite people, which was not an enviable position because it meant that she turned up at my house at any hour that suited her need. Since I could never turn away anyone who was in need, I was frequently victimized into sitting up until sunset listening to tales of Leida's abnormal problems. I can just hear you saying "what's normal?" While I can't set exact parameters of normalcy, I feel reasonably safe in classifying as abnormal Leida's response to a young man's first kiss and declaration of love with an offer to give him an immediate blow job. Right now, I was on her shit list (which usually encompassed half of Vila do Mar) because I was perceived as competitor for her adored Daddy's affection.

Graham and I looked at each other and he rolled his eyes. We knew what Adriaan's frequent trips to Morocco involved. It was common knowledge to everyone but Leida that he maintained a house there only because the area offered a supply of young boys who were readily available at the right price.

Her face now a sullen mask, Leida jumped to her feet in the precipitous manner that governed all her motions. "I have to go to the *correio* now to send a telegram," she said abruptly and yanked the dog to his feet, grabbed the child by her arm, and off they went.

We watched the trio wend its way through the now jammed street. "I think that little girl would be better off being brought up by wolves," I said.

"Why?" said Graham. "You don't think that having a nymphomaniacal imbecile for a mother and an alcoholic deviate for a grandfather is a nice, normal nuclear family? Tsk, tsk, Emma—I do believe you're getting provincial in your advanced years. But also even lovelier, my dear," he added, kissing my hand with an exaggerated leer.

"No P.D.E., Graham," I said. "You know that Public Display of Emotion is a no-no in the town square. People will think you've been jumping my bones."

"Well, haven't I?" he said with a twinkle.

"Last year's news, darling," I said.

"You mean I have to start from the bottom again this year, if you'll pardon the expression?" he answered. "There are no carry-forward privileges?"

I shook my head. "Nope. It's open season. And if you keep pawing me this way word will quickly get around that we're a thing and my possibilities will become limited."

"Capital idea," he said as he stretched across the table and panted a big juicy kiss on my lips.

"Unhand me, you cad!" I said as I jumped up and hit him across the cheek with a paper napkin. "You have compromised my good name. My seconds will call upon you tomorrow morning."

"Not too early, please. I simply can't duel properly until I've had my morning tea. How about dinner tonight?"

"Great," I said. "What time?"

"I'll pick you up at seven."

We both got up and left.

Chapter Two

I HAD FOURTEEN days to resolve the suicide/murder of Peter Belling. I experienced the elation I felt when embarking on a new case and fully understood Sherlock Holmes' fascination with solving mysteries. Working out what really happened, which involved extracting facts from the heads of people who unknowingly had pertinent information, and from those who, for their own reasons, tried to hide the truth, was a challenge that required the analytical skills of a psychologist, the quick brain of a litigating lawyer, and the risk-taking gut of a stock trader, which fit my profile to a T. I still found it hard to believe I got paid for this—and damned well.

The day broke clear and sunny, as usual in the Algarve—perfect weather for a walk into town. I found going on foot far more pleasant than trying to maneuver my car through narrow, cobblestoned, hilly streets that were originally designed for wagons and then having to battle my way to find a parking space. The concept of one-way streets came late to the town fathers, and there were still many on which one often had the choice of driving over a pedestrian on the sidewalk or allowing an oncoming vehicle to rip off your front door.

My casa was in Forte de San Joao, which was a small complex of houses directly overlooking the ocean a few kilometers from the center of town. My walking route took me along sandy dirt paths to the hill leading down into town, which was lined first with yellow limestone one- and two-story buildings with blue trim and then small white cottages with intricately filigreed chimneys and windows that had been edged in bright blues, purples, and reds in order to keep the evil eye away from the occupants.

As I turned into town, I faced the shining blue Atlantic and the small fleet of brightly colored fishing boats that had come in early that morning to unload their catches on the beach. There the fish had been cleaned and then carried to the long, metal-roofed shed that was the local *Mercado de Peixe*, the fish market and heart of every Algarve oceanfront village. The *pescadors* had already set out their fish on crushed-ice-covered stands in unusual displays that each fish seller arranged in his own special style and design for presentation to restaurant owners, big buyers from Lisbon, and local housewives. The *Mercado* was just as it was fifty and maybe one hundred years ago, as were the old women in black dresses and men's black fedora hats tied on their heads with colorful kerchiefs. Some of them had come by car, some by bicycle, and some still use *carinhas*, carts drawn by one or two donkeys. The crews of the fishing boats sat on the beach companionably smoking and untangling and rearranging their large nets, often with the help of small boys who were learning to join their fathers at sea as had their fathers before them. They looked enviably happy and carefree and unconcerned with the stresses of faxes, contracts, and deadlines. They had that dignity and sense of self evident in people content with who they are. Actually, their lives were *muito dur* or, in English, rough going. Out all night in open boats in what could be violent seas and sometimes cold winds, they worked hard, pulling in heavily laden nets if they were lucky, and if they weren't, a catch that could be fairly meager so as to earn them a pittance for the night's work. But there was always tomorrow.

I walked over to the Praia Mar, a small *taberna* along the waterfront, to talk to Miguel Garcia Ozorio. Now, how would the Bellings have known that at ten in the morning, the place to find the *chefe de polícia* would never be the station *esquadra* but at his favorite *taberna* at the fishing beach? After he finished his *café branco* and buttered *paoseco*, the delicious crusty roll that had just come out of the oven of the *padaria*, he would saunter down to the *Mercado de Peixe* where he would be greeted with great deference. The *chefe* would take his pick from the daily catch of mullet, sole, swordfish, sardines, lampreys, octopus, and prawns and would bring it home at lunchtime to Senhora Ozorio, who would grill it to perfection. No escudos would change hands, of course.

I sat down at his table. "*Boa dia, Comandante. Como estas?*"

He rose in his chair to greet me with a big smile and the usual slightly lascivious once-over that attractive women get from all Latin men under the age of eighty.

"*Bem, obrigado; é você?*"

"*Menos mal, obrigado.*"

Now that we had the customary "How are you? I'm fine, and you? Not bad, thank you" Portuguese pleasantries over with and I had declined his offer of joining him for coffee, he looked at me and waited. He knew I wasn't down there to buy fish. But one did not rush into *negócios* in the Algarve. It was considered rude, a cardinal sin in this land of people who had three different ways to say excuse me: *faz favor, con licenca* and *desculpe*, each applicable to a very specific situation. I switched over to English because he spoke it perfectly and liked to show off his expertise. Miguel was in his fifties, and men of his age who grew up under Salazar often did not have the advantage of an education but left school for work at an early age. However, his parents owned a small *supermercado* in town and could afford to send their only son to school in Silves. I asked after his wife and family. He pulled out a plastic folder that displayed photos of sons, daughters-in-law, and grandchildren and beamed proudly as I exclaimed properly over their apparent beauty and intelligence. Then we discussed how nice and peaceful it was now and bemoaned the congestion of the tourist season. I commended him and his *guarda* for their fine control of the onslaught of outsiders who came to enjoy the superb climate and beaches of our lovely town without always respecting its properties.

"That young American who drowned. Why did he have to come all the way here to kill himself?" I shook my head at his lack of consideration.

A slight alertness in his posture showed that he was aware I had now come to the reason for this early morning visit.

"A sad case," said the *chefe*. "That a man so young cannot find something to live for is a tragedy."

"That is just what I find interesting, *Comandante*." (No one but his wife called him Miguel, and I'm not sure even she did.) "You put your finger right on it—the stresses of the world today are sometimes overwhelming. In fact, I'm doing a story on the subject of suicide and what happens to young people who cannot cope. You know, it would be very helpful if I could see your file on that young man. I think it would add a great deal of interest if I were to describe how an efficient law enforcement department handles a suicide case."

The local people believed I was a writer, which seemed an easier occupation for them to comprehend and also explained my sporadic times of residence and sometimes unorthodox behavior. Creative people were given tremendous latitude.

The *chefe* stirred his coffee. "It is against regulations to allow any of our files to leave the *esquadra*, you know."

I was quiet.

"It is also against the rules for files to be out of official hands."

I did not say a word.

"However . . ."

Ah, that was the word I'd been waiting for.

"I do not see anything wrong with my placing the file on my desk where anyone who is at the desk can sit and read it for, say, fifteen minutes this afternoon at three-thirty."

We smiled contentedly in perfect understanding and walked together down to the *Mercado de Peixe* where we both selected an assortment of glistening fish. It was quite an experience shopping with the chief of police. The fisherman whose wares we chose was so honored that he not only refused payment but insisted on delivering the fish to both the *chefé*'s casa and mine on his way home. My *criada*, Gloria, would make a delicious *caldeirada* for dinner. This was the Algarve fish stew version of the French bouillabaisse, and I was already salivating in anticipation of dipping crusty, freshly baked bread into the herbed sauce.

Promptly at three-thirty, I sat at the *chefé*'s desk looking over the file. Peter Belling's body, clad only in jockey shorts, had been found on the beach in the early morning by a jogger who immediately called the police. His clothes were found neatly folded and tucked into one of the rock grottoes that abut all Algarve beaches. His wallet was in a trouser pocket and contained passport, identification, photos, credit cards, and a small amount of escudos. Another pocket contained a handkerchief and the key to his room at the local *pensão*. His shirt pocket contained a note, which was in the file. The handwriting had been verified by comparing it to the signature in his passport and the letter he had sent to his landlady reserving a room. It was very short and damning.

> Please forgive me. I have tried to help, but there obviously is too much that I cannot understand. I am miserable because I know I have failed. Good-bye.
>
> > Peter

The head and body had contusions that could have been inflicted before death, but were not inconsistent with normal battering by sea rocks and the rough surf of the Atlantic.

Drownings were not unusual in a village on the ocean, especially one that attracts thousands of tourists. Suicides were less common, but the local medical examiner, one of the town's two doctors, was very familiar with watery deaths and its manifestations and wrote the death certificates quickly, which usually closed the case immediately. It was fortunate that Peter's body was sent to Lisbon for the autopsy since suitable facilities for such an examination were sorely lacking in Vila do Mar. The one time I had been forced to go to the village's only hospital, I realized that though I prize things quaint and simple, these were not qualities I value in my medical care. The accommodations looked like something out of the Crimean War, and I felt like asking the nurse where they kept the leeches.

There was no doubt that Peter's death was caused by drowning. The level of water in the lungs was conclusive. The contents of his stomach showed that he had eaten dinner about two hours earlier and that he had taken a large amount of cocaine shortly before his death. Given all this evidence, the police conclusion could have been accidental drowning of a man who, befuddled by drugs, made an imprudent decision to plunge into the ocean at night and could not handle the currents. However, the presence of the note definitively made it suicide.

Or did it? There were many questions, such as what he was doing at that beach; his *pensão* was at the other end of town. Was he at some coke-snorting party nearby? Was he the type to be at such a party? If his despair about the breakup with Leida drove him to such fatal despondency, what specific factor or occurrence made him decide that this was the moment to end it all? Was he alone when he made the decision? Wasn't drowning an odd choice of means to do away with oneself when one was as excellent a swimmer as Peter was?

As I walked into my casa, the phone was ringing.

"Emma darling, how dare you sneak back into town and not let us know!"

I dropped down into the comfortable tan leather chair next to the carved wooden chest that was my phone table in the foyer because I knew this would not be a short call. It was the Honorable Dirk Croft, the charming English aristocrat of a certain age who was the de facto social director of Vila do Mar society.

"Ah, the drums have been beating, I gather," I said with a smile. "Who reported the sighting—Graham or Leida?"

He snorted. "Surely you don't think I would place any credibility in the word of the Daft Daughter? Actually, I ran into Graham in the *supermercado*. They just got in my special order of Branston Pickle."

I laughed. "Dirk, you've lived in Portugal for twenty-five years. Surely you've found an equivalent local condiment. I think it's quaint the way you English carry England with you wherever you go."

"This from the woman who has a carton of New York City Hebrew National hot dogs in her freezer at all times?" he said in the drawn-out nasal tone of the upper class.

"O.K., I admit to having powerful yens."

"Don't we all, my darling. And I have one to see you. I'm having a small dinner party tonight. You must come, of course."

I had a dinner date with Graham that night, but Dirk's little social events, usually attended by the leading lights of the English-speaking expatriate community, were fertile territory for the kind of gossip, backbiting, and intimate innuendo that I found repellent when not working and rewarding when I was.

"Will Julia be there?" I asked. She was his current inamorata. The usual term of office as Dirk's Lady was two seasons, which meant Julia would soon be history. As I remembered from last year, she was a meticulously groomed and lacquered fiftyish widow whose hobbies were bridge and bitchery. She had a computer-like mind that automatically accumulated dirty data on people and was a living testimonial to the accuracy of the statement "garbage in, garbage out."

"*Ca va sans dire*, my dear Emma."

Great. One evening with Julia could save me hours of asking around and could accelerate my investigation of Peter Belling's death by days.

"Wonderful, Dirk. I'll be there."

"Remember the rules, my love. Wearers of jeans will be barred at the door. Cocktails at eight, dinner at ten."

Which meant Alka-Seltzer at two. It always took my digestive system about ten days to accommodate to the Iberian dining timetable. I never could understand how the Spanish and Portuguese managed to finish a heavy meal at close to midnight and be at work early the next morning without looking like they'd been up all night with the Pepto-Bismol bottle.

I called Graham and changed the date for the following night. He wasn't in the slightest bit miffed at being postponed. Time was considered of little importance in the Algarve. Today, tomorrow—what's the difference? It was the pleasant easy approach to life that stood in stark contrast to the big city stress of self-imposed deadlines set by people who needed to create false images of their own importance. I usually needed a week of decompression to slow down my inner clock to Algarve pace whenever I arrived in Vila do Mar. It was one of the principal reasons I chose to live here.

Now, what to wear. The casual wardrobe in the closet of my casa needed fairly infrequent replenishment since Algarve style stayed basically the same from year to year. However, the formal clothing section required annual infusions. When Algarve towns such as Albufeira became overrun with pink-nosed clerks and secretaries from all over Europe, the highborn rich and elegant moved up the coast to quiet, and as yet undiscovered, Vila do Mar. There entertaining ran the gamut from the casual chic of Bermuda shorts barbecues to haute cuisine and couture. Tonight would be the latter. My host had a keen eye and an even keener memory for style; not only would he instantly recognize the designer of the dress you were wearing, but he would also recall exactly when and where you previously wore it. It's devilish.

I got there at nine because, not having the booze-toughened liver of the Algarve old timers, two hours of tippling would send me into orbit. Dirk met me at the door, and as he took my pink silk satin notched collar jacket, he looked at the matching sleeveless dress and said approvingly, "Ah, I do like Mizrahi. You're made for his sheath, my dear." Did I know my customers or what? "And those marvelous baroque pearls—I don't believe I've seen them before." I expected him to pull a jeweler's loupe out of his pocket.

His tall, trim figure sported a navy blue velvet jacket, black trousers, white shirt, and Etonian tie. His white hair was brushed back on the sides, undoubtedly with the silver-backed brush set I have seen on his dressing table, and worn with a full wave on top that fell carefully over his brow. He had those clear Inspector Morse blue eyes and, all and all, was a very attractive man of the older English Gentleman genre.

Dirk was the third son of the fifth Duke of Sandringham, which meant he had an Honorable in front of his name but none of the goodies that went with the dukedom. Following the laws of primogeniture, the eldest son alone inherits the title and estates. This keeps him busy and wealthy but leaves the rest of the duke's offspring floating about to find their own ways in the world, hopefully in some dignified fashion. When the estates passed on to his elder brother who became the sixth Duke after their father's death, Dirk was unwilling to lower his sybaritic style of living for any period of time. Instead, he took the risky route of lending his honorable family name to the huge industrial project of a brash but brainy young East End developer who needed the respectable endorsement in order to raise large investment capital. Derided at the outset by his family for being a dupe, he was hailed as a shrewd sage when the development boomed and Dirk walked away with a tidy fortune. He now divided his time between a small elegant house in Cadogan Mews and a huge luxurious villa overlooking the ocean in Vila do Mar.

"I believe you know everyone, Emma," he said as we stepped down into the large living room that covered the entire length of the front of the house. A fire was burning in the huge *azulejos*-bordered fireplace, casting a soft light on the white stone walls and brightly colored handmade rugs scattered about on shining terra-cotta tile floors. Jars of flowers were everywhere, a tribute to the labors of Dirk's much-envied butler-cum-gardener, Francisco, who was now serving drinks while his wife, Maria, the cook and general *criada*, was passing out hors d'oeuvres.

I usually liked to bring my host a small gift when I went to a dinner party, but no one ever brought anything to Dirk. It was impossible. No flowers could equal the exotic rarities Francisco grew so lovingly in Dirk's vast gardens. No wine could match the contents of Dirk's peerless, priceless cellar. He had a case of wine shipped to him monthly from London's posh Shreve and Asbury Vintners. And no one would dare bring a decorative *chatchka* to a home where every single piece had been carefully selected to blend perfectly with the exquisite decor carefully created by the owner.

As the hostess du jour, Julia came forward to greet me with an expertly social smile.

"Darling, how nice to see you. What a divine dress."

I looked at her lavender velvet Chanel with the heavy gold Versace choker necklace and said, "You look lovely, Julia." And I meant it.

The entire town old guard was there, and I went around the room kissing smooth, face-lifted cheeks and making the kind of catch-up small talk one makes with acquaintances after a long hiatus. Sipping champagne and munching on a small square of Maria's wonderful hot *bacalhau* pie, I was content to float around pleasantly and mindlessly until dinner. I knew the conversation then would consist of local gossip and I could easily bring up the topic of Peter Belling.

"Emma, I don't believe you've met my nephew, Mark," said my host, introducing me to a man who looked as if he just stepped from the pages of a Ralph Lauren ad but without the one-day stubble. There was no ring on his left hand nor any indentation indicating recent removal of one. He looked directly into my eyes and I suddenly felt that I might mix unexpected pleasure with business that evening.

"Mark, this is Emma Rhodes, who, if I were twenty years younger, would be the mistress of this house."

"If you were twenty years younger, Dirk, the line of eager competitors for that position would ring the town. As it is today, I think the line extends to the beach." I looked towards Julia. "I see the present incumbent seems happily entrenched."

He made a slight grimace. "Perhaps because she's unaware that a new election is in the offing."

"But she must know that the term of office is limited, Dirk."

He smiled grimly. "After two years, they all get to think they're indispensable, which makes them insufferable and intolerable. Julia is starting to suggest which tie I must wear. What on earth gives her the idea she has that right?"

"Maybe because you fawn all over her and tell her what a delightful creature she is? Maybe because she thinks you care about her and her opinions? I've seen you at work, Dirk. It's a reasonable assumption."

He became indignant. "But that's only polite and gentlemanly behavior. I wouldn't dream of treating a woman any other way."

"Then don't be surprised that they're somewhat shocked when you turn over in bed and announce 'Darling, I'll expect you to be out of here tomorrow.'"

Mark had been listening to the exchange and said with a you-old-devil-you smile, "I see, Uncle, that your reputation in the family is not ill-founded."

I could not believe I was standing there defending a woman who was tough enough to take on Mike Tyson, in *and* out of the ring. But that kind of macho talk usually made me feel like planting a knee to the groin. However, this wasn't the right venue nor, I suspect, audience for feminist consciousness-raising. Besides, Mark had a lovely deep voice that matched the intense virility of his appearance, and I thought I'd rather cast him as an escort than an adversary. So I sent him to get me more champagne.

He brought me another glass and we looked at each other happily.

"Now I know why Uncle insisted I come tonight."

"Had you other plans?" I asked.

"Actually, I told him I did," he said. "You see, I've been to a few of his dinner do's. The food is marvelous, the wines are superb, and the company excruciatingly boring. There are over fifty bars in Vila do Mar and if you extrapolate that number figuring ten attractive women per bar, I'm missing out on at least five hundred opportunities. So I wasn't eager to waste an evening doing family duty, especially when I'm only down here for a week."

"What brings you to the Algarve?"

"The family owns some property in Silves and we have an offer to purchase. In fact, the potential buyers will be here tonight, Uncle tells me."

"Then it's expeditious for your business to be here this evening."

He shook his head firmly. "Business is transacted during business hours. My evenings are my own."

It was good he was in a family business. With that philosophy, he'd be out on his ass in a month if he were working for anyone else. From his Turnbull and Asser shirt and Saville Row suit, it was obvious they weren't hurting for money back at the old homestead. Now all he needed were brains and charm and potentially he'd be my kind of guy.

"And why are you here?" he asked.

"At the party or in Vila do Mar?"

"I'd be interested in your answers to both," he answered with a twinkle in his eye. Hmm. I liked eye-twinklers. It was a point that weighed heavily in his favor.

I explained that I owned a home in town and that turning down an invitation from his uncle was as unthinkable as refusing one from the Queen.

"Uncle tells me you're a writer. What sort of things do you write?"

"Mostly books on psychology and behavior modification," I answered. I found it better to tell people that I produce dry academic tomes so that they weren't tempted to ask to read my nonexistent oeuvre. The instant eye-glazing produced by my announcement proved what I suspected—this is no raving intellectual. He probably thinks Kierkegaard is a smorgasbord restaurant, but he's still damned attractive.

"Dinner is a bit late, my dears," announced Dirk. "We're awaiting two other people. They're coming from Silves, so we'll have to excuse their delay." Just then, the doorbell rang and he smiled. "Ah, there they are." He walked over and opened the door to admit a man and woman whom, after giving their coats to Francisco, he brought to the step at the edge of the living room.

The man was formally dressed and the woman was wearing a long black skirt, white blouse, and a black knit fringed shawl of the type worn by Fado singers.

"Everybody, this is Elizabeth Eddington and Chilton Evans."

I put down my glass and ran up to her. She looked at me in astonishment and her face became suffused with beaming delight as we threw our arms around each other.

"I gather you two have met before," said Dirk calmly. With true British sangfroid, he exhibited absolutely no curiosity about the coincidence. "May I have Francisco bring you some champagne? I'm afraid you've missed the cocktail hour but you must have at least one glass before we go in to dinner."

She and her companion nodded graciously, and as they were waiting, I took Elizabeth aside to let her know that the facts of my true profession were unknown to this gathering, and that to everyone in town, I was a writer. She accepted my statement unequivocally without a question.

"Elizabeth, please introduce me to your lovely friend."

It was her companion, Chilton Evans, who was instantly identifiable as one of those effusive gallant charmers who were highly effective with elderly ladies and a quaint joke to young folk. He looked to be about fifty, with narrow shoulders and the beginning of a paunch. He had ordinary regular features, a ginger-colored brush mustache that matched the thinning hair on his head and would have conveyed a totally nondescript appearance if you had not noticed the greedy intensity of his ever-moving green eyes. His dinner clothing was worn with the self-conscious perfection of one who was not born to it. I liked men to wear scent, but his was a strange combination of lemon and disinfectant.

"Chilton, this is Emma Rhodes," said Elizabeth with a fond smile, "a very dear friend indeed. We met in England last month."

"Ah, you are then perhaps a friend of our poor Hugh?"

I didn't miss the possessive "our." I didn't know where good old Chilton fit into the family picture, but Hugh Eddington was Elizabeth's brother. I knew him slightly; he was involved in the case I was working on and unfortunately ended up strangled in his own bed. I was the one who found his body.

"Let's say more of an acquaintance," I answered. "You, I take it, were fairly close to Hugh."

"We did some business together and, finding we had much in common, became good friends."

Since Hugh's business associations involved drugs, deals, and deception that caused him to be murdered, that wasn't much of a recommendation.

"That's how I met Elizabeth," he said, taking her hand. It wasn't a sexual gesture, but more of a comforting one. The guy reeked of cheap smarm. What was a purely good and intelligent woman like her doing with a putz like him?

As though she heard that thought, Elizabeth said, "Chilton has been raising money for Casa dos Meninos, Emma. He has some wonderful ideas."

I'll bet. Why do I wonder who will be the ultimate beneficiary?

"We've created a foundation for Elizabeth's children's home so that we can draw major contributions and give her wonderful enterprise the support it needs and deserves."

Elizabeth was one of the truly good people who made me feel that perhaps there was hope for mankind after all.

Upon a vacation trip to the Algarve many years ago, she came across a five-year-old girl who had been chained to a tree, abandoned by her parents who were too poor to support her. Elizabeth took her back to her hotel and then decided to stay in Portugal. She bought a house in Silves and began to fill it with other abandoned children, and soon it became an institution named Casa dos Meninos—house of children.

"But I thought you had enough money to maintain the home from the estate Hugh left to you," I said to Elizabeth. "That plus the funds you get from the state should be ample, shouldn't it?"

"Ah, yes—'maintain' is the operative word, Miss Rhodes. But if Elizabeth's good works are to grow as I think they should so that we can save as many children as possible, we'll need far more than Hugh's legacy."

Again it was "we." The guy's presumptuous possessiveness was getting to me.

Like all people too filled with themselves to notice others' reactions, he was totally unaware of my irritation. But sensitive Elizabeth spotted it immediately.

"Chilton's kind offer to take over the fundraising frees me to handle what I'm really there for and do best—taking care of the children." And then her face lit up. "He has gotten enough for us to buy an adjacent piece of land that I've been longing to acquire for years so that we can expand our facilities."

I turned to Mark, who had joined us.

"I think this is your cue, Mark. Elizabeth and Chilton, this is the man who is selling the land you want." Everybody was profusely and politely delighted to meet each other. Then our host announced, "Dinner, my dears. Everyone into the dining room at once, please, or Maria threatens to withhold her soufflé."

There were cries of "Never!" and "Unthinkable!" And everyone trooped into the dining room with good natured alacrity.

Dirk's sprawling white-stone house stood atop a hill that overlooked the ocean in front and the Monchique mountains in the rear. The building consisted of two farmhouses he had connected and totally remodeled. One house was transformed into two huge rooms; the living room took up the entire front half and the dining room took up the entire rear half. The other house contained bedrooms and baths. In the middle was the mammoth modern kitchen that connected both wings.

You couldn't walk into Dirk's dining room without gasping with delight, no matter how often you'd been there. The wall of glass facing you was a fantastic living mural of twinkling lights of houses that studded the mountains beyond. The long refectory table, which he had obtained from a monastery in Obidoes, had a row of votive candles running down the middle illuminating the Baccarat stemware and highly polished silver and service pieces. Each place had a red, blue, and gold Royal Crown Derby bone china dish atop a pewter service plate. Instead of a single large showy floral centerpiece, there were small bunches of flowers arranged with exquisite taste in individual crystal bowls at intervals along the table so that everyone could enjoy their beauty.

When in earlier days I once commented to Dirk about the lack of colorful local pottery and handicrafts on his dinner table, he said with firmness, "Local is for lunch." And that was that.

As we were eating our delicious *creme sopa de mariscos*, a spicy cream shellfish soup filled with lobster and shrimp, table conversation hadn't yet reached the din that forces one to chat only with one's neighbors (God help you if they were boring). It was a good time to bring up Peter Belling.

In order to get everyone's attention so that a topic is picked up by the entire assemblage, it was vital to launch your opening conversational gambit across the table. I was seated next to Dirk, who was at the head, and Julia, as hostess of the evening, sat at the other end.

"Julia," I called across the table, "what do you think of the latest Vila do Mar mystery?"

All heads lifted as I knew they would.

"What mystery?" asked Julia, visibly perturbed at the possibility that she might be out of the loop.

"That young American who allegedly committed suicide in the ocean."

I always giggled when I heard the police department spokesperson as well as the media use the term "the alleged perpetrator" even when there were three hundred eyewitnesses to the crime. They had to conform to the law and be concerned about prejudicing the potential juror pool and inhibiting possible lawsuits. I had no such constraints and could enjoy making any accusation I wished.

"What do you mean 'alleged' suicide?" said Julia. She looked puzzled and upset. Could she have missed out on something vital?

"He was found on the beach, his clothes neatly folded, with a suicide note," said Dirk. "What more proof does one need?"

I knew I was stepping out on a limb. If Peter was indeed murdered, then I was publicly announcing to the murderer that I was not buying the suicide story and he or she should no longer be complacent. Announcing my opinion to this crowd was tantamount to placing an ad in the local paper: it would circulate around the entire community by tomorrow morning and the killer would know that I was roiling the waters. I knew of no faster way to get attention and answers quickly.

"There were too many questions about the whole thing," I answered Dirk. "You know the authorities, not to mention the tourist office, want to avoid scandal. Don't you think it's possible they pushed stuff under the rug just to push *l'affaire* off the front pages?"

"What sort of questions?" asked Julia.

Every spoon clanked to a stop while I ticked off my list of reasons why Peter Belling's death could have been something other than suicide.

"Hmm, for a psychology writer, you make an excellent detective," said Mark.

I heard Elizabeth cough and avoided looking at her.

"It's true that he was staying near us at Pensao de Dom Dinis," said Pamela Cartlington, who lived in a splendid building that was once a twelfth-century church on the Rua da Alegria with her husband, Reginald, a retired planter from Singapore, and four corgis who had a remarkable resemblance to Reginald. "Why, indeed, would he go all the way to Santa Eulalia when we have a perfectly fine beach right below?"

"Perhaps his mind was unbalanced," said Mark. "Suicide is hardly the act of a rational man."

"Let's not forget he was besotted with Leida Van Dolder, proof of an unbalanced mind if I ever heard one," said Dirk.

"In love with Leida?" said Reginald Cartlington in astonishment. "But didn't I hear that he was a vicar?"

"Yes," said Julia. "In the United States they call it a minister."

"You're quite right to be startled, Reg old boy," said Dirk. "A rather unholy alliance."

By this time, the entire table was buzzing with comments. Just the reaction I'd wanted. I saw Elizabeth smiling.

"A man of the cloth, like a doctor, is taught to have a tremendous respect for life," said Dr. Colin Robinson, a retired Harley Street surgeon. "To take any life, even one's own, is almost impossible for someone so trained."

"But why, if he was in love with our Leida, would he want to do away with himself?" asked Julia.

"I think that alone should be reason enough, my dear," said Dirk dryly. "The woman's a witch and whatever rhymes with it."

"Didn't I hear that she, in the crude parlance of the day, dumped him?" asked Dr. Robinson's wife, Sheila. "From what I understand, he wanted to marry Leida and take her back to America. She refused, and it broke his heart."

"Hearts don't break that readily, my darling," said Dr. Robinson.

"Spoken like a cardiologist, Colin, not a romantic," said Julia, smiling.

"Surely the two aren't antithetical, dear Julia," said the good doctor, looking at her in a way that made me feel sorry for Sheila. I looked at Dirk and noticed a small smirk of satisfaction that indicated he fully approved of Julia's preparation for her departure from his establishment.

That's what I found so unpleasant about small-town society—the dearth of participants inevitably results in playing musical beds, with someone always left standing alone.

"But what about the cocaine they found in his body?" said Sheila. "Couldn't that account for his bizarre behavior?"

"Which brings up my question of where he got the drug. Was he at a coke-snorting party? And if so, where and with whom?"

"That's easy," said Pamela Cartlington. "Right along our street there are at least three *tabernas* that are hangouts for the local drug culture."

Drug culture—an oxymoron if I ever heard one.

Francisco had cleared the plates and Maria was now serving her delicious filet of pork stuffed with dates and walnuts and cooked in port wine. As she placed my plate before me, she leaned over and whispered, "*Me encontre na cozinha*"—meet me in the kitchen.

Mmm, that sounded promising.

Conversation came to a virtual standstill as we all oohed and ahed at the flavors and delicacy of Maria's cooking.

"Elizabeth, why don't you tell us about your Casa dos Meninos?" said Dirk. "I don't think anyone here is aware of what simply marvelous work you are doing there."

Elizabeth's face turned pink. She was a shy person, but this was a topic upon which she could extemporize eloquently for hours. She described that she housed forty-three children of different ages, all of whom had been abandoned by their parents. The table was completely quiet as she described how the children came to her. When she told them about the child chained to the tree, there was an audible gasp from everyone. When she mentioned the prostitute in Portimao who considered contraception a violation of church law and so far had abandoned four newborn babies to Elizabeth, there was a great deal of head shaking and mumbles of "poor little things" from the women and "she ought to be horse-whipped" from the men.

"Can't the children be adopted?" asked Pamela.

"Only if there is parental consent, or with court consent if parents are not found." She explained that infants are desirable for adoption, but the older children are not, which means they spend their entire childhoods in Casa dos Meninos.

"Who supports your establishment, Elizabeth?" asked Dirk.

He was prompting her. I got the feeling that this was a planned scenario. Dirk a patron of an orphanage? It seemed so out of character for someone who never dropped an escudo in the hat of a beggar and immediately advised the police to clear off any homeless person he found sleeping in the village square.

Chilton chimed in. "Up to now, Elizabeth has been using her meager income and savings to support the children. The state gives her some money per child but it's a mere pittance." He looked at her with the kind of reverential awe one would bestow upon Mother Teresa if she happened to walk by.

"Chilton tells me you are trying to buy some land adjacent to your place to build an additional facility."

"Yes, for the old people," she said, her face sad.

"People in this country are starting to abandon their old people as well as their young."

There were sharp cries of "No!" and "Barbaric!"

"We now have three elderly—two eighty-year-old women and one ninety-year-old man—living with us. Their families could not afford to take care of them or even feed them. So they just threw them out onto the streets. I want to have a home for them so they can live out their lives in dignity and comfort. And I plan to have the children and elderly living together. It would create a more natural situation and would engender familial relationships that would be good for everyone."

"Capital idea."

"Wonderful."

"However, Elizabeth needs financing to buy and build, and Chilton here has established a Casa dos Meninos Foundation Fund for that purpose," said Dirk. "Chilton is a retired tycoon from Bournemouth, you know, and he's seen fit to start the Foundation and keep it going with his own money."

Wait a minute. He's financing it? Something has to be in it for him. What and when is the payoff?

"Chilton, old chap, why don't you tell everyone about the fund-raising ball that's taking place next week at the Dona Felipa? It's one hundred pounds a ticket, all going to the worthiest of causes. I don't think you've publicized it enough, Chilton, and I'm certain a number of people here would be happy to attend if they knew about it. Julia and I are going, of course."

That answers my question, but also brings up another. What's going on here? Dirk the philanthropist? It's not a fit. Dirk lived one of the most self-centered, utterly selfish lives imaginable and this eleemosynary posture was totally out of character. But it did the trick. Within minutes, every couple there had asked to buy tickets. Chilton's slightly miffed look at Dirk's criticism turned to a 250-watt glow when people began handing him checks. Elizabeth's face reflected quiet pleasure.

When all the business was completed, Dirk rang the little Georgian silver bell next to his plate and Maria came in triumphantly bearing her famous Grand Marnier soufflés. After revelling in this exquisite delicacy, we all adjourned to the living room for coffee. A great meal, great wine, and a good deed are a marvelous combination to make one feel totally self-satisfied. The sense of well-being in the room was almost palpable. Mark came over and I excused myself "just for a moment," which he figured was powdering-my-nose time, but I headed for the kitchen.

Maria pulled me over to a corner of the huge pantry. She and I have been good friends for years. She has a soft spot for me since I gave her the use of my house for her daughter's *casamento* when Dirk refused to allow his home to be used for anything so potentially riotous as a wedding.

"*Meu filho*, my son, he goes to one of the *tabernas* Senhora Cartlington talks about. He is a good boy, a student at the university. He was *amigo* to the *pobrecito* who died."

"Can I speak with him?" I asked. "Will he be there later tonight?"

"*Sim*, he is there every night. It is the Lido Bar. His friends are there, they talk, they sing. They are young and carefree, but Manuel, he is *muito miserio* about the young American's death. He says it is *mal, injustica.*"

"Can you get word to him that I would like to talk with him tonight, Maria?"

"*Sim*," she said, "I will phone him now."

"There's no need to tell Senhor Dirk or anyone about this, Maria. Let this be just between you and me, *muito privado, Pois?*"

She smiled and nodded. I hugged her and returned to the party. I saw Mark sitting with Elizabeth and Chilton. Both men jumped up when I came towards them, and Mark indicated the seat next to him on the couch.

"Since I know you never discuss business after sundown, Mark, I don't need to worry about being an unwelcome interruption, do I?"

"Miss Rhodes, or may I call you Emma—you could never be anything but welcome anywhere," said Chilton with a smile and, incredibly, a small bow. I looked at Elizabeth and Mark to see if they were as amused by his David Niven routine as I was. Not a blip on either face. I couldn't believe it; the guy was positively oozing unction and they were buying it. Or maybe they were too polite to show their feelings.

"Mark is coming out to Silves tomorrow to go over the land and the details of acquisition," said Elizabeth. "Emma, it would be lovely if you could come with him and I could show you the Casa and the children."

"That would be super, Emma," said Mark warmly.

"Yes, indeed, Miss Emma," said Chilton. "Your presence would add a ray of sunshine to the proceedings."

Gag me with a spoon. The guy's incredible.

I said I'd be happy to go. I wanted to see Elizabeth's home and get a closer look at Mr. Congeniality and his Foundation Fund. I told Mark that I was tired and would see them all the next day, said my proper farewells to the guests and my thanks to the host, and headed out.

I found a parking space right on Rua da Alegria, which translated roughly into Street of Joy, an apt name for a strip with four *tabernas*. Like so many of the town's streets, it was an acute hill just wide enough to fit two VWs coming each way or one Mercedes going wherever it wanted which meant I had to park half on the narrow sidewalk, about six feet from the nearest building. I started to walk down the street counting doorways to find the Lido Bar—the third from the top, Maria had told me. You would think I merely had to look for the neon sign that spelled out the name of the establishment. Forget it. The entire street was dark except for street lights.

When I first came to Vila do Mar, I was told that the *carniceiro*, where one bought meat, was right next to the *padaria*, where one got bread, and they were both right next to the *correio*. Well, I figured that would be easy. I knew where the *correio* was because I had been there many times to pick up my mail. I must have gone up and down the street four times looking for signs and storefronts. Forget it. Why did they need signs when everybody knew where they were? Why did they need display windows when everyone knew what they sold? There were doorways—that was it. You found the *padaria* by following your nose to the source of the marvelous aroma of fresh baking. The butcher shop was identified by the beaded curtain in the doorway that was meant to keep the flies out, only nobody bothered to tell that to the flies.

The general attitude toward insects in the Algarve was that if you ignored them, they did not exist. I always tried to adopt the native customs, but tolerance of bug life was one you had to be born to; it was not an acquired taste. I developed a reputation for eccentricity when I brought in a roll of screening and had the local carpenter make screens for all my windows to keep out flying insects. As for prevention against the *formigas*, little black ants that were the scourge of the Algarve, you sprayed Baygon, a Bayer product, and that did the job. You wish. The only thing that worked was eternal vigilance.

I entered the unmarked doorway that brought me into the Lido Bar. The sounds of Willie Nelson resounded off the whitewashed walls, attesting to the international appeal of country western music. A long bar covered one side of the room, and the tables were filled with jeans-clad young people in their twenties who, from the thick smog that hung low in the air, must each have been chain smoking all evening. I could never understand the heavy cigarette use that went on all over a continent of otherwise health-conscious people. Europeans were into yogurt and full-grained breads long before we Americans were. They had always been believers in the therapeutic importance of certain waters and mud baths prevalent in spas throughout Europe. Yet they totally ignored all the warnings about smoking.

I stood at the door of the taberna, hoping Manuel would spot me. Unlike my usual drop-dead-entrance goal when I came into a new room, this time my aim was to be innocuous. I had changed from the pink silk and pearls; if I'd walked in wearing that outfit I'd get lots of comments but no conversation. I'm a tad older (O.K., maybe more than a tad) than the habitués, but with my jeans and cotton sweater plus the twenty-five-watt lighting, I fit in reasonably well with the clientele.

"Miss Rhodes?"

I turned to see a tall young man with a black beard and mustache and those haunting, soft, dark green eyes that make Portuguese men so attractive. He was wearing jeans and a red-and-black handknit sweater with the Portuguese rooster logo. He had an intelligent face that conveyed kindness and a bearing that conveyed strength. I liked and trusted him on sight.

"Manuel?"

He smiled and motioned me over to a table where a young man and woman were seated. I had thought we would be alone, but perhaps the additional company would prove even more productive.

I sat down and he introduced me. "This is Rafael and Brigida." We all smiled and shook hands. Rafael was a dark-skinned, slight young man who looked nervous. The young woman was very pretty, a fact she seemed to be trying her damnedest to counteract in case you should, God forbid, think she was just a frivolous airhead. Her un-made-up face had that intense "I must save the world" look and her long dark hair appeared to be totally unfamiliar with either scissors or comb.

"I thought you might like that they're here as they were also friends of Peter's," said Manuel.

He spoke English with only a slight accent.

"That's fine," I said. But I noticed they looked somewhat blank as we spoke.

"Sorry," said Brigida haltingly, "but we have not much English."

"*Não problema. Falamos Portuguese*," I said.

They looked surprised and delighted. "*Fala bem*," said Rafael. I thanked him for the compliment and told him I speak well because I consider it ungracious to live in a country and not make the effort to learn the language.

"*Não como os Inglesos*," said Brigida, and we all laughed. No, not like the English who can spend their entire lives in a country and never bother to learn more than the working rudiments of the language, just enough to get along with the servants and shopkeepers. Perhaps it comes from the hundreds of years of colonialism when they moved into countries bringing with them the supposedly superior British culture and regarding the locals as ignorant

44

inferiors—so why even bother to learn their primitive patois?

"*Por favor*," said Rafael, "I would like for you to speak English. You see, it is much important that we learn." We ended up conversing in a polyglot Portuguese-English that seemed to work fine for all of us.

"Peter Belling was a wonderful guy. We all loved him," said Manuel.

"*Não dura a bem*," said Rafael sadly.

"Good doesn't last"—a fitting epitaph.

They told me how they had met Peter on the beach one Sunday and had admired his powerful swimming. They struck up a conversation, found him *muito simpatico*, and asked him to join their *sardinhas assadas* barbecue. After that, they became a steady quartet. Peter's *pensão* was three doors down from their favorite *taberna* and they met here often. They developed a tremendous respect for him.

"He was a man of the church and very learned," said Manuel, "but not one of those self-righteous *religiosos* who made you feel sinful. He was just, well, one of the guys."

"What about Leida?" I asked.

Rafael made a grimace. "That *puta*? She is usually spending her time with the other *malcriados*."

Malcriados meant "poorly brought up people" and is considered a major insult in a country where politeness is revered. A *puta* is a whore.

I wasn't surprised at their disdain for Leida, because to know her was not to love her. Except for Peter.

"I heard that he was madly in love with her," I said.

Manuel shrugged. "Yes, he was taken with her. But I think it was more infatuation than love. He had never met anyone like her before."

"Who did?" said Brigida. "She's an *unica*—one of a kind, thank God."

"I heard that he was obsessed by her."

"I think she appealed to the reformer in him, the man of God's wish to save a fallen soul, you know," said Manuel thoughtfully.

"Would he have killed himself if she dumped him?"

"*Nunca!*" they answered in unison. Never. "It is impossible for someone like him to kill himself at all," said Manuel.

"We are all first of our families to attend university," said Brigida. "Our parents have known only hard labor and poverty, and we are their bridge to a world that is incomprehensible to them. It is hard to be a bridge with each foot in a different world, not knowing quite who and what you are. But Peter was a secure, well-balanced man who knew exactly who he was and where he was going." She smiled ruefully. "We all envied him that. Such a person does not commit suicide," she said emphatically.

"But what about the note?"

They looked thunderstruck. "He left a note? The papers never mentioned that."

I told them the contents of the note.

"It is in his handwriting?" Manuel asked.

I nodded. "Unmistakably."

They shook their heads.

"But what does he mean, 'I tried to help and I failed?'" asked Rafael.

"You know how Peter wanted to help everyone," said Manuel. "Perhaps he believed he could not do enough. For a man of God, the goals are much higher than for the rest of us."

"What about the cocaine?" I asked.

They looked mystified. I guess the *comandante* decided to keep a lid on anything that smacked of sordidness so as not to scare off the *turismo*.

"The autopsy turned up a large quantity of cocaine in his body," I told them.

"*Impossivel*," said Manuel firmly. "Peter wouldn't touch the stuff. He hated drugs—which is why he used to get so angry at what goes on over there"—and he inclined his head towards a table in the corner where two men were deeply involved in what looked like a business discussion.

"That's your local cocaine *mercado*," he said disdainfully. "You can buy it like you buy rice at the supermarket."

"If it's that overt, I must assume *el chefe* is aware of these activities," I said.

"Of course," said Brigida. "But he never comes in here. If he did, he might have to take official steps."

"So he ignores the negotiations," I said, "but I'll bet the negotiators don't ignore him."

Manuel said bitterly, "Of course, they have their own cozy arrangement with our *polícia*. That used to burn Peter's ass." (Which is a rather free translation of Manuel's words.)

"Did Peter make his anger apparent to the corner table?" I asked.

"Big time!" said Manuel. "He felt everyone must take a stand against evil and that passivity is tantamount to collusion. We tried to tell him that may go in America, but in Vila do Mar, only silence is safe."

I knew that *el chefe* was not above taking a few escudos here and there to, as he put it, make life easier for people. He had even convinced himself that he was a public benefactor. Closing his eyes to overtime parking, cutting through the horrendous town bureaucratic red tape to get someone a permit, allowing a fishmonger to illegally park his truck at the *Mercado de Peixe*. I always saw it as harmless, small-town crookedness involving victimless crimes, and I not only tolerated it but took advantage of it. Drug dealing, however, was no longer in the realm of petty infractions. Nor was it just simple one-on-one accommodations to a citizen's needs. Drug dealing involved a network, and it was certainly not a victimless crime.

"*Pois*, Manuelito, how did a small sardine like you hook such a gorgeous fish? How about introducing me to your sexy friend?"

It was one of the men from the corner table. He spoke in Portuguese but the leer was international.

I looked at him coolly. "*Mas, senhor, eu náo tenho vontade de conhece-la.*"

47

He turned bright red.

"*Fala Portugues!*"

My three tablemates were grinning from ear to ear.

"The lady speaks Portuguese better than you do, Carlos," said Manuel, "and as she says, she has no wish to know you. So bug off."

He was visibly embarrassed and tried to apologize but I just looked at him silently and he slunk off.

"You know that burro, Manuel?"

"Of course, Emma. This is not New York. Everyone knows everyone in Vila do Mar. Carlos has been a troublemaker since we were kids. He is a stupid burro, but crafty."

"The ideal qualifications for a small-time drug dealer," I said. "But who's the big guy—who is his supplier?"

"That's what Peter wanted to know," said Manuel. "He was in a big anger always to find out where the drugs were coming from. He asked everyone."

"You mean Peter went around town asking people to give him the name of the local drug lord?" I was incredulous. "You mean like you'd try to find a plumber?"

"His approach was somewhat simplistic," said Manuel, "but he was very brave and deeply committed."

"He should have been committed, all right. That's not brave, that's brainless," I said in disgust. "And what did he plan to do if he found the big drug honcho? Make a citizen's arrest?"

They looked puzzled. That wasn't a concept understood here.

"He said he wouldn't bother with *el chefe* but would take the matter at once to Interpol."

It was a wonder Peter Belling lived past the age of twenty-one. It sounded as if he saw himself as a cross between Don Quixote and Batman. That kind of self-righteous pure naïf would not exactly have been Mr. Popularity, especially among those who got their kicks out of living on the edge, which often included a bit of coke snorting, a description that would fit almost the entire crowd

I ran with in the Algarve. I never could understand how otherwise intelligent and often highly achieving individuals had a need to risk their health and lives by shoving an illegal poison up their noses in order to inject a temporary "high" into a life that was usually about as good as you could get.

I learned the futility of lecturing them and instead just got the hell out of any party where nose candy was the treat of the evening.

"Are you thinking as we are, Emma? That Peter's questioning made him very unpopular and possibly dangerous to whoever is bringing drugs into our village?" asked Manuel.

"And that perhaps Peter did not kill himself but was helped to do so?" added Rafael.

Yes, I am, but by whom? Whoever it is, that person is very rich and lives extremely well—and I know everyone in the local area that fits that description. I hate the idea—but it must be someone I know.

Brigida looked at me very sharply. "*Faz favor*, Emma, why are you wanting to know all this about Peter?"

I truly disliked dissembling, but happily was saved by Manuel.

"She is a writer. My mother says she will write a book about it."

They looked at me with respect. People were always impressed with authors, whereas investigators were rated on a par with process servers, bail bondsmen, and washroom attendants. I got up to leave.

"*Ta lug*, everybody. Thanks very much for your help."

"You will try to find out the truth about Peter?"

"I'll try," I answered.

"Please keep in touch with us, Emma," said Manuel. "We cared about Peter and we do not like to think his death should be a lie."

Chapter Three

MARK PICKED ME up early the next morning in one of his uncle's Mercedes. Dirk had three—one for his exclusive use, one for the servants to use for marketing, and a spare for guests.

Mark looked like Ralph Lauren would have wanted his models to look but never could. It took generations of breeding to instill that mien and carriage of total assurance and grace. He wore a gray tweed jacket that undoubtedly had the name of the custom tailor sewn into the side pocket, gray flannel slacks, a white shirt with pale gray stripes, and a red paisley ascot. Not every man could carry this off at nine in the morning, but he looked more comfortably at ease than the investment bankers I knew who wore three-thousand-dollar jackets over jeans in order to achieve the calculated casual egalitarian look but ended up looking like men whose wives forgot to lay out their clothes the night before.

"Mark, you look positively splendid."

He eyed the fawn-colored suede pants I had Gloria help zip me into, the moss-green silk Liberty shirt with Hermes scarf, and the Valentino brown blazer I was wearing and said:

"You look pretty smashing yourself."

If Graham had been picking me up at nine for a trip to Silves, I would have pulled on jeans and a sweater at ten to nine. But for Mark, this was a business as well as pleasure trip and the English of a certain class are still sticklers for proper attire. If I read him wrong and he showed up in true

Alga
seco

mos
clea
that

esca
liter
and
dem
grad
cour
have
you
don
ther
Mod
has
elev
the

Cynthia Smith

inhabitants fled to the castle atop the hill
town, an edifice that still stands to...
bedraggled and overgrown.

The Portuguese are not big on m...
outside of the larger cities. Unli...
French departments of touris...
casual about those relics of...
attract tourists who need...
areas. Silves is a classi...
castle atop the bill, t...
a thirteenth centu...
of the outstand...
Outside of to...
fifteenth-c...
declared...
can't...

Muslim culture and regarded as a more important city than Lisbon. Its fall came about from the mixture of religious fervor and pure greed which characterized the Crusades.

In 1187, after Saladin's defeat and the Saracens took Jerusalem, the Pope appealed to Christendom to save the Holy Land from the infidels and the Third Crusade began. Dom Sancho I, the King of Portugal, shrewdly saw his chance to engage some major help in clearing the Moors out of the Algarve. When a fleet of German and English Crusaders stopped at Lisbon on their way to Jerusalem, he suggested they attack Silves, tempting them with the prospect of loot from the vast riches of this wealthy city, giving them the pious justification of a holy mission to destroy infidels.

On July 16, 1189, the combined fleets of the Crusaders and Portuguese sailed from Lisbon. Five days later, they arrived in Silves and attacked the lower city while the

overlooking the
day, albeit a bit

aintaining historic sites
ke the savvy English and
n, the Portuguese are very
the nation's past that would
raisons d'etre for visiting specific
case in point. Besides the neglected
here are the somewhat tatty remains of
y Gothic cathedral that is considered one
ing religious monuments of the Algarve.
wn a lonely open-air pavilion that shelters a
ntury stone lacework cross that has been
a national monument of incalculable value. If you
ind it, one of the local kids will volunteer as a guide for
w escudos. This kind of laid-back approach to national
monuments is one of the charms of Portugal. If it is a ruin,
it looks like one. I find a special beauty in the simplicity of
an ancient building that looks ancient and untouched, much
like the elegance of an older woman who has shunned the
artificial youth of cosmetic surgery. I enjoy standing in a
quiet ruin and feeling myself back there in time, a sense that
is impossible when you are surrounded by groups of tourists
and the multilingual voices of their guides. I don't need it to
be totally restored and dolled up; I use my imagination to
envision what it was.

The siege of Silves lasted six gory weeks during which
the Crusaders torched the port, the city, and the people.
And when the beaten Moors offered to surrender the city to
Dom Sancho if the surviving inhabitants would be allowed to
leave with whatever possessions they could carry, the holy
men with the brilliant red crosses of God on their chests
refused. Instead they rapaciously stripped the citizens of
everything they had and then sacked the city mercilessly for
three days until a disgusted Dom Sancho drove them back to
their ships. Silves was one of those unfortunate cities that
seemed to invite disaster. Once an imortant port, the Rio

Arade suddenly became mysteriously silted, making it unnavigable, and the great earthquake of 1775 completed the job of destruction.

Now Silves was a lovely, quiet hilltop town with moss-topped tile roof houses, flower-filled gardens, narrow cobbled streets where roosters strutted and dogs slept in doorways. You could tell a lot about a people by their treatment of dogs. I didn't ever remember seeing a scrawny mutt, because the kindly Portuguese fed and romped with the dogs who roamed the beaches and streets.

We arrived in time for the open-air produce market near the medieval bridge that spans the river and picked up a bag of figs and olives to bring to Elizabeth.

She was in the garden in front of Casa dos Meninos when we arrived and came toward us with her arms full of flowers and a welcoming smile.

"Emma, Mark—how wonderful that you got here. And so early, too. How do you like my garden? Aren't my flowers lovely?" she said with pride.

But I wasn't listening because I was lost in the view. The house stood atop a hill overlooking sweeping golden fields and groves of almond trees divided by a random pattern created by old stone walls. Workers were kneeling and some standing in the fields. I heard church bells in the distance, and it all looked like Rosa Bonheur's painting "The Angelus" that hung on my third grade classroom wall.

"It must be enchanting in January when the almond blossoms are in bloom," I said.

"It's a sight I never tire of," she said. "Do you know the legend of how all these almond trees came here? The Scandinavian bride of an ancient Moorish king was so homesick in the palace of Silves that her husband feared she would die of a broken heart. Unable to make it snow in the warm Algarve, he planted groves of almond trees, and the sea of pinky-white blossoms every January and February was so enchanting that she made a miraculous recovery."

Mark was taken with the house. "What a charming place. Was it a farmhouse?"

"Yes," said Elizabeth. "This was once a very large *quinta*. The house and all the land as far as you can see was a prosperous farm that belonged to an absentee owner who lived in Lisbon. I was on holiday here staying at a *pensão* in Silves, walking and bicycling around the countryside. I came upon this house and fell in love with it on sight. Fortunately for me, this was during the 1974 revolution when the communists pushed out the remnants of Salazar's rather repressive regime. The owner, figuring his property would be confiscated shortly, sold it to me quickly and very cheaply. But the Portuguese are such a kindly gentle people, which is one of the reasons I decided to spend my life here. Most revolutions are bloody, but the only red you saw here in 1974 were the red carnations the revolutionaries sported in their rifle barrels. Some farms in the Alenteajo were confiscated by the peasants and eventually returned. But no one ever bothered me."

"And all the land?" asked Mark. I noticed his voice had changed from idle curiosity to professional interest. It was daytime now, working hours for our diligent real estate agent.

"I didn't need nor want that much acreage so the owner sold it to adjacent farmers."

"I bet you're sorry now, Elizabeth," I said. "If you had it, you wouldn't be doing business with Mark for your expansion plans."

She shook her head. "No, those fields wouldn't be suitable for my purposes. They're too far removed from the main house. I need the land and building across the road"— and she pointed to a large sprawling structure that looked like it had once been a school.

"My dear, it's poor business to mention the word 'need' to the seller." There was Chilton upon us with his words of wisdom. "It tends to drive the price up, don't you know?" he said with that self-satisfied smirk often seen on the faces of fools who think they're being shrewd.

Tight little lines formed around Mark's mouth. "I don't know who you are used to dealing with, sir, but we do not do business like a Middle East bazaar. We've given you our word on the price and that's rock solid."

I do enjoy a creative put-down. Chilton's face turned a bright pink that clashed unbecomingly with various shades of orange he was wearing. He was obviously a no-taste type who thought color coordinating an outfit means everything must match instead of blend. I bet myself he was wearing orange socks and brown shoes. I peeked and I won.

"Would you like to see the house?" said Elizabeth quickly. She was one of those nice people who tried to change the subject or venue when she sensed a brewing brouhaha. Me, I adored a juicy contretemps. I would've loved to see Mark and Chilton go at it hammer and tongues. But Elizabeth was our hostess, and we dutifully followed her into the house.

The living room, or what the English refer to as "the lounge," had the warm, inviting look of a place that had been accumulated, not decorated. Natural leather couches and chairs that looked comfortable rather than stylish; colorful Beiriz rugs scattered about on the floors; and walls covered with local hand-painted tiles, colorful pottery plates, and pieces of gilded carvings of saints and cherubs that come from old churches. I recognized some of brother Hugh's lovely antiques and wondered what Chilton would do if he knew what Sotheby's would get for the French desk in the corner.

Elizabeth showed us her bedroom, which was at the other end of the house. It was furnished simply, but with great charm. The guest bedroom was next to hers, but I noted she stood at the threshold to prevent us from entering.

"This is Chilton's, isn't it?" I asked.

"Why, yes," she said. "How did you know?"

"It's that cologne he uses that smells like lemon and disinfectant."

She laughed. "That's not scent, that's Chilton's carpet disinfectant spray. He has mysophobia—fear of getting his feet dirty. That's why I stopped you from going in. No one's allowed in with shoes on. It's a silly harmless thing that's merely an inconvenience for him," she said like a mother excusing her child's mischievous behavior.

The personal profile of this guy gets worse and worse. The adjoining bedrooms made me wonder if Elizabeth was allowing her emotional needs to blind her to her financial responsibilities. If there was another affiliation beyond the business one, then I would really worry about her when she got the inevitable big letdown. I could prevent the damage he could effect upon her business, but not her heart.

We went back to the living room. It was very quiet. "Where are the children, Elizabeth?" I asked.

She looked at her watch. "They should be back any moment for morning tea. They're out on bicycle trips with Chica and Rosa." As she spoke, we heard the sound of excited voices, and in seconds the door burst open and we were suddenly surrounded by what seemed like a hundred children all talking at once.

"*Ajudamos na colheita das frutas!*" they kept shouting in delight.

The short, sturdy dark-haired young woman—who we later learned was Chica—said with a great wide smile that was no less wonderful because of two missing bottom teeth, "Senhor Alvarez allowed them to help him pick the fruit from his orchard."

They all clustered around Elizabeth, intent on telling her joyfully of their adventure, and the love and pleasure in their faces and hers gave me a slight lump in the throat. I remembered when I was a child how important it was for me to find my mother there when I burst in with tales of the day's happenings. I looked over at Mark and saw his face mirroring my reaction. This was no institutional orphanage where the children were merely housed, clothed, and fed. This was truly their home. Mark and I looked at each other in silent agreement: we had to do all we could to keep it going and growing.

"Tell me about the gala benefit you're giving next week for the Casa," said Mark as we sat on the porch later having tea and scones with Elizabeth and Chilton.

"It will be held in the small ballroom of the Dona Felipa in Vale de Lobo," said Chilton enthusiastically. "There will be a superb dinner, dancing . . ."

Mark waved his hand. "That's unimportant. What is important is how much are the tickets and how many have you sold?"

"We're charging one hundred pounds per person."

"And how many persons have reserved to date?"

"Fifty," said Elizabeth triumphantly. "Isn't Chilton wonderful? That means five thousand pounds."

"Musn't forget, dear lady," said the great benefactor with a preening smile, "there will be expenses, of course."

I bet that's where you come in big time, Buster.

"That's a ridiculously paltry figure," said Mark in disgust.

"Mark, this isn't London; it's the Algarve," I said. "There aren't that many couples floating around here who can blow two hundred pounds in a night."

"There would be—if the attraction was great enough," he said with a smile. "How many do you think would come if Princess Anne was the guest of honor?"

There was a dumbfounded silence.

"You'd probably have busloads corning in from Faro to Lagos," I said. Suddenly a thought hit me. "You're Dirk's nephew. He has a number of brothers. Which one is your daddy?"

"The Duke of Sandringham." He paused. "I'm his eldest son."

Which meant Mark would be next in line for one of the oldest and wealthiest dukedoms in England.

I saw the awe on Chilton's face as he realized who Mark was.

"Then you are the Earl of Chelmsford," he said. I fully expected him to tug at his forelock at any minute. The English reverence for aristocracy amazes me, especially with the behavior of the so-called top of the heap, the royal family. It's hard to understand how British taxpayers are willing to bankroll the profligate lifestyle of a pack of fatuous lightweights whose sole contribution to the country consisted of visiting hospitals and opening fairs.

"Princess Anne may be a pal of yours," I said, "and I don't doubt the persuasive power of your charm, your lordship, but wouldn't next week be somewhat short notice for the royal calendar?"

He looked smug. "Right, but it so happens next week she's scheduled to ride with me at our place in the country. We're expecting about ten for the weekend—I could fly all of us down in my plane for the evening." And he looked at me. "And perhaps bring Emma back with us."

The prospect may sound enchanting, but having spent many a weekend at stately country homes, I'd decided no amount of fine wine and broiled kidneys could make up for the lack of central heating. I found I didn't enjoy trying to zip up my evening dress with fingers too frosty to function, and goose pimples tended to destroy the effectiveness of a décolletage. That stiff upper lip the English were so admired for was really, I suspected, just frozen in place. As far as making the trip in a private plane piloted by his future lordship, that was another of my no-nos. When about to be ferried through the atmosphere in a huge tin can, I needed to be secure in the knowledge that the person at the wheel was in tip-top shape and in no way impaired. If they were employed by a major airline, I knew someone was keeping check on them. But with a private aircraft, it was a bit rude to ask your host pilot how he fared on 'his last physical, and rather nerve-wracking to stand around before takeoff watching him knock down five martinis. I would only fly in a plane that had two on the flight deck. In case the top man lost control of any of his vital bodily functions, I would want to know there was a copilot to take over the lead seat.

"Mark, having Princess Anne would be fantastic," I said, ignoring his invitation. I figured we'd get to that later. "Chilton, you'd better get the drums going quickly to get the word out. Actually, all you probably have to do is alert Dirk and you can be sure that every Brit in the entire Algarve with a reasonably comfortable income will know within hours. The others will take out second mortgages. You know how you English love royals. When they hear about Princess Anne, you'll have to fight them off."

Then I had a thought. "Mark, who else will be in your planeload of fun-lovers?"

"Let's see . . ." he began, ticking off his fingers, "there's Freddy . . ."

"And he is?" I asked.

"The Duke of Westminster."

And one of the richest men in England. He owned the land under Harrod's, Liberty, Jaeger, and most of Bond Street. By the time Mark got through with his guest list, I thought Chilton would need a change of underwear. Elizabeth just looked bewildered.

"Chilton, I think you'd better ring up immediately and see if you can move the gala to the Grand Ballroom. With that glittering guest list, I think we can expand our horizons. Don't forget to notify all the international dethroned royalty in Estoril. They dearly love an occasion to wear their ribbons and tiaras."

I could see the cash registers gleaming from his eyeballs as he started to calculate the take from the benefit. I could also see that I'd have to make sure the right person benefits from the take. Elizabeth had told me that Chilton was a retired millionaire, a fine human being now totally devoted to good works, and she felt very fortunate that he chose to interest himself in her little Casa operation. The fact that he dressed like a tout and spoke with the overcareful diction of a person who was new to the use of polysyllables didn't cancel his tycoon credentials; good taste and education were no longer necessary qualifications for making money in England. It was the fine human being in him I couldn't seem to locate.

"I think Elizabeth is marvelous, but I don't share her high opinion of her friend," said Mark as we were driving home. "If that Chilton chap is handling the monies, someone had better be checking on the exchequer."

"It's in the works."

He looked at me quickly. "How?"

"The Casa's account is in Banco Espirito Santo. So are mine."

"Bank accounts are supposedly held confidential."

"Supposedly."

He smiled broadly. "Emma Rhodes, I'm beginning to think there's more to you than meets the eye—which is saying a lot because what meets the eye is pretty bloody marvelous."

The drive back to Vila do Mar from Silves was even better than the drive coming because there was now a relaxed relationship between Mark and me due to a common cause plus my awareness that the man had a mind. One of my failings (and I bet you thought I thought I was flawless) was my tendency to prejudge all members of the nobility and to assume, based on vast experience, that the bigger the title the smaller the brain. I was wrong here; the guy was sharp and what was more, extremely nice. Nice—that may have seemed like a weak and wimpy word that was hard to explain, but to paraphrase Supreme Court Justice Peter Stewart, I couldn't define it but I knew it when I saw it. Mark was bright, which made me wonder what he did besides handle small estate matters. I was a great believer in the direct question approach, but I didn't want to ask for fear he would rightfully demand a quid pro quo, and I was not about to launch into any details about my profession. I only revealed the details of my rather convoluted life to those whom I cared about and who were important to me. He wasn't in that league. Yet.

Chapter Four

AS I CAME into my house after Mark had dropped me off, the phone was ringing.

"Hello, my *hamoodie* cutie," bellowed a familiar voice. "So what's the matter, you don't need me so I don't hear from you? I'm getting Emma Rhodes withdrawal symptoms." It was Abba Levitar, who came after my parents on the list of my favorite people in the universe.

"You sound like a Jewish mother, Abba."

"I'm the next worse thing—a product of one. If I haven't made at least one person feel guilty today, I've failed."

"Where are you calling from?"

"My office. Where else would I be at this hour?"

"In your business, Abba, God only knows."

"In my business today, we can't even let Him know because some of our villains talk to the same God."

Abba was a top-ranking officer in the Israeli Mossad, one of the most effective and respected intelligence groups in the world.

"Listen *bubele*, this time I'm the one calling to ask for something. I'm in big-time need of some R & R. Usually I'm the one who tells my people when to get the hell away for some time off, but this time they're threatening a mass insurrection unless I get off their backs for a few weeks."

"I read in the papers that you're having a bit of bother in Israel," I said.

"So do you have a bed for me? And just so you know how much I need the rest and relaxation, I don't want the bed to be yours."

"Abba, you never have to ask. Come anytime. There's always a place for you."

"You think I'm some peasant putz? Even in Brooklyn we learned it's bad manners to drop in unannounced."

"Of course, Abba. Who could ever fault your impeccable manners? Like the last time I had dinner with you in Brussels and you told the waiter to remove the shredded shit from your plate because you didn't approve of julienned vegetables."

He roared with laughter. "O.K.. so I'm not one of Nature's noblemen. But I'm lovable. I'll be coming sometime tomorrow."

You never asked Abba exact details. First place, he didn't know from hour to hour where he'd be and how he'd get there. And second place, even if he did know, security prevented him from telling you.

Abba was an invaluable and beloved friend. Sex between us was strictly conversational (with him) and utterly unthinkable (to me). Abba was five feet six, weighed 250 pounds and looked like a friendly bear until you noticed the piercing eyes that could shift in seconds from dancing to dangerous. I was delighted that he was coming. Peter Belling's mysterious death was developing avenues of complexity, and now with the artful dodger Chilton to deal with, I could use some expert help. There was no one better than Abba; he was brilliant, discreet, and utterly trustworthy. The phone rang again and it was Graham.

"Hello, darling, it's maid's night out so I thought I'd do a *sardinhas assada* on the terrace." And then he added, "Bring your nightie in case it gets too late and/or you get too tiddly to drive home."

Grilled sardines were the local specialty, and at lunchtime red pottery braziers were outside all doorsteps and at all work sites, creating the literally mouth-watering aroma of charcoal-broiled fish. There were no McDonald's or Pizza Huts in town; the Algarvian working man's idea of brown bagging it was to bring a plastic sack of fresh sardines and grill them for lunch. These were not the tiny sardines you got in cans but were larger, more like smelts. They were taken from the sea and packed in boxes in coarse salt, which you scraped off before laying them on the fire. They required no seasoning or silverware to eat. You merely gobbled them down whole accompanied by chunks of bread to catch the little tickling bones and glasses of Dao red wine to smooth their passage along. Fancy Portuguese restaurants scorned having such peasant fare on their menus, but would supply them, albeit a little unwillingly, upon urgent request from people like me who preferred this simple succulent treat to the sauced-over fish dishes with French names.

"Graham, I accept your invitation . . . to dinner, that is. But about the sleepover, who the hell owns a nightie?"

I never understood why people got dressed to go to bed. The term "bedclothes," I believed, referred to sheets, and that was all I needed. I spent a fortune on Porthault linens because I loved the sybaritic pleasure of soft fabric against my body. If I could afford only muslin sheets, maybe I'd sleep in Dr. Dentons.

We ate out on the terrace next to the pool of Graham's sprawling house overlooking the ocean and beach at Santa Eulalia, which was about three kilometers from the center of town. We were sipping wine, and looking out at the line of fishing-boat lights studding the ocean horizon in a perfect match to the many stars in the sky. The air was so clear that the stars didn't twinkle but remained sharp lights. The marvelous fragrance of eucalyptus and wild lavender kept drifting by with the breeze. These scents are forever evocative to me of Portugal. It was one of those absolutely perfect Algarve evenings that I dreamed of during freezing nights in New York and damp ones in London. Graham and I just sat enjoying the lovely companiable silence of good friends.

"Great! I was hoping I'd get here before you two started fucking."

"Well, if it isn't our darling Leida," said Graham. "Who else would barge in uninvited with such a charming greeting?"

She plopped down on a chair next to Graham, who hadn't bothered to get up, and said, "I've been looking all over town for you two. Then I figured you must be home, near a bed," she said with the infantile giggle of a child who's just learned how to say *shit*.

"Well, I'm glad you found us," I said, and Graham arched his eyebrows incredulously, probably thinking either I'd lost my mind or found religion. "Graham, why don't you offer Leida a drink?"

He didn't move from his chair. "From the look of her, everybody in town has already offered her one. But if she feels she can't go on living without another, she damned well knows where I keep my liquor."

Anybody else would have either kicked him in the balls or departed hastily or both. But how could you take offense when your own offensiveness always provoked this sort of rudeness? You came to assume it was normal.

Leida walked inside to get herself a drink.

"Graham Adams, ever the gracious host," I said.

"To quote my father, who was revered on our street as the neighborhood pub philosopher, if you are shit, you get treated like shit."

"Words to live by," I said. "Please remember to keep me posted on his other eloquent aphorisms whenever they come to mind."

"I'd be delighted to," he said seriously, "but only when they're appropriate, of course."

"Of course."

Leida came out with a tall tumbler of vodka. There were no bubbles to indicate the presence of either tonic or soda. Oh, well; I didn't hear a car so I guessed she walked, which meant she'd be a threat to no one but herself.

"Leida, tell me about your poor lover," I asked.

She giggled. "Which one?"

"The one who killed himself, Peter what's-his-name."

Her face changed suddenly. For a moment, I couldn't read her expression, perhaps because it was unusual to see her exhibit any emotion other than the basics of anger, joy, and lust. Could it be sadness? Then I suddenly realized— my God, it was fear.

"Yes," she said. "It was terrible. He drowned himself." She gulped down half her drink.

I put on my best Riverside Memorial Chapel voice.

"I'm so sorry, Leida. Did you love him very much?"

The question obviously puzzled her. Of course, she didn't understand love. Her only relationships with men were sexual.

"He was O.K." Then she added with a smug smile, "He was crazy about me."

"Then what happened?"

She shrugged. "He just didn't understand."

The words in Peter's note: "There is obviously too much that I cannot understand."

I felt Graham watching me with a quizzical look.

"Leida, love," he said sweetly, "your glass is almost empty. Why don't you go in and get yourself a refill?"

As soon as she disappeared into the house, he turned to me.

"O.K., Miss Rhodes, you're hot on a case, aren't you?"

"How can you tell?"

"You don't give a flying fuck for Leida and suddenly you're acting like her big sister. Unless you've turned into Mother Teresa since I last saw you, your show of deep concern in what she calls a love life must have a reason."

Graham was the only person in Vila do Mar who knew what I did for a living. Our season of intimacy last year made pretense difficult, if not impossible, and also taught me to respect his integrity and discretion.

"Peter Belling's parents are in town and I've agreed to look into their son's death."

"I assume they don't accept the suicide verdict."

"Quite right."

"How much do you actually know about the circumstances surrounding his death?" he asked.

"Just what's in the official police report."

He smiled. "So much for privileged official information. But then *el chefe* always had a soft spot for you. In his case, a hard spot would be more accurate."

"How much do you know about it, Graham?"

"Enough to know the story sounded like a joint effort of the *Política* and *Turismo* so as not to make waves—an apt turn of phrase, you must admit."

He looked into his glass and then looked up at me and sighed. "You're undoubtedly planning to grill Leida mercilessly. Here I planned an evening of hot seduction, and instead it's turning into one of cool deduction."

"If it's any consolation, Graham, your efforts would've been in vain. I'm into celibacy at the moment. That is, until I settle on the designated lover of the season."

"Am I to deduce that I'm out of the running for the job?"

"Do you want me to give you the 'I like you lots and let's be good friends' routine?"

He groaned. "Spare me. I know the speech by heart."

"Yes," I said, "but from giving it, not hearing it. Consider this a learning experience—Graham gets rejected. It's an unprecedented occurrence, but it's time you understood what anguish you've been inflicting upon women for years. I don't know how many you've dumped since I've known you, but I know we're talking double digits."

Leida came in with another tumbler of straight vodka. I didn't know how she managed to stand erect, let alone move about. Perhaps it was genetic—her daddy was known to consume a full bottle in one sitting and still be able to walk away from the table with a semblance of dignity. When I was in Vila do Mar, I could easily handle three to four glasses of wine; you got inured to it very quickly because it was as prevalent in the Algarve as iced tea in Texas. Standing in every kitchen were three five-liter wicker-covered *garafoes* of white wine, red wine, and mineral water *sin gas* (no fizz). The very dry Algarve air had the same effect on your body, so your intake of fluids was necessarily high. Most of us kept sated with wine and water but there were many, like the Van Dolders, who filled their liquid quotas with booze.

"Peter really fell for you the very first time you met—which was right here on the terrace, wasn't it?" said Graham to Leida.

Now that he knew and approved of my mission, he was obviously going to lead the witness for me. She nodded happily.

"As I recall," he went on, "you came on rather strongly to the chap."

"He liked me a lot. We went back to my house after and fucked," she said matter-of-factly.

It wasn't that Leida was a nymphomaniac; she just thought that was what you did with men. Never having received any kisses in her life that were not carnal, she didn't understand affection. All conversation to her was either pre- or postcoital.

"I'll bet you showed him a thing or two, right? Leida knows more sexual positions than the Kama Sutra."

"Who's he?" asked Leida.

For a sweet, sensitive, and somewhat naïve young man like Peter Belling, Leida must have been an overwhelming experience—and highly flattering, no doubt. From what I'd heard of her behavior between the sheets, she undoubtedly introduced him to erogenous zones he never knew he had. The poor guy was hooked—he didn't stand a chance.

"Did you like him?" I gave up on love.

"Sure. He was nice to me. He brought me presents."

That alone would enshrine him in her Lovers' Hall of Fame. The only mementos she received from her usual suitors were black eyes.

"You saw each other pretty often, I bet."

"Oh, sure—almost every night." She giggled. "I told you he was mad about me."

"Did he ever take you to the Lido Bar?"

"Once in a while. But mostly he liked us to be home— you know, near the bed" —and she put on the kind of lascivious leer that was commonly seen in adolescent locker rooms. Graham rolled his eyes in disgust. If Leida's tales of the prowess and performance of her various lovers were true, then the Portuguese were breeding a race of supermen that can do more for the growth and international reputation of their small country than Prince Henry the Navigator and Magellan together.

"He was crazy about Adriana, too," she said. "But he was kind of upset about her," she said, looking puzzled. "That I wasn't married and she had no papa, I mean."

Poor pure, simple Peter. With his kind heart and normal nuclear family upbringing, how could he comprehend Leida's complete unconcern for such details?

"Were you with him the night he died?" I asked.

"No," she said quickly. She was lying.

"Did you ever bring Peter to Adriaan's?"

"No." She began to look slightly frantic. Lie number two.

Then it was as though a dark curtain came down over her face and it took on the look of sullen obduracy one sees on the visages of people of limited intelligence who are frightened. I'd obviously touched a nerve and she was terrified, which meant that further questioning tonight would be useless. But a meeting with Adriaan would not.

Chapter Five

IT WAS EASY for me to get to Adriaan. He was crazy about me. Not sexually, of course—I was too old for his taste. As I'd mentioned, Adriaan's preference ran to youth of any gender. I knew of a Swedish couple who were in the process of buying one of Adriaan's houses. They made the error of bringing along their lovely, blond, fourteen-year-old daughter to the final negotiations. They were about to write him a check when Adriaan said, "That wouldn't be necessary if you gave me your daughter." The nubile young thing blushed confusedly and the parents smiled at the old reprobate, thinking it was just a joke in bad taste. When they realized he was dead serious, they left in a huff with their daughter but without their house. Adriaan shrugged and the tale went into the town's large store of Van Dolder legend.

Adriaan liked me because I was smart; he had an abiding admiration for brains, which accounted for his contemptuous attitude toward his daughter.

I had phoned Adriaan to notify him of my arrival in town and he responded with delight and an instant invitation to lunch. I would have been happy to skip the meal since his table ran to heavy, gravy-soaked meats and fried potatoes. As a daily reader of *The New York Times*, *The London Times*, and *The Wall Street Journal*, all of which he subscribed to, he had to know about the importance of low-fat, high fiber diets. It wasn't that he was unaware of the existence of cholesterol; it was just that he considered himself so all-powerful and invulnerable that his arteries would not dare to fail him.

When I came in, his housekeeper, Santa, led me outside where my host awaited at the stone table on his magnificent balustraded terrace overlooking the ocean.

"Emma—you're looking as lovely as ever." He rose to plant on my lips a wet kiss that reeked of two hours of scotch. In front of him was a silver ice bucket and bottles of scotch, vodka, and mineral water *con gas*. He was dressed in his usual finery of slightly soiled chinos and once-white T-shirt. Vanity was probably the only vice of which he was not guilty.

"You're looking as well as ever, Adriaan, which is miraculous considering your lifestyle," I said.

He laughed. "I think I'll will my body to science. After I die at the age of a hundred and ten, they'll open me up and find out that a regimen of fats, alcohol, drugs, and sex is the secret of longevity that the world has been searching for—and the big killer is deprivation of all of the above."

Adriaan was a tall man in his sixties. His lean body and smooth skin were a tribute to genetics; another man not blessed with such superb antecedents who had lived Adriaan's dissolute existence would have been a ruin. Yet here he was—chipper, stalwart, and slightly smashed. It wasn't fair.

Adriaan was undeniably brilliant, and though every drinker swore that his faculties were totally unimpaired by liquor, Adriaan was the only one I knew for whom that was true. I was with him when he reeled into a local *taberna* where we ran into a smarmy but dull-witted young Englishman who had been renting one of Adriaan's properties for three consecutive summers.

"Adriaan," the Englishman said in a slightly nasal voice that he considered upper class although he sounded as though his sinuses needed draining. "I'd like to talk to you about buying the house I'm in."

Adriaan ordered another drink and then turned to him.

"Jimmy," he said, and the young man paled because he always insisted on James. However, he somehow sensed that this was not the moment to correct his landlord. "You remind me of the story of Lord Duveen and Samuel Kresge. Lord Duveen was the curator for Kresge, for whom he was trying to build an enviable art collection. Well, one day Kresge heard that Gainsborough's *The Blue Boy* was coming up for sale at Sotheby's. He contacted Lord Duveen and asked him to buy it for him. Duveen responded immediately, 'Mr. Kresge, you are not ready for *The Blue Boy*.'" Then Adriaan took a deep sip of his scotch, turned to the young man and said, "Jimmy, you're not ready for one of my houses."

And he didn't even slur a word.

We sat on the terrace while I had soda with vodka—I list the ingredients in order of quantity. I do not share Adriaan's capacity, and more than one drink gives me the lightheaded feeling of fuzziness that alcoholics love and I hate. I'm not a control freak; it's just that I can't bear it when my brain seems to stop communicating properly to my mouth and I get consonation and can't move my vowels. Perhaps if this was a purely social occasion and I was dealing with a less challenging mind I might go for two drinks, but alcohol has always been unimportant to me. I don't need it to switch my vert-button from intro to extra, nor to release my social inhibitions; I'm there already. I was born primed.

"Leida tells me you've been in Morocco."

He made a *moue*. "I tell her when I'm going, but not when I return. That's one of the ways to keep her from dropping in all the time. Tell me, do you barge in on your parents and violate their privacy whenever you feel like it?"

"The situations are hardly parallel, Adriaan. My parents and I usually have an ocean between us so 'I just happened to be in the neighborhood' visits are unrealistic. Leida lives within driving distance."

He sighed. "Yes, that was a big mistake. I thought living in separate houses would allow us to live separate lives. But with her, it would have to be separate cities."

"Unfortunately, that was your unilateral choice, Adriaan. She, on the other hand, dearly wishes to be part of your life. After all, she has lots of fatherless years to make up for."

Hers was the poor-little-rich-girl story with Leida as the pawn of bitterly divorcing parents. Her mother was a member of the archaic Swiss aristocracy and an international beauty who seemed to have trouble grasping the conventional mores of modern life, especially that of marital fidelity. Adriaan's punishment of his wife for her continual cuckolding was to divorce and disgrace her publicly for adultery and deprive her of her daughter by suing for and winning full custody of a child in whom he was totally uninterested. Mission accomplished, he put the motherless little girl into a series of boarding schools, leaving himself free to pursue an increasingly profligate life all over the world. When Leida reached eighteen and there were no more schools for her to attend, he finally brought her home, which was at that time Vila do Mar. Not that he took her into his home, but instead installed her in her own house so that she wouldn't interfere with his unconventional sexual activities. But apparently this wasn't working.

Santa summoned us for lunch and we moved into the dining room and sat on heavily brocaded chairs at his vast dark mahogany table, and I once again marvelled how so intelligent a man could live in so foolishly furnished a home. The house was magnificent, but the decor totally ignored the location. In Palm Beach, Biarritz, the Riviera, and areas where the climate was temperate during the winter and hot in summer, even the most imposing mansion was decorated to give a feeling of cool, light airiness. Here in this huge house, hanging over the beach in a sunny resort town where it was warm most of the year and blazing in the summer, was furniture that he brought intact from his home in Amsterdam. Very suitable to the damp and cold Dutch weather, it was totally inappropriate for here. Faded horsehair couches, heavily carved sideboard and tables, and walls hung with tapestries and large paintings. Of course, the wall hangings were Aubussons and the paintings bore signatures such as Chagall, Rouault, Vuillard, and Matisse. Adriaan was justly reputed to have a priceless art collection and I knew that he, like many museums, had a large storeroom filled with additional treasures for which there was no display room. It wasn't that Adriaan had the appreciative, loving eye and driving lust of a collector; he merely had the greedy heart of an amasser. If something was deemed valuable, he had to have it because no one else deserved it more.

We chatted about world conditions, which was always a hoot because Adriaan's politics were slightly to the right of Attila the Hun. When Salazar died, he went into mourning for a month. Me, I thought dictatorships may have been nice to visit because of the low rate of crime (which, unfortunately, was usually accompanied by the high rate of summary executions) but I wouldn't want to live there, nor could I understand how anyone would.

Santa brought in *calde verde*, the ubiquitous Portuguese soup that was made of kale, potatoes, garlic, and olive oil. Like most peasant dishes, the contents varied with the cook. She went back to the kitchen to get more bread for Adriaan's dedicated mop-up operations when we heard the phone ring, and she returned with the bread and the announcement that Senhor Adams was on the phone. To my surprise, Adriaan excused himself. It must have been important if someone with his old-world manners would desert a guest at the table to take a call. I heard his voice raised but unfortunately couldn't make out any words other than "*milhao* escudos." He returned to the table a number of minutes later looking irritated and so rattled that he forgot to apologize for his absence.

Obviously aware that he had to say something, he mumbled, "Graham asked me to say hello."

"That couldn't have gotten you so upset," I said.

He was taken aback by my direct challenge to discuss the subject of his conversation. Sure, it was pushy, but how else could I collect facts for my mental databank? I knew the correct behavior would have been for me to ignore his change in mood and give him the choice of explaining or ignoring it. But then I might never have known what caused the sparks between Adriaan and Graham. Of course, you could say that was none of my business—but how would I know it wasn't unless I knew what it was? My work was like doing jigsaw puzzles—you fit all the pieces together until a complete picture emerged. The only difference was, nobody handed them to me in a neat package—I had to go out and collect all the pieces.

"Graham and I have some business together. Sometimes we don't agree on terms," he said brusquely.

"Really? I thought Graham retired from property development and management after he made his killing in Praia do Plata."

He was getting irritated with my persistence. Tough noogies.

"It doesn't involve property."

"Aha," I said with a smile. "Just money."

I shouldn't have been surprised at this unlikely partnership. Graham had always admired Adriaan as a businessman but abhorred him as a person. In their world of the high and mighty (high finance and mighty greed) that wouldn't preclude working together. As I learned from the many high rollers I knew, money has no morality and it was perfectly acceptable to make deals with someone you wouldn't allow in your front door as long as it was profitable.

"Daddy, you're home!" Guess who came flying in. Leida, her face filled with joy and love, threw her arms around her father just as the last piece of dunked bread reached his mouth.

Picking the prized tidbit off the side of the table where it had flown, Adriaan's face did not register that of a fond parent.

"What are you doing here?" he asked, glowering at her.

Her elated face disappeared as though he had flicked a remote control, and I felt a pang of pain for her. She recovered in a few seconds and threw some papers on the table.

"I didn't know you were home. I just came by to drop off these papers to show you that Forte de San João made thirty percent more profit this year than last."

She looked at him beseechingly, like a dog seeking its master's approval.

His face cleared instantly and he smiled broadly.

"Well, that's very fine news. Well done, Leida."

She had learned to press the right button, which, although it might not get his affection, was certain to get his attention. Money.

When Leida first arrived in town five years ago and Adriaan was finally forced to make the acquaintance of his daughter, he looked for signs of his intelligence in his only offspring. But Leida's mother suffered from the usual family brain drain caused by too many years of intermarriage. As inevitably must be faced by brilliant men who married beautiful but brainless women because their egos needed the buttressing of having showpiece wives, the punishment was having dumb children. They seemed to think that the sheer magnitude of their intelligence would overcome the dilution of their smart gene pool and were furious and incredulous to find that Nature was a greater power than they. Leida was heavily deficient in the brain department, but Adriaan finally found one area of expertise—her mind worked like a cash register. Joyfully and with relieved parental pride, he put her in charge of running one of his rental villa developments. She fulfilled his fondest hopes in the ledger sheet department but was a total bust in the people relations department. She handled money like a whiz but didn't have a clue about handling human beings and soon succeeded in antagonizing staff, suppliers, and guests. Like all minimally capable managers who did not know how to motivate people by direction and leadership, she thought bullying conveyed authority. Her method of dealing with those who worked for and with her was to bark orders and cruelly demean them publicly by bellowing blame for real or fancied errors. This method of management could have played havoc with the business but for the fact that the dignity and strong work ethic of the Algarvians resulted in their resolution to do their jobs well and ignore her totally.

"Just a chip off the old block," I said.

Leida's face became suffused with such joy that I stiffened to face what daddy dearest might say to her next.

"Well, she had better be. After all, when I die, she'll have to manage everything."

"Oh, Daddy, please don't say that," wailed Leida. "You know how upset that makes me when you talk about dying!" And the poor thing ran out of the room sobbing and soon we heard her car start and then take off.

He smiled with total self-satisfaction. "That's always a good way to get rid of her, I find. She gets very perturbed whenever I talk about death."

"Adriaan, when they open your body up when you're a hundred and ten, they may find all your other organs normal—but they'll find your heart is made of stone."

It didn't bother him a whit. "Oh, come, come, she's a grown woman—she should be familiar with life and death."

"The only thing she's not familiar with is love. You're her father, for God's sake—she cares about you; you're all she has. Her mother is dead—she lost you once before when she was a little girl—now she's dreadfully afraid to lose you again. That shouldn't be so hard to understand, Adriaan. You may be heartless, but you're certainly not brainless."

I may be the only person who, to use up my cliché quota for the week, tells it like it is and doesn't pull any punches. Adriaan Van Dolder was the largest owner of town real estate, which included stores, restaurants, and housing developments plus a few small factories producing furniture and local crafts, which meant half the town residents worked for him and the other half wished they did. Like many shrewd, successful entrepreneurs, he had learned the power of money in manipulating people: pay them generously so that they become accustomed to a more luxurious lifestyle and they soon become enslaved by the fear of losing it. Not only had his employees fallen into that trap but so had village officials who had become used to the pleasures of his largesse. Did I leave anybody out? Adriaan had a ferocious temper and was rumored to have whipped a local man to death and escaped punishment by paying a large sum to the victim's family and making a huge contribution to the *policía*'s benevolent association, which at the time had the chief of police as the sole member. He affects such a lord-of-the-manor pose that I would have expected him to demand wedding night *droit du seigneur* of the young maidens in town except they were no longer his gender of preference. Everyone was afraid of him and no one dared to disagree or challenge or criticize him. Except me.

"Perhaps you're right, Emma. Maybe I am a little hard on her. But to tell you the truth, I'm not sure I really love her. I sure as hell don't like her—who could? All and all, she's not the kind of daughter I would have wanted."

I shook my head in wonder. "And whose fault is that? You sent her away to be brought up by lord knows who, ignored her for most of her life, and now you're displeased with the results? You owe her big time, Adriaan. You can't fake feelings that aren't there, but at least you can treat her with some small degree of kindness."

"Emma, you're a very wise person and a very good one. I, too, am brilliant—but I make no claims to goodness. You care about all people—I am concerned only with those who interest, stimulate, and entertain me." Then he threw open his arms and said with a big smile, "Which is why *you* are here."

Santa brought in flan for dessert—that creamy custard Iberian delicacy that I adore.

"Oh, Santa, that's not fair. I never have dessert for lunch, but who can resist your flan?"

She beamed.

I sighed. "You know this means an extra mile of running tomorrow."

Adriaan shook his head. "The only health reason for running is if someone is chasing you with a knife. The body is your life machine and, like all machinery, gets worn down by too much activity."

"What about the brain?" I asked.

He smiled at me as one would at a precocious child who had asked the right question.

"Very good. That's the one piece of our equipment that requires constant use to keep it honed. Which gets us to your activities, Emma. What are you working on at the moment?"

Adriaan also believed I was a writer. This gave me the opening I'd been looking for.

"I'm working on an interesting project, Adriaan. It's a story on suicides. As a matter of fact, I'm including someone you know, that young American of Leida's."

There was that flicker of something in his eyes.

"Sad case," he said. "But I didn't really know him. He was Leida's friend."

"It seemed a strange thing to do for a young man who had, as they say, everything to live for."

"I guess when Leida wouldn't have him, he just couldn't handle it. Apparently he just couldn't deal with rejection. I think it's a sign of the weakness and breakdown of current society. Young people today just don't have the moral fiber and strength we did."

I suppressed my inclination to comment on the claim to moral superiority of a man who regards perversion as commonplace but I didn't want to break his chain of thought.

"You really think that was the reason he killed himself?"

"Well, didn't his note say as much?"

How did he know the contents of Peter's suicide note? Of course, Adriaan had access to any official file or information he wanted. But why would he want it?

"Did you ever meet him?" I asked.

Slight hesitation, almost imperceptible. "No." Then he added, as though an afterthought. "Wolfie and Andries knew him fairly well, I believe."

"I heard they were in South America, staying at your ranch in Uruguay," I said.

"They'll be back next week."

This was a gay German couple who were both good friends of mine. They were friends of Adriaan's as well, but most of their get-togethers ran more to the orgiastic rather than the convivial. They were wonderful guys who had a real *joie de vivre* and a knowledge of village activities that was encyclopedic. If ever you wanted to know who was doing what with whom, to whom, and why, one visit to their home could save you hours of local bar-hopping. I made a note on my mental calendar to call them next week.

When I got back to my house, I found Abba stretched out fast asleep on a chaise on my front patio. He was wearing very brief swimming trunks fully exposing as much of his body to the sun as his black hairy covering would permit. I looked down at him fondly.

"You're undoubtedly thinking I'm living substantiation of Darwin's theory," said a quiet voice.

I jumped. "I thought you were asleep," I said as I leaned over to kiss him.

"With two eyes, yes. But in my business, the third eye is always open." He looked me over carefully. "You look good enough to eat, sweetheart. And I may do just that. I'm starved. Where's that jewel of a housekeeper when I need her?"

"Gloria had a few errands in town. She should be back soon. Why didn't you just help yourself?"

He shook his head. "I never forage in strange houses since I ate a whole pot of stew out of Shimon Meyer's fridge and found out later it was the cat's dinner."

"Come on in. I'll fix you something."

I took out the *caldeirada* and put it into the microwave.

"You sure you know what you're doing, my darling *motek*? That looks just like the stuff at Shimon's."

"Trust me," I said as I laid out a plate, bread, and silverware.

He laughed. "The last Jew who listened to a woman who said that was Sampson with Delilah. In my country, we've learned to trust no one."

When I put the bowl of steaming fish stew in front of him, he attacked it with the kind of joyful relish that warms the cockles of every hostess's heart. Not until he had mopped up the last of the sauce with the fresh brown bread did he look up. I always found it funny that the Portuguese call whole wheat bread *pao segundo* which means "second bread." It's a carryover from the days when no one appreciated the healthier value of whole wheat and white bread was the preferred product.

"Thank you, *motek.* That was truly a *meichel*—a delicacy. I'll have to trade recipes with Gloria. I'll give her mine for *gefilte* fish if she gives me hers for *caldeirada.*"

I ground some Angola coffee beans and we took our cups of black coffee out to the terrace.

Abba sighed with contentment. "This has to be one of the most beautiful views in the world. And I've seen many."

My house overlooked the ocean, which was usually the unique shade of blue that reflected a clear cloudless and smogless sky. Right in front were my own little Grand Canyon configurations of red-gold limestone cliffs of sea-carved grottoes that had been enisled by years of assault from the waters of the Atlantic. In the distance, you saw the colorful boats lined up on the fishing beach and the multilevels of sun-baked, red-tile-roofed white houses that were built into the hillsides surrounding the town. It was a view of which I never tired.

"So where are you coming from, all dolled up?" he asked.

I looked down at my outfit. I was wearing a chino skirt, sandals, and a striped beige-and-white linen shirt. "This you call 'dolled up'?"

He gave out a booming laugh. "We're together twenty minutes and already you're talking like Jackie Mason. You're not wearing jeans and you are wearing eyeliner, which as I recall usually doesn't get applied until sundown."

"Ah, elementary, my dear Watson. That detecting eye for detail never gets turned off," I said playfully, "even on vacation."

"That habit has saved my life more than once," he said soberly.

"I had lunch with Adriaan Van Dolder."

"Aha, and how is our friendly neighborhood fascistic pederast these days?"

"Flourishing," I answered. "He's a grandfather now, you know. Leida has a two-year-old daughter."

"I fervently hope the doting deviate is not given baby-sitting privileges."

"I admit the man's a bit of a satyr, but he has a brilliant mind and is never boring."

Abba snorted. "They said that about Dr. Mengele."

"But this is a man who helped Jews escape from the Nazis in Amsterdam. He's honored on the Avenue of the Righteous in Yad Va Shem."

He was incredulous. "Adriaan Van Dolder? How do you know this for a fact?"

"It's one of the givens in town—everyone knows it."

"I never accept givens. I'll have to check on it someday." He eyed me narrowly. "Was this just a social call or did you need him for something?"

"A bit of both."

He took a big sip of coffee and then sat back in his chair. "You told me you were coming here on vacation. I've heard the American term 'a working vacation' but I never believed in it. You are working, aren't you?"

"I did come here strictly for vacation, but then something came up, some people who need help . . ."

". . . And can afford the assistance of Emma Rhodes, Millionaire Private Resolver."

"Don't you think tragedies happen to rich people as well as poor? Aren't they entitled to have their pain alleviated? Listen, my dear Abba, you're sitting right now and enjoying the fruits of my lucrative labors—so don't knock the importance of money."

"Whoa—who's knocking? Don't get so huppity-puppity. I love your money and I love you. You've got an incredibly fast and fertile mind and you deserve every kopek, franc, escudo, and pound they pay you. Now tell me all about it."

So I did.

When I came to the part about Peter Belling being terminally smitten with Leida, he shook his head in disbelief. "The poor deluded schmuck. He probably saw her as Mary Magdalene, but they don't teach you how to reform a piranha in theology school."

When he heard about the cocaine and my visit to the Lido Bar, he became angry. "Goddamn drugs again. I hate them. You just got through with a drug bust in Belgium—now you're involved again in Portugal."

Talking about my last case in Belgium reminded me about Elizabeth Eddington and I jumped up.

"I nearly forgot, I have an appointment with the bank manager at Espirito Santo. I have to find out about Elizabeth Eddington."

"Wait a minute, *tsotskele*, what the hell is she doing here?"

Abba knew Elizabeth as he had been involved in the affair in Belgium. I gave him a brief rundown on the Chilton Evans story and then took off for town.

Senhor Carlos Goncalo Mareiros came out of his office to greet me extremely cordially as befitting one of the bank's larger depositors. He led me to his impressive office, which was heavily furnished to show that he was a man of great importance, and offered me a seat facing his monstrous mahogany desk. I accepted his offer of coffee, which I didn't need or want, but I had become reconciled to its being part of the procedure of doing business in the Algarve. One never plunged directly into the reason for the visit but engaged first in pleasant, low-key social chatter while sipping. This ritual used to drive me nuts because I suffer from Minimal Focal Faculty. Don't bother looking the term up in any psychology or medical book—it's a name I made up in high school to keep from being badgered by teachers who kept telling my parents that their 165-I.Q. daughter was not working up to her brilliant potential. It's amazing how simple it was to sucker educators with psychobabble. Like with the emperor's new clothes, they were too insecure to admit their own ignorance so they bought my mythical diagnosis and left me alone to pursue learning on my own terms. What it actually meant was that I had no patience. I was born with instant comprehension and if a subject didn't interest me, I knew it at once and I was out of there. My teachers expected great things from me, which was a major pain for someone with no desire to restructure the Internet or develop a drug that dissolves calories. My motto has always been if it's worth doing, it's worth doing well—but only if it doesn't take all day. That's why I had difficulty adjusting to the Algarvian way of doing business, which required that social amenities be observed before one got down to the nitty-gritty. I learned to slow down my internal meter when I was in Portugal. Time was not of the essence here and the attitude was that there were few things that could not await the passing of pleasant preliminary civilities.

"I hope everything is all right with the service you are getting from us," said Senhor Mareiros.

Ah, that was the cue I'd been waiting patiently for. Up to this point, we'd been chatting about town gossip and the weather. Now we were finally ready to get down to business. I discussed with him the possibility of speeding up the transfers of pounds and dollars into my accounts so that they would convert into cash more quickly. He had a few suggestions and we worked out a way this could be achieved. I was most grateful for his help and told him how pleased I had always been with the way his bank worked with me. I never ceased to be amazed at people's susceptibility to praise no matter how extravagant. I laid it on with a trowel and he was positively preening with pleasure. Now that I'd softened him up, it was time to go for the gut. (Sure it's coldly calculating, but the man was beaming with delight and I'd made his day. He'll go home happy, which will make his wife happy because maybe he wouldn't notice the new dent in her car, and his children will be happy because maybe he wouldn't bother to ask about their school grades. So what was the harm?)

"As a matter of fact, I think so highly of your bank that I recommended to my friend Elizabeth Eddington that she place her Casa dos Meninos Foundation account with Espirito Santo in Silves. Would you know if she's done so yet?" I asked, smiling winningly.

He accessed his computer and said, "Yes, here it is."

"There's probably a sizable amount in there now, but you know it will get far larger after the benefit ball next week," I said.

He had not yet heard about it, so I gave him all the details, for which he was most grateful, because it was incumbent upon an important man of *negócios* like him to lend his presence to such a significant affair.

"Well, there has been a lot of activity in the account," he said, looking at the screen.

Much as I would have liked to, I didn't ask for the current balance. That would be pushing discretion too far for Senhor Mareiros and I wasn't yet ready to risk losing him.

Now it was time to get to the important information I came for.

"I know Miss Eddington"—*Ms.* doesn't hack it here—"planned to establish a double signature requirement between her and Mr. Evans so that both would have to sign for all transactions in the account. But she's not a person accustomed to dealing with such matters," I said with a confiding conspiratorial smile implying that the poor little woman was not as sophisticated and knowledgeable as he and I. "I hope she did it correctly."

Once again he touched the keyboard and looked at the monitor.

"No, the terms are that only one signature, either hers or his, is required for deposits and withdrawals."

That wily son of a bitch. He could clear her out in a minute—and was probably waiting for the time when the balance had burgeoned, like after the ball.

"Oh, dear, I'd better talk to her about that," I said. "Thank you so much for your time and help, Senhor Mareiros."

I was seething so much as I drove back that I passed Sir Barry's bar before I realized Abba was sitting there. I figured I could use a belt at this moment so I parked, walked over, and sat down at his table.

"You're damaging my action," he said. "How can I get any passing *chaticha*'s attention when a beauty like you is sitting with me?"

"If I remember my Israeli slang," I said as I motioned to the waiter, "*chaticha* means babe, or dish, or hot number. With that outfit, you shouldn't have any trouble snagging a sweet thing even if Kim Basinger were with you."

"What's the matter, you don't approve of my man-of-action clothes?" He had on the well-worn, battle-scarred uniform of an Israeli soldier replete with a hat that sported two bullet holes. "It gets me women all over the world."

"Emma, darling!" Dirk stood at the table. He looked at Abba and his eyes slowly scanned the full black beard, the girth that hung in rolls over his belt, and the three empty glasses of *cerveza* that sat in front of him.

"And who might this Falstaffian gentleman be?" he asked with a slightly condescending smile.

Abba lifted his fourth glass of beer and said in ringing tones, " 'Thou seest I have more flesh than another man, and therefore more frailty.' "

Dirk's eyes opened wide and a wide smile suffused his face.

"Well I'll be dashed. A man who knows his Shakespeare. Act three, scene two, *Henry the Fourth*."

"Correction, sir," said Abba. "Act three, scene three."

Dirk thought for a moment and then said, "By Jove, I do believe you're correct. May I join you?"

Abba waved grandly. "Of course. 'Small cheer and great welcome makes a merry feast.' "

"*Comedy of Errors*—correct?" said Dirk.

"Right you are, sir. Get this man a drink, forsooth," said Abba.

Dirk's eyes were dancing with delight. "The last thing I ever expected to find at Sir Barry's was a Shakespearian scholar, no less one dressed like a cross between Moshe Dayan and Ernest Hemingway. Sir, this less than humble establishment is honored by your presence."

Abba doffed his hat and bowed.

"Egad and gadzooks, Abba," I said admiringly. "I thought you were a psych major at Brooklyn College. Whenceforth comes this knowledge of the bard?"

"I minored in English Lit. In fact, I was a member of the Shakespearian Drama Society." He turned to Dirk. "I played Falstaff three times."

"A man of many parts, obviously. By the way, I'm Dirk Croft. I think our friend here has been too dazzled by your performance to introduce us."

"Quite right, Dirk. This is Abba Levitar, a very dear friend of very long standing. He's staying with me for a while."

"Well, I am exceedingly pleased to meet you, Abba. May I gather from your clothing that you are Israeli? And if the uniform is indeed yours, as it must be since there cannot be many more of that size in your much vaunted army, then you must also be somewhat of a hero."

"Everyone in the Israeli army is a hero, Dirk. We're a nation of amateur soldiers who win because we fight like hell. We know this is our final battleground; we have no place else to go."

I finished my white port and tonic and got up to leave. "Look, guys, I see you're having a fine old time, so let me take my leave. I have chores to do. Abba, I'll see you back at my casa."

"Emma, darling," said Dirk, "I gather you're having dinner tonight with my nephew, which will leave your houseguest at loose ends. May I invite you to dine with me this evening at my home, Abba?"

I could see that was not exactly the kind of night Abba had envisioned for himself, but I also knew how much he enjoyed good food and erudite conversation.

"Abba, just in case you're worrying that Dirk is one of those Brits who lives on mutton and boiled sprouts, I want you to know that his palate is as sophisticated as his language. In fact, you are fortunate to be invited to the finest table in Vila do Mar. There are those who have thought of taking out a contract on Dirk in order to get Maria, his cook. She produces food that's equal to any four-star restaurant in Lyons or Brussels."

I knew that would get him. He loves sex; he loves good conversation—but he adores good food.

He stood up, doffed his hat, and with a deep bow said to Dirk, "Milord, I would be delighted and honored to accept your kind invitation."

I left the two of them engaged in animated dialogue and felt the satisfaction of having made a successful match. As I got into my car and started up the hill leading out of town, I spied two familiar figures in the car coming towards me. I slowed down and called to them.

"Anne, Martin—hello."

Their sad faces lit up as they stopped their car next to mine. Luckily, there were no other cars in either direction at the moment.

"Emma, oh, we've just been talking about you," said Anne. I could see they were bursting to ask questions, but were too well-bred to break their word.

I'd have had to have a heart of stone to ignore the plea in their eyes. "Look, I have some stuff to tell you. If you're not doing anything right now, why don't you just follow me to my house and we'll talk over a drink."

"What an enchanting spot," said Anne as they stood awestruck on my seventy-five-foot terrace.

They oohed and ahed at the house, which was white with a red tile roof, aqua shutters, and a beautiful filigree chimney. From the outside it looked like any of the fishermen's cottages seen in villages throughout the Mediterranean and Aegean seasides; the inside had the stark structural beauty of those primitive homes with the convenience of modern amenities that blended rather than overwhelmed the simple feeling of the dwelling. Sliding glass doors opened from the terrace into a living room with a red tile floor and a fireplace bordered with blue *azulejo* tiles. Since stone was the available—thus less costly—material, the kitchen counters, bathroom walls, and floors were real marble. The house had two bedrooms, each closed off in a separate suite arrangement with its own bathroom and its own door to the outside to afford total privacy, a necessary commodity given the lifestyle of me and my friends.

I'm a firm believer that a home should reflect its function. My Algarve casa was a beach house set in a resort community and was used basically as a rest and relaxation base. I furnished it with local materials and pieces. Rough-hewn tables, beds and chests, leather chairs, and walls hung with samples of local arts and crafts. It was simple, colorful, and comfortable. However, since I didn't suffer the pressured nine-to-five life (or eight-to-eight, as was demanded by the fancy legal sweat shop where I used to work before I discovered the talent for my unique profession) I didn't need an escape hatch from the world. I liked to keep in touch, which accounted for the presence of current communications equipment in each of my three homes: an answering machine and the latest computer containing a fax and copier.

We sat on the terrace and enjoyed the colorful display of flowers bordering the entire area as well as the mimosa and almond trees that provided welcome shade against the hot sun. Gloria brought us drinks and the usual Algarve hors d'oeuvres, sardines and sweet local onions that you could eat raw and not have to remember for hours, bread chunks, and a plate of green and black olives.

They commented on the unusually brilliant light in the Algarve.

"It's so clear and absolute," said Martin, "it always seems as though you just took off sunglasses."

"Doesn't it ever rain here or get cloudy and overcast? It's been perfect every day we've been here," said Anne.

I told them that it was guaranteed not to rain for ten months of the year and the temperature ranged from fifty degrees to the eighties.

That was why it was such a popular resort spot for the Dutch and English, who lived under cloudy and rainy skies so much of the year.

"Peter wrote us about the climate. It seemed incredible, but it is true," said Anne, looking at me. She was too polite to demand information, but this was a hint.

As a rule, I kept away from clients while working on their cases. I gathered all the information I needed from them at the outset and thenceforth worked unfettered by their anxieties. As I told them, I delivered results, not reports. However, since I made the rules, I could break them. To lose a child was painful enough, but to grieve alone in a strange country without the support system of friends and family was inordinate anguish. I felt the Bellings desperately needed to be involved in solving their son's untimely death so as to lessen their sense of living in a state of isolated limbo. However, I had to be selective in the information I revealed. I wouldn't tell them about Manuel and the Lido Bar for fear they would be drawn to the place and go around asking questions that might alert the very people I want to keep off guard. As for Leida Van Dolder, with luck these nice people might never have to know that their son's last days were spent wasting his love and attention upon a dysfunctional harridan.

I told them, in censored form, of the contents of the police report. I gave them a copy of the note I had committed to memory when I read it—did I mention I had a photographic memory? They were stunned.

"Are they sure it's Peter's handwriting?"

I assured them it was and explained how they had compared it to his *pensão* registration and signature on his passport.

"It does sound like Peter," said Martin slowly. "He was always sort of excessive in his emotions. But to say he failed—failed at what? According to his personal goals, or anyone's for that matter, he was a highly successful human being."

"When will they release his—his body to us?" Anne said with a break in her voice, and Martin reached over to touch her hand.

I explained that official procedures in a town such as Vila do Mar creaked along at a pace that infuriated Americans who were used to a degree of efficiency that was viewed here as totally unnecessary. There would be no point in trying to accelerate matters; they would only get the usual answer: "These things take time."

"What about his personal effects?" asked Martin. "We don't even know what they were."

I had written down the list for them. Unless you were Agent 007 and carried things like miniaturized cameras hidden under your fingernails, a photographic memory was the next best thing.

They looked at the list. "His glasses," said Anne. "I don't see his glasses on this list."

"That's right," said Martin. "Peter couldn't see two feet in front of him without his glasses. He was never without them."

The first oddity—a flaw in the perfect police picture. It was common procedure for suicides to remove glasses before doing away with themselves. Of course, there were no inviolate rules when you were dealing with what could have been an unstable mind, but given the fact that Peter's clothes were not tossed at random but neatly folded, careful premeditation was indicated, which should have meant eyeglasses on top of the pile, as though they were the last item shed. Where were they? It wasn't the greatest clue in the world, but it was a start, and it did leave the Bellings with a sense of hope.

Chapter Six

NOW I HAD a few details to take care of before Mark arrived.

The gala was just days away and my dear, I didn't have a thing to wear. I kept Algarvian casual and Dirk dress-up clothes in my casa closet, but ball gowns had never been required. To most women, this would ordinarily mean immediate panic. But not little Emma. I had already clipped out of *Elle* magazine the photo of a black satin Givenchy gown that was form-fitting, low-cut in the front, and virtually nonexistent in the back that had the knock-'em-dead look I thought suited the occasion. I walked it over to the fax machine and sent a copy to my *modista* in Lisbon who has a dressmaker's dummy of me standing in her workroom. She also has a fax machine that I bought for her for just these sorts of situations. Mariana Alcoforado had the same kind of talent as my grandmother who used to say, "anything my eyes see my hands can do." Mariana could create magic merely from a picture and would FedEx the completed gown to me within three days. The gown would be made that swiftly because she liked me and because she had refurbished her entire home with the latest modern conveniences, including a microwave and a hot tub, due to the lavishness of my compensations for her labors. It was truly wonderful how easily things could be accomplished when you worked with efficiency, organization, and a helluva lot of cash.

AS MARK TRIED to maneuver his car down the sandy road, I heard him cursing under his breath.

"These roads were made for mule carts, not Mercedes," I said with a smile. I hated people who said "we should have" so I didn't mention that if I had known we were going to Antonio's on the beach, I would've suggested we take my VW with the stick shift. I also might have told him that his pale blue silk shirt, navy blue ascot, fawn slacks, and blue blazer were not exactly suitable garb for a beach bistro, especially Antonio's.

At the restaurant, I was greeted with a big hug and then Antonio looked Mark up and down and shouted, "*Que beleza!*" I didn't think Mark would like to hear he had been called a beauty, but from his sudden flush I could see that he caught the message. When Antonio led us to one of the long wooden picnic tables, Mark hesitated before sitting on the plain, not-too-clean bench. Antonio, who was a grizzled, puckish man of an indeterminate age ranging possibly from fifty to seventy, took the ever-present, not-too-clean towel off his shoulder, grandiosely wiped off the bench, and waved Mark to be seated. All the guests at the other tables cheered and applauded. Instead of sitting, Mark bowed, first to the applauders and then to Antonio. The whole place roared its approval and Antonio smiled broadly and enveloped Mark in a bear-like *abraço*. I was sorely tempted to do the same.

When he sat down, I leaned over and kissed him.

"What was that for?" he asked with a smile.

"For falling into the spirit of the Algarve."

"Instead of acting like a perfect prat, you mean."

"Instead of refusing to rest your bum on the bench and stomping out of here in high dudgeon, as would so many of your countrymen."

"My dear, you're forgetting the marvelous British sense of humor. We're the nation that gave you *Monty Python* and *Fawlty Towers*. We English love to be tweaked."

"Not if it's a member of the lower class who's tweaking a member of the upper class."

"You're suggesting that we are not a classless society. Are you in America? Somehow I can't imagine Donald and Marla Trump having dinner with their plumber and his wife."

"True, but that's the distinction of money, not birth. If the plumber hit the lottery and started contributing to the correct charities, he could break bread with Brooke Astor. Whereas in England, it's family, not finances, that determines your status forever."

He took my hand across the table. "The devil with politics. Let's talk about you and me."

"Like what we should order for dinner?" I asked as one of the waiters stood at our table.

"But we haven't seen a menu," he said, puzzled.

"The menu is those big grills over there and the marvelous aromas. The selection is a whole *linguado*, which is sole, one-half *franga*, which is chicken, or *gambas*, which are shrimp. For drinks, you have a choice of red, white, or rosé wine. I warn you that the rosé is the management's own mixture of all the leftover reds and whites. I must also warn you that everything is brushed with *piripiri*, which is a delicious but fairly strong Angolan spice. They lay it on lightly here but there's a *piripiri* chicken restaurant in Monchique that's famous for its aftermath effect, which is indelicately known as 'ring of fire' and 'ice in the bidet.'"

The waiter brought a huge basket of bread, a plate with a full bar of sweet butter, and a large salad bowl filled with lettuce, sliced green tomatoes, and sweet onions dressed with wine vinegar and heavy, dark-green olive oil. Mark was delighted.

"I think I'll have the sole," he said.

"*Linguado para el senhor,*" I told the waiter, "*y gambas para mim. Y vinho branco, faz favor.*"

I loved to order shrimp in Portugal because you got so many of them. Everyone has some crazy petty economy: Edsel Ford was reputed to check that lights were out in all rooms in his mansion every night; mine was that I wouldn't order shrimp cocktail in a restaurant because I couldn't bear to know the unit cost. Six dollars for a shrimp cocktail containing six shrimp meant I was paying a buck a shrimp, which struck me as outrageous.

By this time, two other couples, who nodded to us with a smile, were seated at our table, which startled Mark. I explained to him that one ate family style at Antonio's.

"I wanted us to be able to talk alone," he said ruefully.

"Don't worry, Mark. By the time the second glass of wine is consumed and the decibels of sound increase accordingly, no one sees or hears anyone else—we'll be as private as in the fanciest Mayfair restaurant."

I looked around fondly. This was one of my favorite eating places. "By the way—who told you about Antonio's?"

"I was sitting next to this chap at Sir Barry's and I asked him where to take a friend for dinner. He asked if my friend had élan, which I thought was a rather piquant question. I told him more than any other woman I had ever met. He then emphatically suggested Antonio's."

When the food arrived, we both tucked in with enthusiasm and there was no conversation as he carefully boned his grilled sole and I shelled my shrimp. After we finished eating and were on our second bottle of wine, we felt the sense of well-being and ease that led to a freedom of words and thoughts. The breezes and sounds of the ocean created a soft and sensual background that was conducive to revelations of feelings and memories that seemed to emerge naturally from both of us. For the first time in years, I felt I was falling in love.

"Emma, I think I'm in love with you."

His timing was perfect.

He drove me home and came in for coffee—and breakfast.

Chapter Seven

WHEN I WALKED into the kitchen the next morning, I saw Abba and Mark on the terrace having breakfast, deeply engaged in conversation.

"I see you two have a lot to talk about," I said as I kissed them both and sat down with my cup of coffee and roll with *queijo fresco*, which is a delicious cream cheese made locally of goat's milk.

"Not really," said Abba. "So far all we've talked about is you. The guy's asked a lot of questions but don't worry; all I gave him was name, rank, and serial number. You can tell him about the three husbands and five kids."

As Mark choked over his coffee, I said to Abba, "You caused it; you give him the Heimlich."

We all chatted for about ten minutes until Mark looked at his watch and jumped up. "I must go. I have an appointment with the solicitor in town who's handling the sale to Casa dos Meninos. Will I see you later, Emma?"

"You won't be able to, Mark. The meeting with your solicitor will last hours, and then there's the notary who must be involved. This isn't London. A land sale in the Algarve can take days, weeks, or even months."

He looked shocked. "But all the papers and titles are in order. The solicitor assured me everything would go through quite normally."

True, except that the Algarvian version of normally varies slightly from yours. For instance, last year an American in town sold his house to an Irish national. The price had been agreed upon as well as the stipulation that payment would be a fixed amount of dollars. The first time they were about to go to contract, the notary found some small item that didn't conform to his interpretation of the law. By the time that had been corrected, the exchange rate on dollars had changed so the papers had to be redrawn with the new price. The second time, the Irishman's local lawyer questioned the conveyance of some of the furnishings, and by the time that was straightened out, the exchange rate had changed again, and so on. Weeks turned into months and then, by the time everything was in order, the exchange had dropped radically and the Irishman, who was buying his dream house for retirement with his life savings, found he didn't have enough money. His first reaction, as would be that of any red-blooded Irishman, was to go off on a two-day bender in town. When they finally scraped him off the barroom floors, his wife had gone back to Ireland and returned with the additional funds and the sale went through." I paused. "And this was considered a normal real estate transaction."

"I think if Mark could say 'oi veh' he'd say it now," said Abba.

"You mean this matter could conceivably drag on for quite a long time?" asked Mark.

"Yes, boychik," said Abba, "and I see from the changing expression on your face that you have suddenly realized the significance of this fact—yes, you'll be able to spend more time with Emma."

Mark looked at me with such delight and love that I just wanted to throw my arms around him and shut the world out. I saw Abba looking at me—his keen eyes missed nothing, which was apparent when, after Mark had left, he said in a soft voice:

"So this one is different, my little *ahuvati* sweetheart."

"Abba, I do believe I'm in love."

"So what's wrong? That's great. Of course, he's not Jewish, but then neither are you. Does he have a mother?"

"Yes, he talked about her. He loves her very much. His father, too."

"The father I'm not concerned about—all men go nuts for you on sight. But the mother may have a different head. You certainly don't fit the image of the nice, manageable, empty-headed, horsy baronet's daughter she's probably had in mind for her darling sonny boy's wife. You're strong and gorgeous, which means she'll be strictly backseat from now on."

"Ridiculous. First place, basically I'm just a nice, home-loving gal from Rye, New York . . ."

". . . with a mind like a steel trap, a face like a madonna, and a body like Demi Moore."

"Secondly, who's thinking marriage?"

Abba looked at me. "You are."

"Why is it you always seem to know what I think even before I think it?" I asked.

"First place, I have twenty-twenty insight courtesy of my psychology degree from Brooklyn College. Secondly, you've been rubbing the goddamned third finger on your left hand for the last five minutes."

We both began to laugh so hard that Gloria came out to make sure we were O.K. After we both got through wiping tears from our eyes, I asked about his evening with Dirk.

"Very charming, learned, and interesting guy is our Honorable Dirk," he said. "His wines are superb; the two bottles we drank would be a month's Mossad salary. Do you know he gets a case a month shipped to him from his own special vintner in London? And the food was glorious. That Maria is a magician." He looked self-consciously at Gloria. "Almost as good a cook as you, Gloria." Gloria smiled with pleasure and I was going to suggest to Abba that he join the diplomatic service. Comparing Gloria's plain cooking with Maria's sophisticated presentations was like comparing McDonald's to Lutece. "She made an Iberian bouillabaisse that was like nothing I've ever tasted. I ate so much of it that she loved me. She took me into the kitchen to show me how to make it."

My mouth dropped and Gloria gasped. She knew enough English to understand that Maria had given him her fabled secret recipe.

"*Diga-nos*, tell us," we pleaded.

"Well, she didn't swear me to secrecy, so I guess I can share it with you, as they say in current yuppy circles. What ever happened to 'telling' people things? Today everybody 'shares' information. You know, that doesn't make sense? You 'tell' someone a fact and it's finished. To 'share' it with them means a joint activity. If I 'share' the recipe with you, does that mean we have to cook it together?"

"Abba, enough of the William Safire lecture on language. The recipe, please."

He pulled a grungy piece of paper out of his pocket.

"O.K. You take about three-and-a-half pounds of fish— she used snapper—cut into two-inch slices and make a stock out of the bones and trimmings. Sauté two minced onions in olive oil and butter, add two large tomatoes that you've peeled, seeded, and chopped and simmer about five minutes. Add the fish stock, two tablespoons of minced parsley, one bay leaf, one pinch thyme. Bring to boil and add salt and pepper to taste and two cups of dry white wine. And don't use cheap wine like a lot of people do for cooking. What they don't realize is the alcohol cooks off and all you're left with is the shitty flavor. Good wine enhances the food, lousy wine kills it. Simmer for fifteen minutes. Meanwhile, preheat the oven to 400° Fahrenheit. Now chop two cloves of garlic and eighteen blanched, toasted almonds and grind them into a paste that you add to the wine sauce."

"Aha," Gloria and I said in unison. "That's the secret ingredient—almonds!"

"Pour the sauce over the fish slices and bake for about one half hour.

"O.K., now that my Craig Claiborne schtick is over, let me tell you a few other things I picked up last night."

It seemed Abba followed the same routine I took after dining at Dirk's. He went to the Lido Bar.

"Were you able to get those kids to talk to you?" I asked.

He looked at me scornfully. "Have you forgotten what I do for a living? I can make anybody talk."

"Is the Mossad now issuing battery-operated genital squeezers?" I asked.

"One doesn't have to resort to primitive torture devices when you have that famous weapon, a *Yiddishe Kopp*. I walked in and two minutes later, the kids were falling all over each other to talk to me. From your description I figured they're all the kind that if they had cars it would take ten minutes to read the bumper stickers—'stop acid rain,' 'save the whales,' 'no nukes,' 'preserve the rain forests.' Peaceniks are always fascinated with warriors so I wore my battle fatigue outfit with the bullet holes. The assumption that I inflicted an untold number of deaths creates awe, and the fact that I narrowly escaped death as proven by the bullet holes in my hat creates sympathy. I tell you, it's an everyone-wins situation."

"You had no trouble with the language?" I asked. "Of course, a number of them do speak English."

"Emma, didn't you know South America is the Fourth Reich? The continent is crawling with ex-SS men, concentration camp commandants, and lots of other Nazi animals. Speaking Spanish and Portuguese fluently comes in quite handy for we Israelis who love to hunt."

I asked him if he met Manuel.

"No, I was more interested in that cocksucker Carlos, the slimy little bastard selling drugs in the corner. Do you know he's not running a supermarket—it's a fuckin' mail-order business."

"You mean like Land's End and Lillian Vernon?"

"You're not too far off—only he doesn't even have the expense of printing fancy catalogs. The putz just takes orders for drugs—any kind, any quantity. He writes it down, gives you the price, and collects full payment in advance, plus shipping. The other difference is he doesn't deliver—you pick up at the bar. There's a regular schedule—the end of every month."

"But where does he get the stuff?"

"It's all done by mail. He put all the orders in a five-by-seven green envelope that was addressed with a thick brown marking pen."

"To whom?" I asked in excitement.

"Sure, honey, the drug supplier's name, address, zip code, blood type, and phone number were right on the envelope along with an invitation to drop by when I'm in the neighborhood. You think the guy's some kind of dumb fuck? It was to a post office box."

"That's smart," I said. "That means Carlos can't identify him because he doesn't know who he is. You didn't happen to be able to read the box number, did you?"

Abba clasped his heart. "*Hamoodie*, my love, you wound me. You think I just got hired last week? Carlos and I became asshole buddies—he was so anxious to impress this fearless hero of desert wars, he couldn't wait to show off every detail of his marvelous system."

"So?" I asked.

"It goes to post office box seventy-seven in Faro. He's mailing it this morning."

"How does he get the merchandise to fill the orders?"

"Within five days, he'll pick it up at his post office box right here in Vila do Mar. The envelope will have the drugs and his payoff. Pretty neat. No face-to-face, no one knows anyone, and it's all done with the unwitting cooperation of the Portuguese post office."

"Carlos' package will arrive in Faro in tomorrow morning's mail. I'll be there."

"What do you plan to do then, Miss Marple?"

"Follow it," I said simply. "What are your plans for the day, my hero?"

He looked very pleased with himself. "I have a date."

"That's fast work; you just arrived yesterday."

"We met at the farmer's market in town. We were both buying figs."

"Ah, companions in constipation. What a romantic bond."

"Don't mock. She's gorgeous. Her name is Inga."

I groaned. "Not another one of your six-foot, blond Swedes, Abba."

He smiled and got up. "What can I tell you? They just adore short, dark, hairy Jewish men. It must be a refreshing relief from all those acres of colorless, pale-skinned Scandinavians. I think they see us as fierce and exciting—a blond schlong must be pretty uninspiring."

"Abba, you've got a mouth like a sewer."

"Such an accusation from a Sarah Lawrence girl? The maidens I knew who attended your fancy college used language that would have made a longshoreman blanch."

"With us, it was only an affectation of rebellion that helped us vent. With you, it's a way of life."

"Right, *tstotskele*, but given my way of life, I need all the venting help I can get." He waved as he got into his rented car and drove off.

I headed into town to the *farmácia* to replenish our Alka-Seltzer supply, which had been severely depleted by my last night's houseguests. I made my selection and noticed they now carried Rennies, the very effective antacid tablets that grace the medicine cabinet in every English home, and I reached for a package.

"I see you're familiar with the basic accompaniment to English cooking."

Dr. Colin Robinson smiled at me.

"Here it's not so much the food as the hour," I said. "Although *piri-piri* requires heroic measures."

As they wrapped my purchase, he suggested we go for morning coffee, one of the requisite pleasures of living in Vila do Mar. Although it was cool, the morning sun made it pleasantly possible to sit at one of the sidewalk tables and enjoy the popular village sports of people-watching and being watched. When the waiter brought our *café brancos*, the doctor looked around the table for sugar.

"I see you forgot that these days you have to ask," I said. In previous years, there had always been a generous bowl of individual packets of sugar on every table. (Village cafés refused to recognize the existence of anything so unnatural as artificial sweetener. After watching people slather butter on their rolls plus devour a number of sweet almond cakes, I could understand why restaurants might consider Sweet'N Low unnecessary.) When the packets of sugar began to disappear in far larger quantities than could possibly be consumed at the table, the restaurateurs realized that the large population of transient vacationing renters found it preferable to fill their larders with piles of these little free packets from the restaurant rather than pay for two-liter bags of sugar from the *supermercado*. Sugar rations were now only issued upon demand.

"How is your book coming along?" he asked.

I didn't mention that I had a book in progress at Dirk's dinner party, which meant he'd discussed me with someone. I hope it was merely idle curiosity rather than personal interest because I had an intense dislike for womanizing doctors, a type of which he appeared to be a slimy shining example.

"I think I may be able to help you. I've had a number of patients who were suicides. Perhaps we can work together," he said, and laid his hand on mine.

So we're already collaborators, are we? He could probably see his name on the book jacket, undoubtedly on top of mine, and a successful tour of all the talk shows, for which I admit he has just the right glib handsomeness. I removed my hand and pointedly did not use it to pick up my coffee cup to make it plain that I didn't need it but just preferred it elsewhere.

He recognized my gesture, but the egotistical smarmy sucker just smiled because he viewed it as a coy ploy rather than a sign of rejection.

"Young Peter to my mind was a classic case," he said.

Now we're talking. "I didn't realize you knew him."

"He came to me professionally a few times. I'm basically retired, but I had so many pleas from people—you've seen the deplorable medical facilities here—that I set up a small clinic in my home."

"I thought you were a cardiologist."

He waved his hand. "My specialty, yes—but I am a medical doctor fully trained in all areas."

"What was Peter's problem?"

"Since he's deceased, the oath of patient confidentiality no longer applies so I can speak freely of his treatment."

Somehow, doc, I think you regard all oaths as subject to your own flexible interpretation, the marital one especially.

"Actually, he was concerned about his heart. He had experienced pains in his chest."

I sat up straight. "And was it?"

"No—tests showed nothing. I diagnosed it as stress. He seemed terribly agitated about something. I prescribed an antidepressant but he wouldn't take it. Said he's adamantly against drugs of any kind."

"But isn't everyone?" said a cultured voice. It was Dirk. "May I join you?"

"We were talking about Peter Belling," I said after he had ordered his coffee. I wasn't going to let this conversation get supplanted by the kinds of trivial exchanges of gossip that Dirk adores. "If he was so much against drug-taking, how do you explain the autopsy showing a heavy intake of cocaine?"

"Colin is a cardiologist, not a psychiatrist, Emma. Who can explain the vagaries and vacillations of the human mind?"

"Well, he was very upset," said Colin. "It's not impossible that given sufficient cause, he could have been pushed over the edge to seek relief."

"And what could have been a more sufficient causation than Leida?" said Dirk. "She would have hit an innocent like Belling like a thunderbolt."

"You knew him, Dirk?"

He hesitated. "Well, I guess I ran into him a few times."

"Where?" I asked. "It's not like you ran into each other's shopping carts at the *supermercado*. Somehow I can't imagine how your paths would cross."

"Well, we certainly didn't frequent the same barber or clothier. He was one of those scruffy jeans-wearers who confused good grooming with capitalistic oppression."

"You met him at the Fera dos Santos, Dirk, remember?" said Colin. "He came over to our table at the town fair with Leida."

"That's right," said Dirk. "I recall now—he was a minister, which surprised me."

"Why?" I asked.

He was thoughtful. "Clergymen are usually rather calm. They are people who have found their own centers and are therefore more secure and content than most of us sinners. But he seemed unsettled and unhappy." Then he smiled. "But of course, he was American. Given the complexities of your multilayered ethnic, racial, and economic society, even a man of God could be confused." Then he added, "But if he wanted cocaine, he just had to reach into little Leida's larder."

"Where does she get it from?"

Dirk glared at me. "I don't know if I'm more bothered that you ended your sentence on a preposition or that you assumed I would know her source for drugs."

Not wishing to be out of the conversational loop, Colin contributed: "Most likely her father is her donor. He's a large user, I fear."

"You may fear," said Dirk dryly, "but Adriaan fears nothing and no one. I've left our table in restaurants when he took out his little snorting kit after dinner. He may have no compunction about committing illegal acts publicly but I'm not as tight with the *polícia* as Adriaan—who is?"

"I didn't know he was into the heavier stuff," I said. "I know he's been a pot smoker for years."

"That may have been his last year's drug of choice, my dear, but most vices seem to have time limits. The high of the initiate eventually gives way to the boredom of the reprobate." Then he turned to Colin. "I was so pleased that you and Julia had a lovely lunch at Quinta do Lago the other day. I do so approve when my friends enjoy each other's company."

These were two old hands at little games like adultery and mistress swapping. Dirk's implicit message of full approval of the takeover was instantly recognized and acknowledged with a nod from Colin. Julia would probably pitch a hissy fit if she knew she was being passed along like a used car, but then she might not want to risk disturbing her eye job.

"Emma, have you ordered a gown yet for the ball?" asked Dirk. "Just about everyone will be there."

Colin looked a little confused about the rapid change in subject, but he didn't know Dirk as well as I. When he was bored with a topic, it was over. It was a natural part of the imperious nature of the nobility to be not unconcerned so much as totally unaware of the interests of anyone but themselves. It was just one of their unlovely qualities that made me worry about the possibility of Mark and I ever making it as a couple. I haven't seen manifestations of this trait in him, but it may be inevitable given his upbringing.

"It was good of Mark to offer to bring the Princess. She's rather a handful, you know, but Mark has always been such a darling boy, no one could ever refuse him anything," Dirk said proudly. "Chilton tells me the place is almost entirely sold out."

"What?" I said in amazement. "It's not even a full day since Mark made the commitment."

"My dear, I only had to make five strategic phone calls last night and *après moi le déluge.*"

"Are we expecting a flood? Shall I start to build an ark?" Graham plopped down at our table.

That was one of the things I loved about life in Vila do Mar. It was so *gemütlich*. If you sat in the town square long enough, you were sure to see everyone you already knew and got to meet those you wanted to know. Graham leaned over and kissed me full on the mouth. Dirk's face tightened in disapproval, which obviously pleased Graham. I remembered there was a minifeud running between them due to a business glitch wherein Dirk was ousted from one of Graham's deals for conduct unbecoming to an investor like demanding better terms due to the luster of his name. Graham told him that his consortiums never needed window dressing and he either chips in equitably or ships out.

Dirk stood up and said, "I must go, my dears," and walked away.

Graham looked after him and then down at the table. "He didn't leave his share of the bill, of course. He still thinks the pleasure of his aristocratic company is something others should pay for."

Colin reached into his wallet indignantly. "I'll be delighted to do so."

"Loyalty to friends is a lovely thing, indeed," said Graham with a smile. "Watch out that he doesn't draw upon it too often."

Colin suddenly found reason to do things elsewhere and left.

"Well, Graham, now that you single-handedly, effectively offended two of my friends, what shall we talk about?"

"I did a pretty fair job of getting rid of those bloody buggers, didn't I?" he said with a broad smile. "Anyway, they're not your friends. The doctor is a pompous ass who thinks he's a cross between Louis Pasteur and Sean Connery. And Dirk is Dirk. Now I am your true friend. Of course, you may not want to bother with your old friends when you become a duchess, which I gather is not an unlikely possibility."

"I had just been thinking how nice this everyone-knows-everyone, small-town living is—now I'm beginning to wonder if the coziness is worth the total loss of privacy and personal freedom."

"But darling, it's not the size of the town that makes you so visible—you're a bit of a knockout, you know, and you and his young lordship make a smashing couple that would stand out in the Savoy. By the way, I happen to think he's a rather lovely chap and I'm envious as hell. But if you prefer not to discuss your love life, which is a great disappointment to me, how about your professional life? How are things going with Peter Belling's case?"

I shook my head. "Nothing much has turned up yet." I felt a pang of guilt at withholding information from Graham, but as fond as I am of him, his business-is-business attitude, which allows him to work with a corrupt miscreant like Adriaan, makes it possible that he could be mixed up in anything, drug distribution included. Then I told him my suspicions about Chilton's chicanery. He became infuriated.

"The bloody prick—to steal from abandoned children. That has to be an all-time low in morality. What can I do to help block the bastard?"

"Talk to your buddy Senhor Mareiros at Banco Espirito Santo and get him to put some kind of lock on the account."

I knew I'd never be able to convince Elizabeth Eddington of Chilton's nefarious purposes in time to prevent him from withdrawing the monies amassed from the gala. She'd have to suffer the emotional consequences after he defected, but I sure as hell won't allow her to suffer the financial ones. Graham got up from the table, threw down money for the check, and said:

"I'll go over right now. From what I hear of how ticket sales are going, Chilton might decide to clear it out before the event takes place."

"It's possible, but I'm betting on the power of pride and greed. I don't think he can resist the chance to mingle proudly with royalty and revel in the role of benefactor. And I think greed wouldn't allow him to leave without getting every last escudo. Besides, he has no reason to run now. He has no idea that anyone suspects him. Actually, I have no proof other than my gut feeling that he's a rogue. My guess is that he'll take off right after the ball and stiff all the suppliers who haven't demanded upfront payment for their services."

Graham leaned down and put his hand on my midriff. "Emma, love, you have an eminently trustworthy, not to mention lovely, gut. It has more sense than most people have in their heads. I'll get Mareiros to put a lien on the account immediately."

When I returned to my casa, I phoned London.

"Detective Chief Superintendent Franklin's office," answered a brusque voice.

"Hello, Sergeant Jarvis, this is Emma Rhodes."

His tone changed to friendly. "Oh, 'morning, Miss Rhodes. The Superintendent is right here."

"Emma—hello. How are you, where are you, and is this purely a social call, or is that too much to hope for?"

"To answer your questions in order, I'm fine, I'm in Portugal, no, and yes. And if this convoluted questioning is Scotland Yard's latest interrogation technique, I think you'd better go back to rubber truncheons."

I could hear the smile in his voice. "Actually, we're considering reinstating the rack—we still have a few in the basement left over from the War of the Roses."

I could hear Sergeant Parnell's guffaw.

"You mentioned that you were going on holiday to Portugal after that whole business in Belgium," he continued. He was referring to my last case, which took place in both Brussels and London, where we met.

"Do I take it that your usual penchant for involvement in foul play has cropped up once more?"

"Yes—you could say that."

"And you're turning to me for help?"

"Yes again."

"I'm flattered, albeit a trifle disappointed."

If you noticed that his turn of phrase indicated an educational level above that of most policemen, it was because he was a graduate of Cambridge and the son of schoolteachers. His swift rise to the top level of Scotland Yard was regarded as remarkable in a police force that was suspicious of elitely schooled men and biased against people of color. But Caleb Franklin was an exceptional man. Charming, erudite, and possessed of a keenly analytical mind, he was the descendant of an American slave brought to London by Benjamin Franklin, who taught him to read and write and then freed him, whereupon he married an English schoolteacher and sired many generations of schoolteachers. The current Caleb is the first member of the family to follow a profession other than education.

"I'm looking for information about a man who calls himself Chilton Evans. He's a devil with ladies of a certain age and I suspect he may have a pattern of flattery and fakery that ends up in his walking off with their life savings."

"We have a batch of files on those types; it would take you a day to go through them, Emma. But I happen to have a shortcut for you sitting right next to me. Sergeant Parnell is a walking computer of mugs and buggers, so why don't I put him on the line with us? Can you give us anything more specific than the fact that he dazzles and does in older women?"

"Yes, he's mysophobic about his feet. Spray cleans the carpets constantly and won't allow anyone in his room with shoes on."

"Squeaky Ebersole, sir, that's who it is for sure. Name's Charles Ebersole."

Eureka! I felt relieved because although I'm smart and strongly confident in my conclusions, I'm not so blindly arrogant as to believe I'm infallible. I was fairly certain Chilton is a predatory phony, but it's good to have it confirmed.

"Does he have form?" asked Caleb.

"No, sir, he's been brought in over and over again but never gets charged. Some old pussy complains he done her out of a pile of money; we got him dead to rights—but he never makes it into a courtroom."

"Why not?" I asked.

"'Cause, miss—when it comes down to it, the old pussies refuse to testify against him. Don't know what he's got; he don't look like Paul Newman to me, but no matter what he done to 'em, they're over the moon about him and always say they don't want to get him in trouble."

"Where did he get the name Squeaky?" Caleb asked.

"The lads named him that for Squeaky Clean. The first time they brought him in, he wouldn't go into the interview room; made a right fuss, he did, until they sprayed the floor with some kind of disinfectant. Said the place had bugs and germs and the like and he don't want them on his shoes."

"That sounds like our boy. Chilton Evans, Charles Ebersole—he doesn't even have to change the monograms on his shirts," I said. "I must say he isn't the grubby criminal type. In fact, he's quite acceptable socially, but I guess that's required equipment for a con man."

"That's right. Con men have to be polished and charming in order to ply their profession, which requires mingling in moneyed circles," said Caleb.

"He come from good family," said Sergeant Parnell. "Not one of them homes where Pa's forever taking a strap to the young 'uns and Mum loves her whiskey a sight more than her kids. Squeaky's Dad was manager for one of the Boots chemist stores and missus was a nice lady who stayed home and took care of her kid. He was an only son and they give him everything—but it waren't enough. He went to university—red brick, though, not a fancy one like the Superintendent, but he's educated. He's just a wrong 'un, broke their hearts, he did."

"What's his usual M.O. —how does he make his killing? So far it's been fairly small potatoes—he's been putting money into the account and taking money out."

"That's how con men work, Emma. They build the victim's confidence by contributing their own funds to whatever the cause, meanwhile constructing a major event that will bring in the big money—and then they abscond."

"The gala." I told them about the ball that had already attracted five hundred guests at one hundred pounds each.

Sergeant Parnell whistled. "That'd be fifty thousand quid. I hope, miss, you figure a way to stop him from getting his mucky maulers on that."

"Not to worry, Sergeant. He has to deposit all the checks and await clearance before he can withdraw cash. But the account's been blocked by a friend of mine who's put a lien against it. He won't be able to touch a single escudo."

"Well, that sounds quite efficient," said Caleb.

I didn't tell him that Senhor Mareiros would never ask to see the legal lien papers for the unpaid loan Graham would claim was due him from the Casa dos Meninos. He knew he could always say they had been misfiled or misplaced, a not-too-rare occurrence in his small understaffed bank.

"I'll bet the weather is sunny and blue skies in Portugal," said Caleb. "As I look out my window all I see is pouring rain and people hugging themselves to keep out the cold damp."

That sounded very much like a hint for an invitation, one I would've jumped on a week ago. Caleb and I have unresolved sexual sparks floating between us. The juices flowed the moment we met, but I was involved with someone else at the time and I am a firm practitioner of sexual monogamy. This would have been the ideal way for us to find out if we could have a great thing going together, but having a very sexy, attractive detective living in the next room while I was trying to sort out my feelings about Mark would never do.

"There's a much nicer view from my window, Caleb. I'd invite you down to share it, but my guest room at the moment is occupied by Abba."

I heard a small sigh. "I seem to have very rotten timing. Do you suppose there's a cure for this condition?"

"Persistence."

He laughed. "Your prescription gives me hope. How is Abba?"

"Right now he's off somewhere with a Scandinavian Amazon doing whatever is possible between a five-foot-six man and a six-foot-tall woman. Actually, the only activity that such a disparity makes difficult is one Abba does very poorly."

"What's that?"

"Dancing."

"That's a base canard," roared a voice at my elbow. It was Abba. "To whom are you conveying this slanderous accusation? I may not be twinkle-toes with a waltz, but I'm hot shit with a hora."

"It's Caleb Franklin." And I handed him the phone.

"Caleb, old son. What are you doing in the gray, wet wastelands of London? Come to sunny Portugal . . ." I waved my hands and shook my head furiously. "I'd suggest you come here and share my bed in Emma's lovely casa, but the position has already been taken."

After we both said our good-byes and hung up the phone, Abba smiled at me.

"Uh-oh," I groaned, "there goes that Ann Landers look. What sagacious love life advice do you have for me now?"

"I'm a psychologist and you dare compare me to some rich *yente* with a blond bouffant?" he said indignantly.

"Abba, aren't you the one who told me that the practice of psychology is ten percent education, ten percent luck, and eighty percent *sechel*, which I believe is the Yiddish word for common sense? According to that definition, I'd say Ms. Landers is eminently qualified. You also said that psychology is an inexact science and results rather than means are the measurement of success. By that gauge, I'd say she's a winner."

He shook his head admiringly. "You argue like a Talmudic student. If you weren't a gentile and a woman, you'd be a big hit in Crown Heights."

He sat down on the chair facing me. "All I wanted to say is that if you put off a spectacular hunk like Caleb Franklin, you must be pretty hot on milord Mark. Have you thought what it would be like to be Lady Emma and spend your days opening local fairs, raising money for the Girl Guides, overseeing an army of servants in a massive, stone, cold house that requires wearing heavy tweeds indoors nine months of the year, and producing an heir?"

"You certainly know how to paint a vivid word picture, Abba. Have you ever thought of going in for politics?"

He made a terrible face. "God forbid. In Israel, that's the kind of suggestion you make to your worst enemy."

"Yes, I've thought about the kind of life Mark leads and what might be expected of me if I join up with him."

"And?"

I shook my head. "I think I'd be climbing the moldy walls in a month. But I really care about this guy. Abba, he's the first man I've ever met with whom I could see myself spending the rest of my life. I don't know if I want to lose him."

Instantly he was at my side with his arm around my shoulders.

"*Motek*—if you really love him, then marry him and it will all work out."

"And if it doesn't?"

"Then at least you'll never have to spend the rest of your life saying the three saddest words in the English language: 'I should have.'"

I hugged him. "I love you, Abba."

"I know," he said with a sigh, "like a brother. O.K., as long as it's not like my brother."

I was surprised. "I didn't know you had a brother, Abba. In fact, I don't know anything about your family, even that you had one."

"Did you think I sprang forth full grown from the waves like Aphrodite? My mother lives in Florida with her third or fourth husband; I lost count. My father died twenty years ago, which was when my brother stopped talking to me."

"Why?"

He snorted. "If I knew why, I could maybe do something about it. I used to laugh at relatives who were tied up with feuds—Tante Ruchel doesn't talk to Uncle Sol; Sam doesn't talk to his sister Molly. I thought it was some sort of familial carryover from the *shtetl*. Usually it either started from some miniscule fancied affront, or it happened so long ago no one remembers the origin. I never envisioned it could happen to me."

"What brought it about?"

He shrugged his shoulders. "Beats me, honey. All I know is that my father was in Florida dying of cancer and I kept flying down from Brooklyn, even though I was a student at the time and didn't have a pot to piss in. But my father was sick and my elderly mother was alone down there with a dying man, so I went. My brother made one trip early on in Dad's illness—it took over a year and a half for him to die. The last time I saw him, I knew I'd never see him again. When I came home, I reported that fact to my brother, who then decided the situation required another trip, so he went for two days. After he returned from that visit, he refused to speak to me. My father died the following week. I alone made all funeral arrangements."

"You were the son who took care of his parents and your brother is the one who's angry? Shouldn't you be the one to be resentful that he abandoned them and left total responsibility to you?"

"You'd think."

I was silent for a moment. "Is that when you went to live in Israel?"

He nodded.

"I've been taking care of my mother ever since—my big brother calls her on Mother's Day and sends birthday cards. That's his idea of maintaining good family relations."

"I love these kinds of stories because they make me feel delighted to be an only child. But you're a psychologist, Abba—what's your take on your brother's behavior? Actually, this one's so easy that my Psych I course covers it."

He laughed. "O.K., Sigmund, so tell me."

"Your father probably said flattering things about you to your brother, like what a wonderful son you are, and your brother realized his father would die without giving him the approval every son craves. So of course, it's your fault. How'm I doing?"

"A-plus, sweetheart. Now that we have my family problems resolved, let's get to yours. So what are you going to do about Mark?"

"Something very uncharacteristic for me—wait. We've only known each other for—my God, is it only two days? I'm seeing him tonight . . ."

"Which means also tomorrow morning," said Abba.

"But only for a very short time tomorrow. I have to be in Faro at the post office to see who picks up those drug orders Carlos mailed this morning. I checked—the mail gets distributed to the boxes at ten."

Chapter Eight

I HAD FORGOTTEN how the Portuguese adore Beethoven. As I entered Cidade Velha, the old town of Faro, through the beautiful eighteenth-century town gate, the Arco da Vila, I was surprised by the absence of bustle and traffic until I saw people sitting in sidewalk cafés in the Largo da Se grand square clustered around radios, and the glorious sounds of Beethoven's Ninth filled the streets. When you couldn't get a cab or a waiter in Portugal, you knew it was either a soccer game or a Beethoven symphony, and you just had to wait until the broadcast was over before you got any action.

Faro was the town everyone went through to get to the beach towns to the west. The southernmost extremity of Portugal, it was the provincial capital of the Algarve and the site of the airport. To my mind, the city offered only two items of interest. The nucleus of Oxford University's famous Bodleian Library was created with books looted by the Earl of Essex on his Cádiz expedition of 1596 from Faro's magnificent library that had been built up by Bishop Jeronimo Ozorio. It always pleased me to think that Essex was a selective looter who didn't only go for the gold but also valued the importance of literature and erudition. I had a soft spot for Essex since I saw an old film on the AMC channel in which that handsome actor Errol Flynn portrayed the dashing aristocrat lover of Elizabeth the First, who must have been totally bonkers. Anyone who would have a gorgeous swashbuckler like Errol Flynn executed had to be certifiably insane. The second item of interest was the eerie bone chapel, a small chapel with walls entirely made of the skulls of the monks who lived and died there, which I always regarded as the epitome of recycling.

I parked near the main post office, went inside to the postal box section, located *Numero 77*, and then walked over to the counter marked *Servico dos Correios.*

"*Faz favor, quero uma caixa. Numero 78, se possível.*"

I paid for my box, opened it, slipped in the pile of letters I had brought, locked it, and waited. At ten o'clock, a postman came over with a bag and began filling the boxes. I saw a green envelope addressed with a heavy brown marking pen go into the adjacent box. At ten past ten, a man approached. He slipped a key into Box 77 and withdrew the green envelope. I fiddled with the key to my box as I noticed him slip the envelope into another, slightly larger, green stamped envelope addressed in heavy brown pen and seal it. I immediately opened my box and proceeded to drop all my mail on the floor.

"*Deus!*" I exclaimed as I stooped to pick everything up. He immediately bent to help me, as I knew he would, politeness being an inbred quality of the Portuguese. As he leaned over, I read the address on the bigger envelope.

"*Muito obrigado.*" I thanked him and he left to walk over to a nearby postal box where he dropped his envelope.

Brilliant. The guy who was running this operation had worked out a distribution design that had the most important asset of any plan—simplicity. The address was to another postal box in Lagos, which was in the western part of the Algarve. The drug orders and cash were sent from anonymous box to anonymous box; nobody knew anybody— except the last person in the chain who would take the money, fill the orders, and mail them off to Carlos, the final recipient, who would mete out the stuff at his little drug boutique in the Lido Bar. The system had all the earmarks of a superb tactician, for whom I felt a reluctant admiration. He seemed to have thought of everything.

"He"? For shame on me. Was this the product of a feminist mother and Sarah Lawrence College talking? "He" could very well have been "she." Whatever, or whoever—I had to find this bastard who was poisoning my town and perhaps responsible for poor Peter Belling's death. Tomorrow I go to Lagos.

I RARELY PLAYED the car radio. Driving time for me was the chance to think quietly and without interruption. Each trip was assigned a subject. Now, don't take me literally; I wasn't one of those compulsive-obsessive nerds who charted her days. But I found my time behind the wheel an excellent distraction-free opportunity to mull and muse about a topic that needed a clear head and quiet analysis. The thinking subject for the trip to Lagos was Mark. We had dinner at home last night; Gloria made *cochifrito*, a dish she learned from her Spanish grandmother. It was actually fricassee of lamb with lemon and garlic and was well within her culinary ability, and even mine. It was easy to make, fast, and very delicious.

You had to brown two pounds of cubed, boneless shoulder of lamb, well-salted and peppered, in a very hot quarter cup of olive oil, then add one cup chopped onions, and half a teaspoon minced garlic. Cook for five minutes, then add one tablespoon paprika, two tablespoons minced parsley, and two tablespoons fresh lemon juice. Cover tightly, reduce heat, and simmer for about an hour, or whenever the meat was done to your liking. This should serve four normal eaters, or two like Abba. It was best served with rice or fresh Portuguese bread, a salad, and lots of Dao red wine. Last night Mark and I sat outside with our coffee, watching the lights from the fishing boats moving along the ocean as the fishermen pushed on to different spots that might yield more plentiful catches. We talked until late about everything but The Big Issue—us and our future. At the moment, neither of us wanted to have any major confrontation that could force us into taking definitive steps, like getting married or breaking up.

Like all little girls, I dreamed of someday coming down the aisle swathed in white tulle with a handsome, Ken doll look-alike awaiting me. That image began to fade as I grew up and found I was enjoying my free life, where I made my own decisions solely based on my needs and pleasures. The reasons for women marrying have radically diminished within one generation. In my mother's day, women married to have their own homes (good girls lived with their parents), to be supported, to have sex, to have families, and to have the pride of derivative status if they married well. Only one of those reasons to marry remained today—having children, although many single women were disregarding that reason. Now we moved out of our parents' homes to go away to college and rarely returned. We supported ourselves, sex was readily available without benefit of wedlock, and we didn't need to marry status—we were the doctors, lawyers, tycoons. So the fact was, if you didn't need sperm or support, why marry? I'd been in and out of love countless times; I'd had twenty-two marriage proposals, and never did I even consider them, maybe because I didn't encounter anyone for whom I was willing to alter my lifestyle and— maybe more important—I never met any man whom I felt I really could not live without. Until now. It could have been that the moment had come when I was subconsciously ready to give up my freedom and wanted to have kids and Mark happened to be the man around at that time. Were his wealth and title affecting my judgment? I wasn't impressed by the aristocracy—I had met many of them and found they tended to be boring, aimless, and insufferably rude to those they considered of the lower social orders. However, I knew it would give my mother rapturous satisfaction to mention her daughter, the duchess, at meetings of the Rye Women's Club—especially to that snotty Mary Burgess, who never let anyone forget that her daughter married a DuPont. The idea of mothering little "honorables" and possibly a duke was sort of intriguing. The only real benefit to marrying into the upper classes—other than the money and power stuff—was the permissive freedom within the relationship. Middle-class couples did everything together except for his or her bowling night, but the rich gave each other a great deal of latitude. He was off to a golfing or hunting weekend, she was off on a trip to visit friends in the Bahamas; he was dining at his club, she was having dinner in town with friends. The idea of not being joined at the hip to a husband made marriage to someone like Mark a big plus for someone like me who bridled at all constraints.

As I approached Lagos, I remembered the last time I was there five years ago, when I'd decided this was indeed the last time. The city had some lovely beaches and the eighteenth-century baroque Igreja de Santo Antonio, a magnificent church decorated in a riot of gold from Brazil with beautifully carved cherubs and angels exploding all over the walls. But these attractions were not sufficient to overcome the overwhelming touristy touch to the town that resulted in streets leading off the central Praca Gil Eanes that were jammed with shops, restaurants, cafes, and bars.

I found the main *correio* and went through the same routine as in Faro—bought the adjacent postal box and waited. I was tense; this was probably the final destination of the drug orders and money, and I was prepared to follow the courier to his point of delivery, which would be the supplier. If this individual learned that Peter was nosing around town to discover his identity, it would have been simple to arrange to have Peter murdered. I was relieved that he/she was a Lagosan rather than a resident of Vita do Mar, which meant my friends were out of the picture.

A short, dark man approached and opened the box. He removed the green envelope, and I already had my car keys in my hand, ready to follow him out, when to my shock, he produced yet another, even larger, green envelope in which he slipped the one he had just received. I quickly opened my box and clumsily dropped the contents all over the floor. He smiled and helped me pick up my scattered letters, and I noted the address on his outgoing envelope—another postal box, but this one in Lisbon!

This was the end of the line for me. Who knew how many more trips that envelope had to take before it reached home base? I could see myself running a merry chase from *correio* to *correio* all over Portugal. This guy was cautious to a point of paranoia, and I would bet that his ultimate delivery would be arranged so convolutedly that it would be virtually impossible to follow it. I'd have to find another path to his door.

Chapter Nine

ABBA WAS IN his favorite chaise longue around the pool when I got back home.

"You're back early and I don't see any prize pelt strapped on top of your car, so I guess you didn't have a successful hunt," he said.

When he heard the story, he agreed that we'd have to flush out Mr. or Ms. Big some other way.

"Speaking of Mr. Big," I said, "have you found a tuxedo your size that you can borrow? The ball is tomorrow night, you know."

He shook his head. "You still don't think I can come in my army fatigues so they'll think I'm Castro?"

I phoned Mariana Alcoforado, who told me she would FedEx my gown to me within hours. I asked her to rent a dress suit and accessories in Lisbon to include in my package.

"What size are you, Abba?"

"Forty regular, fifteen neck shirt."

I looked at him. "In your dreams, darling. How would you plan to cover the other half of your body?"

He threw up his hands. "O.K., O.K., so maybe you'd better make it forty-four suit, sixteen neck shirt."

Mariana assured me that everything would arrive tomorrow, "*não problema.*"

"Do you have black shoes?" I asked.

He sat up indignantly. "Do you take me for a complete savage? Of course I have a pair—for funerals. In the business I'm in and the country I come from," he said wryly, "black shoes get a lot of wear. I brought a full wardrobe with me to be prepared for your mad social whirl here."

"Five T-shirts, two sweaters, two pairs of jeans, and sneakers might constitute an extensive wardrobe on a kibbutz, Abba. Here it's bare bones coverage."

He walked over and dived into the pool. When he came out, he saw me looking at his very hairy, five-foot-six, two-hundred-fifty-pound body.

"Not to worry, *ahuvati*—I'll make an adorable escort. You'll be surprised how great this bod looks in clothes."

To my surprise and delight, it did. The suit fit him well and the cummerbund performed highly effective gut control. He stood up when I came into the living room the next evening in my black satin faux-Givenchy.

"Wow!" His mouth fell open and he just stared at me. It was a highly satisfactory reaction. The dress had a deep horseshoe-shaped neckline in which my pearls nestled and a form-fitting long waist leading to a very full balloon-shaped skirt. There was virtually no back. I spun around to give him the full effect and he gasped.

"You're too good for that Mark guy."

"Who is good enough for me?"

He shook his head. "The man hasn't been born yet."

I smiled and kissed him and we were off.

As we approached the Dona Felipa, the hotel was aglow. Tiny white Christmas lights covered every tree and bush. Through the windows, you could see a series of gleaming crystal chandeliers. Kleig lights were making a moving arc across the front door.

"It looks like the opening of a Hollywood delicatessen," said Abba.

We got at the end of the line of cars that were slowly approaching the front door. As we reached there, an elaborately uniformed doorman opened the car door and assisted me out. Another colorfully costumed attendant waited on top of the steps to lead us to the door of the ballroom where two more brightly uniformed footmen were checking tickets against the list of names before them.

Abba whistled. "Looks like they cleared out the trunks of a 'Student Prince' road company."

We walked inside and immediately spotted Elizabeth and Chilton, who were greeting guests at the front of the ballroom. Chilton was impeccably dressed and Elizabeth was unrecognizable. She brought to mind those old movies in which the plain girl whipped off her glasses and was suddenly transformed into a raving beauty. Elizabeth's drab brown hair, which she always wore pinned up in an untidy bun, now hung in a shiny mass on her shoulders. She wore light eye makeup that emphasized her clear blue eyes and touches of blush that accentuated her lovely English complexion. The big surprise was her smashing figure which was displayed by a simple, form-fitting gown of beige lace. I suddenly realized she was probably not much older than I, which would make her about thirty-seven or -eight, and was a very attractive woman, a fact attested to by Abba's admiring glance that bordered on the lascivious.

"You look absolutely beautiful, Elizabeth," I said, kissing her. "As do you, Chilton," I added, turning to him and bestowing a minimal peck on his cheek. I introduced them to Abba. As they moved on to greet the next guest, Abba said:

"Look at the shoes that Chilton putz is wearing. I think they came from Hercule Poirot's closet."

"Those are patent leather dress pumps," I said, "very suitable for the occasion."

He snorted. "If he wore them in Brooklyn, his balls would be in jeopardy."

"Emma, my dear, you are exquisite." It was Dirk with Julia. "And Abba, you look positively acceptable."

"Is that your example of damning with faint praise?" asked Abba.

"Julia—you look lovely," I said admiringly. "What a great gown." Her dress had a tight lace bodice and a full black-and-white checkerboard gazar skirt. Dangling diamond earrings matched the necklace of a simple strand of pearls and diamonds.

"It's a Galanos," said Dirk proprietarily. I guess he was not yet ready to transfer ownership of Julia. "I haven't seen you around town the last two days, Emma. You've not sealed yourself in your house to work, have you? It would be a pity in this perfect weather."

"I am working, but not indoors, Dirk." Then I tossed out my bait. "I've been to Faro and Lagos doing some research."

Not a ripple or a flicker. His face indicated nothing more than polite interest in my itinerary.

Suddenly there was a rustling of activity at the door to the ballroom and there they were—Princess Anne, Mark, and assorted young nobles. The ballroom became totally silent as Her Royal Highness entered on Mark's arm. She was better-looking than her pictures, or perhaps it was the blue beaded Valentino gown and the splendidly glowing sapphire-and-diamond necklace and tiara. Mark looked around, spotted me at once, and sent me a loving smile that the Princess noticed and reacted to by fixing me with a hostile glare.

"Methinks you made the royal shit list," whispered Abba. "If her mother were Elizabeth the First instead of the Second, you'd be on your way to the Tower in five minutes."

I felt an unusual sensation. Good lord, it was jealousy.

"Obviously Her Royal Lowness has the hots for your loverboy."

"That's ridiculous," said Julia. "The Princess is married, and only a few years ago. She's practically a newlywed."

"My dear," said Dirk, "with the younger members of the House of Windsor, it would be possible for the bride to go off with the rector after the ceremony to have a saucy romp in the apse."

The royal party walked up to stand along the side of the room where people lined up to be presented.

"Come on, Emma, let's meet the Princess," said Abba enthusiastically.

I wasn't eager to render any homage to this lady, but Abba was like a little boy waiting to see Santa Claus.

"I never met a real live princess," he said. "They ran out of stock in Brooklyn just before I was born."

We got on the line, and when I reached the Princess, who stood with Mark at her right, Mark said:

"Your Highness, this is Emma Rhodes, a very special friend of mine."

She eyed me balefully as I curtsied. "I can see that, Mark." Then she slipped her arm through his in a decidedly proprietary manner and looked at me with smiling defiance as if to say, "Bug off, girl—you're minor league."

I responded by deepening my curtsy to give Mark a more generous shot at my décolletage. When I arose, he was looking at me with an intense love and lust that Her Highness couldn't miss, and I walked off with a contented smile. Abba thoroughly enjoyed the entire little exchange.

"Royal, shmoyal—that *meiskite* doesn't stand a chance. You're a gorgeous, glamorous creature with a brain and she looks like she should be mated with a horse, if she hasn't already. Don't they have plastic surgeons in England? For God's sake, someone should take an inch off her nose and put it into her chin."

"Princess Anne is not some young woman from New York's West Side who is seeking to marry a doctor," said Dirk stiffly. We hadn't noticed them standing next to us. "She has no need to transform herself into someone she isn't."

"You mean like Jewish girls who try to look like WASPs, Dirk?" asked Abba in a quiet voice. "You're right. Flawless features can't camouflage a flawed soul. There would be no point in your Princess making any exterior alterations; it's really the interior that needs work."

Dirk's face darkened, Julia looked bewildered, and I figured I'd better head off an imminent holy war so I pulled Abba onto the dance floor.

"The guy's an anti-Semitic prick," said Abba angrily as he maneuvered me clumsily around the floor.

"I wouldn't be surprised. He's anti-everything and - everyone who doesn't meet his Olympian standards in the only two areas he recognizes—class and intellect. You passed muster on the second but flunked on the first. Then you had the temerity to be derisive about his royal family."

"I didn't say anything against the queen," he protested. "I think she's a neat lady. I feel sorry for her. I've seen it plenty of times when a nice, sweet woman turns out a bunch of fucked-up assholes."

"And if you dared say anything bad about that nice woman's rotten kids, she'd tear your heart out. That's a privilege that belongs only to her. The British are allowed to criticize the royal family because it's *their* family. But they won't take it from an outsider."

"May I cut in?"

It was Mark. Abba bowed out graciously and Mark took me into his arms and both of us were lost. I had a sensation of deep sexual pleasure as I felt his hand moving over my bare back. As our close bodies moved around the floor, it was apparent that he was experiencing the same sensation.

"You look absolutely stunning, my darling. Will you come back with us tonight after the ball?"

I shook my head. "I can't. Besides, I wouldn't risk being in the same plane with Her Royal Highness. She may have me tossed out as unnecessary ballast."

He grimaced. "She's always been that way. We used to play together as children. I soon learned that any little girl I took a fancy to was banished."

"From the kingdom or just from the castle?" I asked.

"She's been married twice, but I guess old habits die hard."

He looked behind me. "Let's dance over to that door and slip out."

The moment we entered the garden outside, he began to kiss me until I was breathless.

"When are you coming back to Vila do Mar, Mark?" I asked as soon as I could breathe.

"I have to fly the group back and then stay a day or two with them. I'll return as soon as I can."

I didn't want to tell him not to rush back for fear it would hurt his feelings—but as much as I loved him, I needed time to resolve my case and I'd just as soon he not be here impinging on my time and emotions. He didn't know my profession and I wasn't about to divulge it while knowing so little about him. You're not the only one to consider the possibility that he may have been in some way mixed up in the matter. I wouldn't have been this successful if I didn't regard all angles completely dispassionately. I dislike cynicism but it's a necessary occupational requirement and I initially distrust everyone until proven otherwise. Remember how Humphrey Bogart in *The Maltese Falcon* made the mistake of believing in Mary Astor? Or don't you watch old classic movies like I do? I knew that I was in love with Mark, but I could not allow emotion to cloud my judgment.

I smiled and snuggled up to him. "Hurry back, darling."

When we went inside, I saw Chilton fawning over various members of the exiled nobility who had come down from Estoril. I recognized Nicholas Romanov, who called himself Prince of Russia; Prince Michael of Greece, his wife Princess Marina, and his daughters Alexandra and Olga. Chilton was beaming with pride and incredulity—pride for being accepted by the elite and incredulity that they did so. Elizabeth stood quietly at his side, smiling, at him with the fond look one bestows upon wonder-struck children on Christmas morn. I felt a twinge of sadness when I thought about how hard they would both come down. I hated to see people hurt—it tore me apart to think of how betrayed and violated Elizabeth will feel when she finds out how she'd been used.

"Ah, Miss Emma, so nice to see you. You look absolutely witching." It was *el chefe* Miguel Garcia Ozorio. I knew he meant to say "bewitching" but his English was not quite as good as he thought it was, and I would never offend his Iberian macho by correcting him.

"Good evening, *Comandante*. You're looking quite splendid yourself."

He was wearing a dinner jacket of black silk shot through with a pattern of silver threads that made him look like the maitre d' at an expensive Lisbon restaurant.

"And where is Senhora Ozorio?"

His face clouded. "She was unfortunately called to Monchique to be with her sister, whose son just died of an overdose of drugs." Fury crossed his face. "I detest drugs— they are destroying our young."

Then why, I wondered, *do you permit its distribution right here in your own town? Is it possible that you don't know about it?*

We chatted and were soon joined by *Senhor e Presidente de Camera* of the *Concello de Vila do Mar*, which is the Portuguese term for Mayor, and Senhor e Juiz Firmino Cavalhos, the local judge. Senhor Mareiros of the Banco entered our group and shortly I found myself surrounded by the powerful local quartet of politics, police, justice, and banking. I amused myself by watching them try to avert their eyes from my bosom.

Abba waved as he danced by with some lovely young thing. I saw Pamela and Reginald Cartlington; the good doctor Colin Robinson with wife, Sheila; and Sir Barry and his wife, Iris. In fact, every single member of the British community was there.

I wondered if Graham had come—and there he was with a stunning young woman who was, of course, about half his age.

"I'd love to hug you, Emma love," he said, "but I fear to disturb the gravity that keeps your dress up. That is one drop-dead gown. You look positively gorgeous."

"Thank you. You look pretty sharp yourself." His dress suit hung where it should and clung where it should, the mark of a fine custom-made garment. Graham had the kind of trim figure that made him the joy of his Saville Row tailor. "I would introduce you to Helga here, but she doesn't speak English. She even smiles in German." He looked around the ballroom appraisingly. "There's nothing like a royal to bring my countrymen out in droves. I bet Chilton is surprised at the fantastic turnout." Then he smiled mischievously. "But that's nothing to the surprise he's going to get at *el banco*. By the way, you are certain he's a rogue?"

I told him about my conversation with Caleb Franklin.

"You know the golden boy of Scotland Yard? I am impressed, but not surprised. Nothing you do surprises me, Emma. You're the only woman I know whose postcoital conversation is just as pleasurable as the previous activity. Are you sure we can't turn the calendar back a year?"

I shook my head. "You know I'm strictly monogamous, Graham. Anything else is promiscuity."

Graham stopped a passing waiter and picked glasses of champagne from the tray, which he gave to Helga, who smiled (in German, of course), me, and himself.

"Speaking of sexual depravity, Leida has been looking for you all over town. How have you been so clever as to avoid her?" he asked.

"I've been in Faro and Lagos," I said. There was no reaction on his face, but that told me nothing. Graham's years of wheeling and dealing taught him to have the best poker face in the western world. If he was involved in the drug trafficking, he'd have gotten the message that I was getting close. Shaking up the suspects may be dangerous, but it could accelerate results.

Much as I disliked Chilton, I had to admit he knew how to throw a smashing party. When two liveried servants dramatically swung open the doors to the dining room, everyone gasped in delight. The huge crystal chandeliers were dimmed to set off the effect of a hundred tables bearing candlelit centerpieces of a blue papier-mâché British lion and a red-and-black Portuguese rooster. The crystal stemware gleamed and the hotel had laid out its best blue-and-gold Spode china. The room looked like a fairyland.

"Who's responsible for these imaginative decorations?" I asked Chilton.

"These two charming ladies," he said, putting his arms around Pamela Cartlington and Sheila Robinson, who were standing at the door with him. They flushed with pleasure.

"No matter where we are, even in the remotest corner of the globe, British style and good taste prevails," he said grandiosely.

Maybe it was time someone explained to him that they lost the empire. Both women looked at him with the adoring eyes of a cocker spaniel, although Sheila would more likely have been compared to a rottweiler. She was tall and thin with that stringy build that looked best in riding clothes and tweeds and worst in a ball gown, especially the unflattering lace-trimmed mauve satin that looked like it came right off the peg at Selfridge's and made me want to flog the saleswoman who let her walk out with it. Mauve is a tough color for most complexions to handle, especially the weather-beaten skin that attested to Sheila's devotion to golf. She looked like one of the many neuter gender English women who bestow all their interest on sports and animals, but the look of determined longing she cast at Chilton indicated she had room for other passions.

Chilton was one of those seemingly ordinary men who had the ability to be strongly attractive to women. Their secret, of course, was the level of women they courted. The method was to be extremely attentive to plain women who were not used to the admiration and flattery that he used to persuade them to do his bidding. This was an invaluable trait in Chilton's business, where winning confidence was a necessity. His M.O. was to use them and then take off, but I suspected that Sheila would not be that easy to shed.

The dinner was superb. The hotel wisely had used the services of both their Portuguese and English chefs (yes, there was some excellent British cooking going on throughout the isles these days.) The menu consisted of *linguado* sautéed with grapes (sole Véronique), rare roast beef, Yorkshire pudding with wild asparagus and chantarelles from Monchique, and Portuguese salad (green tomatoes, onions, and lettuce with vinaigrette dressing). For *doce* they quite appropriately served *bolo real do Algarve*—royal cake of the Algarve made with sugar, almonds, egg yolks made into a paste with pumpkin squash and then covered with icing and bound with egg whites. Trolleys of all the best cheeses of Portugal were wheeled around and a fine wine of Portugal was served with each course.

By midnight, I had had it and was ready to leave. I approached the royal table to say good-bye to Mark and waited politely for him to complete his conversation with Her Royal Highness. When he saw me, his face lit up and he asked the Princess's leave, which she grudgingly gave. He left the table to take me to the door and we kissed good-bye. Then I went hunting for Abba and found him surrounded by a group of adoring women who were hanging on his words.

"What on earth were you regaling them with? They seemed enthralled."

"I'm a fascinating guy, Emma. You're the only woman who can resist me."

I gave the parking slip to the valet at the door and within a minute, my little VW came roaring towards us. We got in and I drove out to the main road.

"That was a marvelous party, sweetheart," said Abba. "Beautiful women, great food, and good wine. What more could a man want?"

I looked over at him. "From that slack jaw and slurred diction, I can see you had more than any man should have."

He sat up indignantly. "Let me take the wheel. I'll show you how sober I am. I drive better when I've had a few."

"That would make a great epitaph," I said as I made a turn into the steep hill that led down to the ocean. I tapped the brake to slow down and suddenly my face got hot and my body got cold. No brake.

"Hey, slow down, cowboy," said Abba. When he saw me shift into neutral and pull the emergency brake, he knew what was happening. We must've been doing seventy—it was a very acute hill—and the ocean cliff loomed ahead. Neither of us said a word but I knew his body was pumping adrenaline and fear just like mine. I suddenly remembered a small road to the right that went back uphill and took the turn at seventy miles an hour. The car shot uphill with an impetus so great that it carried us up almost to the top of the hill before we slowed down. When the car came to a stop, we both slumped back in our seats.

"It's a rather radical method to sober a guy up, but I gotta admit it's fuckin' effective," said Abba. He started to get out of the car and I stopped him.

"Either the brakes were cut or the fluid drained. No need to look under the car. Besides, remember you're wearing an expensive rented suit."

He nodded and got back in. "Who?"

"I bandied it around that I've been in Faro and Lagos. I assume the alleged perpetrator got wind of my trips, figured I was getting too nosy and perhaps too close, and arranged to have my activities curtailed—permanently, I'd say. And you happened to be along for the ride."

"Yeah—just lucky, I guess. So this is your technique to flush out the bad guys. Set yourself up as bait and see if they bite. Simple but dangerous."

"And expedient. Can you think of a faster way to find out if the drug distributor is here in town and not in Lisbon?"

"Well, he or she is apparently a local who knew you'd be here tonight. Which narrows our suspects down to just a few hundred. And means you have to watch your ass every minute. Great."

We drove home silently. Abba checked the doors and windows and we went to bed.

Chapter Ten

I DREAMED ABOUT high school, and the change of classes bell was ringing. It was the phone. I reached for it and looked at the clock—3:00 A.M.

"Emma, I'm so sorry to disturb you at this hour."

It was Elizabeth Eddington.

I sat up. "What's wrong?"

"I'm calling from the police station. They've arrested me. I'm sorry to bother you, but I didn't know who else to call."

Abba came into my room and I pulled the sheet around me. I don't wear a nightgown.

"What's the charge? Why have they arrested you, Elizabeth?" I was now talking for Abba's benefit, too.

"For Chilton's murder." Her voice broke a little. I could hear that she was fighting to hold herself together.

"Chilton murdered?" I asked.

Abba's face took on the alertness of a professional.

"Elizabeth, who's your attorney? Call him at once. I'll be there in fifteen minutes."

"But I can't call Dr. Batalha at this hour, Emma. He has a family—I'd wake everyone."

"Elizabeth, this is not a parking ticket. That's his business. Call him!"

Abba and I were at the station *esquadra* in ten minutes. Elizabeth was sitting at the policeman's desk in the reception area with her head bowed. She was still in her lace ball gown. I could see into *el chefe*'s office; he was there talking to the mayor and the judge, all still in the formal dress they had worn to the ball. I went right over and put my arms around her and she looked up and the tears she had been suppressing started to come.

"Chilton's dead, Emma. They think I killed him. Why would I ever do that?"

When *el chefe* saw me, he came right out. He looked deeply harassed.

"Senhora Eddington called me, *Comandante*. I am a close friend and I would like to help all I can."

I could see a ray of hope in his eyes. "This is a very serious charge, Miss Emma, a highly delicate matter. Anything you can do to shed light" —he shook his head dolefully—"would be valuable."

I could well understand his consternation. Law enforcement officials everywhere, but especially in small villages like Vila do Mar, were extremely sensitive to political connections and public opinion. Not only was his prisoner a beloved, almost saintly, figure in the community but he had just come from a ball where he witnessed the extent of her support by the rich and powerful.

"May I speak with Senhora Eddington somewhere private, *Comandante*?"

"Certainly." He took us to a room with a table and four chairs. His quandary in dealing with a prisoner of Elizabeth's social standing was apparent in the respectful way in which he led her into the room. Abba followed us in and we shut the door. No one mentioned anything about the unorthodoxy of this procedure or questioned Abba's identity or reasons for being there.

As soon as the three of us were seated I explained Abba's presence as a friend who could be helpful. She smiled and nodded, the reflex action of a well-mannered person. The glazed look in her eyes indicated she was in shock and she would have been equally polite had I brought along King Kong.

"First, Elizabeth, did you call Dr. Batalha?" In Portugal, as in many other European countries, lawyers bore the title of doctor. Actually, lawyers in the United States were

justified in using the same title since they now received J.D.
—Juris Doctor—degrees.

Elizabeth nodded. "Yes, I phoned. I got his wife. She
said he's in Portimao at a professional symposium and she'd
reach him there."

That's lucky. Portimao was the next town, which meant
he should be here soon. If he were home in Silves, it would
have taken over an hour.

"Now, tell us what happened, slowly and from the
beginning."

She sat staring into her lap for a few minutes. I waited
silently. Questioning an agitated person before she had a
chance to compose herself was a tactic used by interrogators
who wanted to unsettle the suspect into making statements
that could be used to convict. To give it the most favorable
view, they wanted the straight story before the person had a
chance to concoct lies. They usually did not know the actual
character of their prisoner, and from long disillusioning
experience had learned not to trust anyone. I wanted truth,
not evidence, and I knew my witness's moral values; I fully
trusted that Elizabeth's version would be honest even if it
were self-incriminating. All she needed was time to calm
herself so that she could recall those facts clearly. Suddenly
she sat up absolutely straight.

"I'm all right now," she said in a strong voice. "I'll tell
you exactly what happened as I remember it. I was in my
room, too exhilarated to go to bed yet, just sitting and
reviewing the whole wonderful evening. It was wonderful,
wasn't it, Emma?" She smiled sadly.

I nodded. "Indeed it was."

"Chilton was next door. The Dona Felipa gave us two
adjoining rooms at no charge since we were the hosts of the
ball. I heard his outer door open and close, and another
voice talking. I couldn't tell if it was a man or woman. I
paid very little attention; I was off in my own little world,
you see. I really can't say how much time passed when I
think I heard his door again. I remember thinking his
visitor didn't stay long. Then I heard noises, like someone

kicking the floor and some sort of yelling. I hurried into his room through our connecting door and saw him on the floor. He was dressed in his bathrobe and slippers, thrashing about, gasping and sobbing and screaming."

Her voice broke and she was shaking. I put my hand on her arm. "Do you want to stop for a moment, Elizabeth?"

She shook her head and I could see her battling inside to collect herself. She paused for a few minutes and then went on.

"I didn't know what to do. I've seen enough of them to know it wasn't an epileptic fit. He was gasping, wheezing for breath like he was struggling for air, and choking. He was sobbing and screaming, which he couldn't have done if it was food blockage, in which case I would have used the Heimlich maneuver. I saw a glass on the table half filled with what looked like water. I figured that might wash down whatever was causing the trouble, and I put the glass to his lips." She stopped. "But of course, it was too late. He suddenly went limp and then he was dead. He died just as they came in," she said with a flat voice.

"Who?"

"The manager and the chambermaid. Chilton probably tried to call for help and knocked the phone off the hook and I suppose the operator who heard his screams called the manager. When he saw us on the floor, he told the chambermaid to call a doctor. I told him it was too late, to phone the police instead."

"Why did you do that?" I asked.

"Bitter almonds . . . I suddenly got the smell of bitter almonds and I knew he had died of cyanide poisoning. I smelled it on his breath and then in the glass."

"You could detect the smell?" asked Abba. "Not everyone has the ability to smell cyanide."

She nodded. "Oh, yes. The *chefe* asked me the same question. I told him I'm familiar with it because we keep cyanide in our garden shed to use as a fumigant and an insecticide."

Abba sighed. "I guess Miranda is only known here as a nineteen-forties Brazilian singer who wore fruit on her head."

"Didn't *el chefe* caution you that you didn't have to say anything without a lawyer present?"

She looked surprised. "Why would he do that? He asked me what happened and I told him. He was merely doing his job and it was my duty to help him as much as I could, which meant giving him a clear picture of the facts."

"No matter how much they may affect and possibly incriminate you," I said.

"No matter," she said firmly. "The police's function is to find the person who killed poor Chilton. I want to help them. Surely you can see that."

"Yes, of course, Elizabeth. But if all the facts point to you as the murderer, they will have no reason to look any further. Which means the guilty party will remain safely undetected because you have in effect discouraged the police from seeking out the real murderer."

Pretty nifty persuasive logic, eh? From Abba's admiring smile, I could see he was impressed with my tactic.

"Good heavens," said Elizabeth. "I never thought of it that way. Of course, you're right."

"Right now, you've given them everything they need to declare you the killer. You were seen administering the poison, a substance to which you admitted having ready access. All they need is a motive and the case is as good as closed."

"But what motive could they possibly conjecture? I cared for the man—why would I kill him?" she cried.

"I could think of two right off the top of my head," I said.

Her eyes widened. "What are they?"

This was the part I liked least in my work. I hated being the bearer of unpleasant news and when I saw the anguish that my information frequently created, I understood the impotent fury that made men of yore kill the bearer of bad tidings. Nevertheless, it was better that she heard it first from me to prepare her for the inevitable use of it by the police as a disarming accusatory device.

"First, on the lighter side, Elizabeth, they could say you were a woman scorned."

"A what?" she said, stupefied.

"I saw Chilton dancing with at least six different women tonight, as did *el chefe*. The police can be very simplistic." She laughed, which I knew she would and hoped it would soften her up for the zinger I was about to drop on her.

"Chilton loved the ladies—he was a real charmer who really enjoyed pleasing women. But it was entirely innocent. He truly cared about the Casa dos Meninos, you know—and me," she added shyly. "Now what's the second motive? I hope it will be as easy to dispel as your first one," she said, smiling.

Damn Chilton; damn all rotters who spent their lives preying upon the innocent goodness of people.

"I'm afraid this one won't go away, Elizabeth."

When she saw my expression, her smile died instantly. I told her the truth about Chilton Evans. When she heard of his past, which indicated that hers was a familiar modus operandi, her face took on a look of stunned shock. But when the full realization that his interest in the home was bogus, and his feelings for her were apparently shammed, the pain in her eyes was so agonized that I had to turn away.

She was quiet for a few moments. "I see. If the police think I knew the truth about Chilton, or whatever his real name was, they could well believe I killed him. But I didn't know—how could I have?"

"The same way you just learned it—from me. They may not believe that I didn't tell you until now."

"And where, when, and why did you learn it, Emma?"

"Forgive me, Elizabeth, but my profession has taught me to be suspicious and to notice things others may overlook. I hated to hurt you, but I had to protect you." And I told her of my conversation with Caleb Franklin and the Banco Espirito Santo.

"And when did you intend to tell me, Emma?"

"After Chilton made his attempt to clear out your account. Knowing your forgiving nature, I was afraid his past transgressions wouldn't convince you that he hadn't reformed. I wanted to wait until I could present you with positive proof that he was still a bad guy."

I had once before been forced to give Elizabeth Eddington bad news that concerned the true nature of her beloved brother, and I was impressed with how her strength and pragmatism took over after a progression of shock, then acceptance. I watched and marveled to see the same procedure take place.

She got up and walked around the room, then came back and sat down.

"Now I understand why they arrested me and why I must be more discreet."

The door flew open and in bustled a small, dark, mustached man wearing a black fedora hat and a dark grey Chesterfield coat and carrying a black leather attaché case.

Elizabeth jumped up. "Dr. Batalha, how good of you to come."

He bent over to kiss her hand. "Senhora Eddington, I am here to help you. This is a tragedy, a tragedy." Then he noticed me and Abba. "Who are these people?"

She introduced us and explained our relationship. He smiled. "It is good to have friends to raise your spirits at a sad time like this. *Muito obrigado*, thank you so much." And I could see he was waiting for us to leave. I figured he'd better know that we were more than good neighbors bearing sympathy and chicken soup.

"*Doutor*, we are not just friends of Elizabeth's. We are also here to offer professional help. Since she is your client, I can assume that what I will tell you now comes under the heading of 'privileged information' and is not to be divulged elsewhere since we prefer to operate sub rosa. I am an attorney and also a private investigator" —and I looked over at Abba, who nodded his permission to reveal his identity— "and this is Senhor Abba Levitar, who is a highly placed officer in the Israeli Mossad."

Both Dr. Batalha's and Elizabeth's eyes widened and they looked at Abba with a touch of awe.

"Now won't you sit down, *Doutor*, and let me bring you up to date."

I gave him all the facts as Elizabeth had reported. He winced when he heard of her admission of her knowledge of and easy access to cyanide.

"Perhaps it looks better that she told them it was in her garden shed before they found it themselves. They're going to be examining her every action."

"Which brings me to a question that may come up," said Abba. "Elizabeth, how come you didn't call for help when you first came into Chilton's room?"

"There was no time. I could see he was in extremis and needed immediate attention." She smiled grimly. "That sort of medical response is impossible in the Algarve."

"How long did it take for the police to arrive?" I asked.

"Within minutes." She made a face. "It's ironic that authority responds quickly for a dead person who is beyond help and slowly for an ill one who needs it."

"It's the Rhodes' Reverse Ratio Theory of human motivation: a sick person demands a lot of work and little time to do it in, whereas a dead one requires minimal activity and lots of time to do it in."

There was a knock on the door and *el chefe* entered accompanied by the mayor and judge. Dr. Batalha stood up and smilingly invited them to join us at the table. It was all so polite and pleasant, you would've thought he was hosting a dinner party.

"Senhor *Comandante*," the doctor began respectfully, "I see no reason to hold Senhora Eddington here. At present, you merely suspect that a murder has been committed, but you cannot be certain until an autopsy."

El chefe smiled. "Senhor *Doutor*, I am merely *chefe* of *polícia* in this small village but I have been highly trained in law enforcement and forensic techniques in Lisbon. The description of the victim's last torturous movements are typical of cyanide poisoning, and the odor of bitter almonds further proves it."

"Could it not have been suicide?" asked Dr. Batalha.

El chefe hesitated. "This is not a usual way that suicides choose to die, *Doutor*."

"But it is possible, no?" persisted Batalha.

Ozorio nodded.

"*Comandante*," I said, "what about the visitor Senhora Eddington heard in Senhor Evans' room?"

"Correction: the person she said she heard," he said with a rueful smile.

"You haven't yet had time to question the hotel staff to back up her statement. Nor have forensics checked for fingerprints on the glass and throughout the room."

"*É verdade*." He nodded. "True. However, we find her holding the poisoned glass to his lips—and poison, you know, is a woman's weapon."

"Is it?" I asked. "Perhaps in the times of the Borgias, *Comandante*. But these days we've achieved equal rights to kill just like men. If you check the records, I say with no pride whatever, you'll find that the female weapon of choice today is more likely to be a knife or gun, whichever is handier."

"Senhora Eddington has been totally cooperative with the police in every possible way, *sim*?" asked Batalha.

El chefe nodded.

"I understand you might be interested in her as a material witness, but that is no reason to hold her. *Primeiro*, as you admit, there is much to investigate before you can truly justify an arrest. *Segundo*, she is not some foreign visitor or transient. She is a highly respected member of the Algarve community with many friends."

The guy was good, all right. He knew just which buttons to press to achieve the results he wanted. The word "friends" was not used to prove Elizabeth's popularity but to emphasize her powerful connections, a fact of which *el chefe* was uncomfortably aware.

"May I suggest that you release her in her own recognizance? She has deep roots here and would never leave her *meninos* at the Casa. You certainly can trust her character to know that she will make herself available whenever you wish."

El chefe hesitated.

"I would like her to be closer," he said. "If she were here in Vila do Mar instead of in Silves . . ."

"She is welcome to stay with me as long as she wishes," said a voice at the door. We all turned to see the Honorable Dirk Croft. "I heard about this terrible affair and came down to see how I can help Senhora Eddington."

I looked over at Abba and saw him grinning. The casual informality and the way people drop in and out of this place at four in the morning makes it seem like a neighborhood bar instead of a police station.

El chefe looked over at the mayor and the judge and they both nodded. The strength of Batalha's arguments plus the endorsement of one of the town's most influential citizens did the trick.

"Very well, *Doutor*. If Senhor Croft is willing to vouch for her, she is free to go."

Chapter Eleven

I WAS DRINKING my morning coffee on the terrace at 8:00
A.M., even though I had finally gotten to bed at 5:00 A.M.
which caused no problem for me—I could get along on one
hour of sleep.

To me, there was nothing more soothing than an ocean.
It was a windy day, which meant the sounds of the waves
and the lulling visual consistency of the rollers were almost
mesmerizing. The total effect cleared my head and allowed
my mind to consider single issues as though nothing else in
the world existed at that moment.

My working project was to find the true circumstances of
Peter Belling's death—and I had little more than a week to
complete the case. Protecting Elizabeth from being wiped
out by some conniving creep was merely a small side issue
that I regarded as the duty of a friend. Chilton's murder had
transformed the situation into something major, and there
was no question that I had to get her out of her position as
number-one suspect. I said I didn't do pro bono work,
meaning pro bono *publico*, for the public good, in other
words—free for everybody. However, I would always do pro
bono amicus work—free for my friends. Perhaps I wasn't
noble enough to feel responsible for those I did not know, but
I had a very strong belief in the need to give all the help I
could to those I did know.

Oh, well, if everything went along following a personally
convenient timetable, life could get pretty dull. Actually, I
thrived on dealing with the unexpected—I found it got the

juices flowing. If I could solve one murder in two weeks, why not two?

I looked out at my beautiful view and remembered the sad Bellings who, only a few days ago, had stood here admiring the beauty of the ocean that had taken the life of their son. I phoned them.

A half hour later, they were sitting with me and I told them about Peter's concern with the heavy drug distribution in town.

"I'm not surprised," said Martin. "He was so dead set against drug use he'd do almost anything to stop it."

"It is possible that he did almost something," I said.

Anne looked at me. "And that got him killed," she said flatly.

"Possibly. Let's just say at this time, it's an avenue being pursued."

They looked so bleak that I thought a little love interest might perk them up. As long as they didn't know her, they could hold the illusion that Leida made their son's last days pleasant rather than filled with the ugliness of violence.

"Your son spent many happy days here in Vila do Mar. He was in love."

They were astounded. "In love? But he never wrote us a word."

I wasn't surprised. How could he have hoped to describe Leida to such nice, conventional Protestants from Larchmont? I sure as hell did not intend to try either. If ever there was a time for me to exercise my need-to-know information policy, this was it. I told them she was Dutch.

Anne was delighted. "She's Dutch! Of course, Peter's best and oldest friend is Joshua Van Wyk who lives next door. Mr. Van Wyk is a Dutch Jew who escaped from Amsterdam, but his entire family was wiped out in Auschwitz," she added sadly.

"He's a rare book collector; he's the one who got Peter interested. Peter was an avid bibliophile," Martin said proudly. "He had a wonderful collection. He spent as much time in the Van Wyk house as in ours. Mr. Van Wyk's stories fascinated him."

"Especially the one about how his most precious volumes were stolen by a Nazi," said Anne, shuddering. "Peter used to get so upset talking about it and what they did to the Jews."

"Van Wyk had a Gutenberg Bible and a first edition of Martin Luther's Book of Concord. They were the pride of his collection. He said they were particularly valuable because they had flyleaf notations," said Martin. "Those two volumes had been especially precious to him."

"Mr. Van Wyk was in the Underground," continued Anne. "A man in town the people called '*De Verrader*,' which means 'traitor,' betrayed him to the Gestapo and they came for him one terrible night. As they were dragging him out, Van Wyk saw the despicable *De Verrader* take his books. Peter used to get livid whenever he talked about it." She was silent for a moment. "He despised injustice."

"He sounds like a marvelous young man. I wish I could have known him."

"Do you think we could meet this girl, Peter's friend?" asked Anne.

That's what I was afraid of. But I was prepared.

"You will, but not yet. Right now, contact with her could put all of you in danger."

"Of course," said Martin. "With all these rough elements possibly involved, we wouldn't want her to get hurt."

After they left, Abba walked out on the terrace.

"I assume they were the Bellings, that poor kid's parents?"

I nodded.

"Some vacation you're having. You came for a rest and now you're up to your pretty ass in two murders."

If you thought this was one of those books in which Abba's statement led the protagonist to have one of those premonitory flashes in which she suddenly realized how the two murders were connected—forget it. I was too young for hot flashes. Besides, there wasn't a shred of evidence that there was any other relationship between the two deaths other than that they presented the rare probability of having two foreigners killed in this small village within weeks of each other.

I got up and said, "See you later." One of the reasons Abba and I got along so well as hostess and guest was that neither one expected to be briefed on the other's movements. As Abba put it, we were each in business for ourselves.

When I came to the room in the Dona Felipa Hotel, the manager opened the door to let me in. I had called *el chefe* for permission to inspect the room, so was admitted with no difficulty. I'd always read how various fictional English inspectors stood still in the room where the murder occurred in order to gain the "feel" of the room. Maybe I wasn't that intuitive, but all I got was the usual hotel smell of furniture wax and soap plus that same odor of disinfectant carpet spray I had noticed in Chilton's room at the Casa dos Meninos. Everything had been left untouched, of course, after having been thoroughly gone over by the forensic people. There was some residue of the powder used to find fingerprints. It was only in rare cases that sophisticated laser equipment was needed and even the crack Crime Scene Unit of New York City's Police Department more often used the old-fashioned feather duster and powder to do the job.

I wasn't looking for anything specific nor expecting to discover a red hair clinging to the headboard; those forensic guys are incredibly thorough. What I was really seeking was an anomaly, something missing or unexpectedly present. I had an advantage over the police in that I knew the victim and would be more likely to spot something out of sync.

I looked in the drawers and the closet. All I got from this inspection was that Chilton was obviously a neat freak, which would be appropriate for someone with mysophobia. His underwear and socks were lined up in the drawers grouped by color, for God's sake, as were his shirts, jackets, suits, and shoes in the closets. Shoes. Where were those patent leather pumps he wore last night? Elizabeth found him in his robe and slippers, so where were his shoes? The dress suit was hanging in the closet; the dress shirt was in the laundry bag. But no shoes. I wasn't about to go crazy here and think the absence of Chilton's shoes compares with the absence of the dog's bark in Sherlock Holmes. Right now it was an oddity and until I checked out all the commonplace explanations, like the police took them for some reason, or Chilton lost a heel and gave them to the concierge to send out for repair—it wasn't a clue.

I drove over to see Elizabeth. I found her on Dirk's back patio having a cup of tea—the Brits' staunch buttress in times of disaster. She was calm and composed, but her eyes showed sorrow I hadn't seen before and her pinned-up hair and unmade-up face made her once again a plain woman of no certain age.

"Sit down, Emma. Won't you have a cup of tea?" I refused the tea but took the seat.

She started to thank me and I stopped her. "Please, Elizabeth, I've done nothing more than any friend would do."

"But so rarely does," she said with a wan smile.

"I've been sitting here thinking through all that's happened and wondering how I could have been such a fool."

"But you weren't," I said firmly. "You were dealing with a skilled, experienced con man. They prey upon people's greed by offering them shortcuts to prosperity. Except in your case—the greed wasn't for yourself but for the Casa."

"He seemed so sincere, so helpful, so dedicated. I thought he was God-sent." A cloud passed over her face. "And he seemed so genuinely fond of me. Emma, could I have been that wrong about his feelings?" she asked pleadingly.

"No, Elizabeth. A woman can tell those things. From what I saw of his behavior, he truly cared for you."

I wasn't lying. I was sure his psychosis made loving her a temporary reality for him. What point would there have been in telling her that, like other such people, Chilton fell into his role as though it was another skin? Like any psychopath, while he lived the part, he actually believed it was true.

"He started the Foundation with his own money," she said. "He was so enthusiastic, so spot-on about the entire project."

"That's the pattern, how they lull you into security. What better way to prove their good faith than by investing their own money?"

"He never intended to give us the money for the land across the road, did he?"

I shook my head. "According to his previous scams, he keeps infusing and raising small sums for the Foundation to make you trust his sincerity. It's all a calculated build-up to the Big Bang."

"Like the Gala Ball," she said.

"Exactly—the major event that brings in a sizable amount of money and makes his whole effort worthwhile. Then he takes off with the takings. Only this time his scenario didn't work out as planned."

"The *Comandante* told me that he found Chilton's attaché case in his closet filled with checks people paid for tickets. He deposited them in our account."

Usually all currency involved in a murder is kept for a time as evidence. I guess the important names on the checks plus a lack of confidence in the *policía*'s facilities for securing the money made him decide that banking would be the safest way to be sure all monies were accounted for.

"I assume there will be enough to buy the land from Mark's family."

She smiled broadly. "Mark assured me that whatever we took in would be acceptable and sufficient to make the purchase. He's a lovely man, Emma."

Didn't I know it. I missed him more than I thought possible, but I hadn't yet had the time to think the whole matter through.

"I've been trying to figure out who could have killed Chilton, or whatever his name was," said Elizabeth. "Everyone seemed to like him."

"Perhaps someone liked him too much," I answered. "Don't forget that his absconding would make public and perhaps private fools of many people."

She smiled grimly. "You mean besides me."

I noticed Elizabeth shudder. "It's a bit chilly out here, Elizabeth. Why don't we go inside?"

As we entered the living room, Dirk entered the front door.

"Emma, good morning. How nice that you've come to help Elizabeth over these trying times."

He walked over to kiss her. "I've assured her this nightmare will soon be over and she's more than welcome to stay here until then. They'll either find the true perpetrator, or more likely, given the skills of the local constabulary," he said with a tinge of sarcasm, "will just let the case slide into obscurity along with the many other unsolved crimes that occur around here with, fortunately, not-too-great frequency."

"Yes, but isn't it just those limited skills that will make them place the entire blame on me? Why look further when they have such a likely candidate?" said Elizabeth.

I looked at her admiringly. Her mind was working clearly; the gal was a survivor.

"Nonsense," said Dirk. "If you were some ignorant *jardineiro* who tended gardens for a thousand escudos per year you might be in the dock tomorrow. But you are an Englishwoman with powerful, wealthy friends, Elizabeth. They wouldn't dare take any steps until they are absolutely positive of their evidence."

She looked at him calmly. "Then I'm sad for the unfairness to all the poor *jardineiros* in the world who don't have my advantages."

He walked over and took her hands in his.

"Your feelings do you credit, my dear. But where is it written that life is fair? The fact is, my dearElizabeth, we are not all born equal, which is why I have always regarded the American Bill of Rights as an eloquent but naive piece of fiction. You may as well sit back and enjoy the benefits of your position."

"I don't think I can when I know others are not beneficiaries of the same privileges. Perhaps there's something I could do someday to try to correct these inequities," said Elizabeth.

How can you not love such a woman? "But you already are, Elizabeth. You're giving a bunch of potentially lost children a chance for a solid future. That's more than most people do."

Dirk walked over to a small table and picked up a cigarette.

"Ladies, do you mind if I smoke?"

"It's your home, Dirk," I said. "You don't need permission to pollute your own air and destroy your own lungs."

Both Dirk and Elizabeth laughed. As he lit his cigarette, he said, "I realize, dear Elizabeth, that you are probably grieving for our friend Chilton."

I gave her a warning glance with a slight shake of my head that was fortunately obscured from Dirk by his first puffs of smoke.

"Yes, of course," she said.

I didn't want to reveal anything about Chilton's real identity to Dirk or anyone at this time, or, more important, let anyone know of Elizabeth's awareness of the facts.

"He was a good friend of mine as well," he said sadly. "I shall miss him. I can't imagine why anyone would want to kill such a dear man. Perhaps it will just turn out to be some unfortunate accident. But how wonderful that he left you that wonderful legacy of all the money from the ball. I assume you've received it all."

"Yes, the police have deposited it in the bank for me."

Dirk looked at his Rolex. "I'm meeting Colin at Sir Barry's in a few minutes. Why don't you ladies join us?"

"No, thanks, Dirk. I have a million chores to do. I just stopped by for a moment to see how Elizabeth was faring and I'm on my way."

Elizabeth shook her head. "Thank you, Dirk, but I think I'd rather have a lie-down in my room for a bit."

The door opened and Julia came in, still in her negligee.

"Oh, hello, Elizabeth and Emma. I thought I heard voices. Dirk darling, could I take one of the Mercedes? I have a hairdresser's appointment soon. Have to wash out this formal coiffure and reset for daily use, you know," she said with a trill. He reached into his pocket and handed her the keys. "Of course, dear."

He shook his head and looked after her. "I thought for sure she'd be off with Colin Robinson by now. But Sheila, who hasn't paid any attention to her doctor husband for a month, suddenly took hold this morning. The woman's a barracuda; she'll never let him go now. I was hoping to do the severance in a gentlemanly way, but now it looks like I'll have to resort to less pleasant means. Oh, dear, I do hate those confrontations." Suddenly he pulled out another set of keys from his pocket. "Damn, I gave her the wrong keys. I don't want her to go near my car. I'll see you ladies later." And he dashed out of the room.

"What on earth was that all about?" asked Elizabeth.

"Oh, just another episode in Vila do Mar's *Melrose Place*," I answered.

Francisco came in with some small packages and Dirk's mail, which he placed on the foyer table. I'm chronically nosy—or to use my mother's euphemism, curious. I feel that the best way to get to know someone quickly is to look at the books on his shelves and his mail. I don't mean steam open envelopes, of course—I consider that an unforgivable violation of privacy. Besides, it's tacky. I like to look at return addresses to know the sort of people and institutions with whom he corresponds. That can tell quite a story and doesn't hurt anyone. I wouldn't have done it with Elizabeth watching, of course. I just knew she had the kind of scruples I talked myself out of years ago. But she went into the kitchen to return her tea cup so I had a chance to sidle past the table for a quick glance. I froze.

There among the pile was a large green envelope bearing the number of a post office box in Vila do Mar inscribed in heavy brown ink.

Chapter Twelve

"*QUANTO CUSTA?*" I asked Mario, the proprietor of my favorite antique shop, as I held up a small pewter jug.

Vila do Mar's main square was bordered by a mix of glossy-looking shops selling the usual Portuguese specialties of blue-and-white Delft-looking pottery and lace tablecloths that, like most souvenirs, could lose their tackiness and look far lovelier at home on your own table when viewed away from the mass of their look-alikes. Nestled among these emporiums were a few somewhat dingy stores that carried fine antiques and maintained their unappealing facades in order to discourage the casual souvenir seeker.

True antique shoppers would be instantly at home in the jammed poky interior of Mario's shop; their bargain-hunting antennae would immediately start to quiver as they examined the dusty treasures within, as did mine whenever I entered the place.

Mario looked at the small jug and looked at me with the smile that displayed (I once counted) six teeth. We were old adversaries and both enjoyed the buying battle. He was a small, dark man who was extremely proud of his robustness and always asked people how old they thought he was. The first time he asked me, I said, "*Cinquenta e seis*" (fifty-six), at which point he laughed proudly and said, "*Setente e dois*" (seventy-two). And I shook my head in honest wonderment because to me he looks like eighty-two.

I repeated, "*Quanto*, Mario?"

He mentioned a many-thousand-escudo figure.

"*Ridículo!* " I shot back. I showed him how dull and scratched the finish was.

He snorted. "*Não e nada.*" And he took it in the back to polish it up, as I knew he would. Ten minutes later I walked out with my now shiny and tissue-wrapped little jug in a small paper bag.

I walked to Sir Barry's and looked around and saw Rafael and Brigida, Manuel's friends from the Lido Bar, at one of the tables. I waved to them and remembered Sir Barry's allegation that if you occupy a seat in his bistro for three hours, you will be sure to see everyone in Vila do Mar. Then I spotted Dirk and Colin, who waved me over.

"Dirk, what do you think of my purchase? You're an antique expert." And I handed him the pitcher. I ordered a *café branco* and watched him remove the wrapping, turn the piece around in his hands, and then stand it on the table.

"Very sweet," he said. "But I do hope you didn't pay more than ten pounds."

I replaced it very carefully in the tissue and put it back in the little bag.

"Then I guess I did O.K.," I said with a smile.

I PUT THE bag on *el chefe*'s desk. I had driven over right from Sir Barry's and was fortunate to find him in his office.

"We have interviewed all the staff at Dona Felipa and none saw a visitor going to Senhor Evans' room," he said as soon as I sat down facing his desk.

"I'm sure someone will turn up, but right now, I am not here about that. You told me you detest drugs—this is true?"

His face hardened. "*Com intensidade*," he said firmly.

"*Desculpe*, then how can you tolerate the drug-selling going on at the Lido Bar every night?"

He waved his hand. "Ah, that is nothing serious. My man who covers the area tells me it is students selling the little marihuana they grow in pots on their window sills. I would not ruin a young person's life by arresting him for this."

"Your man is either blind or getting paid not to see."

He sat up in fury. "You are accusing my *polícia* of corruption? This is a serious charge."

"So is the wholesale dealing in cocaine that is really going on."

I told him the entire story. When I came to the end, the part about seeing the green envelope at Dirk's house, he gasped and fell back in his chair.

"*Meu Deus*—you are telling me that Senhor Croft is the main drug distributor of the Algarve—a man, I might add, we have been seeking for months—the one who is responsible for the death of my wife's *sobrinho?*"

"Yes, and I think this little jug can prove it."

According to the timetable as Carlos had told Abba, he should have been receiving his shipment in the Vila do Mar post office box the next day, the day after Dirk received and filled the orders.

"I will be there personally at the post office at that time," said *el chefe* firmly. Then he looked at me appraisingly for a few seconds. "*Diga-me*, Miss Emma, what involves you in all this?"

The time for truth is now. "Because I am searching for the murderer of Peter Belling."

His eyes widened.

"This is all for your book?"

"No, for the parents of Peter Belling, for whom I am investigating the truth of their son's death, which I think ties in with drugs."

He smiled. "Ah, I see. You are like the lady Jessica Fletcher on that *Murder, She Wrote* television show?"

I sighed. There was no escape but the whole truth. After I got his assurance of total confidence, I told him my real profession, and I could see his expression change from mild amusement to annoyed skepticism. Law enforcement people did not look kindly on private investigators, especially unlicensed ones who happened to be female. Time to call for backup.

"*Comandante*, you now have before you two serious matters involving subjects of another EC country. Might it not be a courtesy, and possibly a help, to inform the British police about the criminal activities of their citizens?"

I could see that the thought had not entered his mind.

"Especially if it is more than likely that you are going to arrest a highly placed member of the English nobility; I think Scotland Yard would appreciate being involved, and could possibly be extremely helpful."

Like any law officer in a small town, the possibility of working with Scotland Yard intrigued him immensely. There was great ego appeal in the image of working side-by-side with a member of that legendary organization.

"May I suggest you phone Detective Chief Superintendent Caleb Franklin now. You can tell him it was at my suggestion."

"You know this man?" he said, slightly awed.

I knew that Caleb was an international celebrity in law enforcement circles.

"Yes, I know him." Though maybe not quite as well as he would have liked me to.

I smiled inwardly as I watched *el chefe* straighten his tie, pull down his uniform jacket, and sit up in the chair when his secretary notified him that she had Senhor Superintendent Franklin on the line. He told Caleb the entire story. After mentioning my name, he sat and listened for a few minutes and eyed me. Then he handed me the phone with a smile.

"The superintendent wishes to speak with you."

"Well, Miss Rhodes, I recall once saying that you have a talent for being where things are happening and wondering if you are the catalyst or just an unwitting bystander," said that resonant, deep voice that got me every time I heard it.

I laughed. "And I remember telling you that I could never be an unwitting anything."

"Knowing you now, I quite see that. I gather our chum lately known as Chilton Evans is now our late chum. There won't be any tears shed for him here. Sergeant Parnell will be happy to close out his dossier. But Elizabeth Eddington suspected of the murder—the lovely lady who is the sister of that rotter from Wycombe?"

"Only suspected, Caleb, far from proven," I said. "The full range of possibilities has barely been tapped. But the Duke of Sandringham's brother—that may present far greater complications."

"Now that's a scandal our press will adore. A member of one of the oldest, most important families in England—I can just see the headlines: 'Duke's Brother Deals Drugs'—it certainly has a ring to it."

"If it pushes the antics of your royal family off the front pages, it may even perform a national service," I said.

He laughed. "That's one of the things I always loved—er, I mean, liked about you, Emma—the side of you that always sees brighter aspects of a situation. Happily, I will be seeing all sides of you soon, because I accepted the chief's kind invitation to come there tomorrow."

My heart jumped. Caleb Franklin was one of the most attractive and interesting men I'd ever come across—and I'd come across plenty. As I mentioned earlier, we never really got a chance to probe our mutual attraction when we met because I was involved with someone else at the time, and I'd always been a mite sorry. I was not one to mull over lost opportunities and was a great believer in fate, kismet, Batshert, or whatever the various religions use to explain inexplicable twists of destiny. The fact that Caleb was turning up in my life again at this time was perhaps the sign for me to evaluate my true feelings about Mark. If it turned out that Caleb turned me on, then marriage may not be for me.

"I'd offer you my guest room, Caleb, but as you know, Abba is the current resident. Of course, you could always camp on the couch."

I could see *el chefe* enjoying the intimate conversation, and his estimation of me was going up with every word.

Caleb laughed. "Thank you for your generous offer, Emma. But I'll find other accommodations that will be convenient but I'm sure far less amusing. This is a serious matter that will undoubtedly involve the home office. The Yard will pick up my expenses without question. Farewell. I look forward to seeing you and Abba tomorrow."

Caleb coming tomorrow, Mark returning in a few days, Dirk to be detected tomorrow—life was getting hectic—just the way I liked it. I could deal with aggravation, stress, and all kinds of pressures—the only thing I positively could not bear was boredom.

I headed right for the *supermercado*. Did I ever have my priorities right? With all the guests I expected in the next few days, not to mention the voracious capacity of my present boarder, I figured I'd better replenish my larder. As I pushed my small wagon along the aisles, I came upon a young man stocking the shelves. It was Rafael.

"*Bom dia*, Rafael. We see each other again today. *Como estas?*"

He stood up and smiled. "*Menos mal, senhorita. É você?*"

"*Bem, obrigado.* I didn't know you work here."

"I come sometimes to help my uncle, who owns the store. Being a student, I work part-time whenever I can. Like at the Dona Felipa last night—I saw you," he said with a smile. "You looked very beautiful."

"Thank you. What do you do there?" I asked.

"I help my brother Jorge with the shoes."

In European hotels, guests customarily placed their shoes in front of their doors at night and found them polished and cleaned the next morning.

"Jorge shines them; I return them."

"I suppose the police questioned you about the man who died there last night."

He looked puzzled. "No, why would they?"

"It's just routine. They were questioning all hotel employees to see if they saw anything that might help solve the mystery of how the man died."

"That's why they wouldn't get to me," he said. "I am not an employee of the hotel—only of my brother. When he has too much to do, he pays me to help him out. There were many shoes to be shined last night—it was a very full hotel."

Then his face clouded. "Perhaps I should tell them about the *ladrão de sapatos.*"

I stiffened. "The shoe thief? What do you mean?"

"I was returning the shoes this morning—I saw this man standing in the hall. He was wearing those fancy suits you wear for jogging so I figured at this hour, he's probably waiting for a friend to run with. After I put out all the shoes, I looked back and saw him pick up the shoes in front of the dead man's door and put them in the bag he had strapped around his waist, the kind that joggers carry water and things in."

"Didn't you think that was a little strange, Rafael? Why didn't you stop him?"

He smiled ruefully. "I am not supposed to be there. I didn't want to get Jorge in trouble. Besides, the man was such an elegant gentleman, I figured he probably had a good reason for doing this."

"Would you know him if you saw him again?" I asked.

He looked at me strangely. "But of course. So would you. You were sitting with him just before at Sir Barry's . . . the man next to Dr. Robinson."

Chapter Thirteen

CALEB AND I sat in the front seat of my little VW in front of the post office the next morning. We were able to persuade *el chefe* of the folly of using his large official Mercedes, but since we couldn't talk him out of the fancy, impressive uniform he insisted on wearing even when the temperature hit ninety, we stowed him more unobtrusively in the back.

I had never seen Caleb in casual clothes and he looked smashing. The red Ralph Lauren Polo shirt displayed pecs and arms that indicated daily fitness activity, and the color looked great against his coffee-colored skin. Impeccable as always, his chinos were smoothly pressed, his Reeboks fashionably worn but clean. He had arrived late last night and had breakfast this morning on my terrace with Abba and me. They were obviously both very pleased to see each other again, although it was always hard to tell from the usual say-nothing male greetings that men give whether they hadn't met for five days or five years.

"Hello; great to see you. How's it going?"

"Pretty well. You?"

"Keeping busy."

"What's happening in your life?"

"Not much, more of the usual."

"Me, too."

I'd heard that kind of exchange between males who run across each other in the street and was always amused to hear the conversation end with, "Nice talking to you," which made me want to ask, "About what?"

We had checked and knew the post office box mail would be distributed at ten, and sure enough, promptly at five of, Carlos arrived.

As soon as he went inside, *el chefe* stepped out of the car. A few minutes later, Carlos emerged carrying a large package wrapped in green paper and addressed in brown ink. He didn't see *el chefe* until the last minute and he froze. The policeman merely took him by the arm wordlessly and led him to the car where he pushed him into the back seat. Carlos looked terrified.

An hour later, the green wrapping paper and glassine bags of cocaine had been inspected carefully for fingerprints, which were then compared to those on my little pewter pitcher.

Two hours later, Dirk Croft was sitting in the esquadra interview room, thoroughly relaxed and self-assured. He didn't seem surprised to see me there and greeted me with a kiss. However, when Caleb introduced himself, he was a bit shaken but recovered quickly.

"Senhor Croft, you apparently have been in a business of which we were unaware." *El chefe* spoke softly, with a good-natured smile.

"And what is that, *Comandante*?" said Dirk, matching smile for smile.

"Distributing cocaine." The smile was now gone.

Dirk did not stop smiling. "That's quite a serious accusation, *Chefe*. I assume you're prepared to back up this ludicrous statement with something resembling facts and proof."

"Mr. Croft," interrupted Caleb, "perhaps you would prefer to have a solicitor present."

Dirk waved his hand arrogantly. "Certainly not, Superintendent. I see no need to dignify these proceedings with such attendance. This is merely the idiocy of a small-town policeman who has overstepped his capability and is probably seeking to bolster his failing reputation by the grandstand play of arresting a prominent citizen and a member of a noble family."

Ozorio flushed and I saw Caleb's lips tighten. To malign the dignity of a Portuguese male, and in front of a respected colleague like a Scotland Yard official, is about the cruelest thing you could do. It was callous and stupid and lost Dirk any friends he might have had before in the room.

I could never understand gratuitous inflicting of pain, but I wasn't surprised at his cool assurance. He had evolved a clever system whose assets were simplicity and the safe method of anonymity whereby no one member of the network knew another. The seemingly convoluted technique of sending orders from city to city made tracing difficult if not impossible. Even if any one of the couriers got greedy and curious to know the source, all he would find was another courier who knew no more than he. There was no way to trace any of the transactions to him.

The door opened and a uniformed policeman came in, had a whispered conference with Ozorio, and left quickly, returning almost immediately with a box, which he placed on the table in front of *el chefe*.

"I think, Senhor Croft, that it is you who has failed. First, we have this envelope that we took from your garbage." And he pulled out the green envelope I had seen on Dirk's table.

"How dare you go through my garbage?" he said in a fury of indignation. "I'll have you fired for this violation of my privacy and rights."

Ozorio ignored his outburst and went on methodically.

"Which matches the wrapping and addressing of this package of drugs we took from your courier's hands a short time ago." And he placed the packet and contents on the table. "All upon which, Senhor Croft," he said with grim satisfaction, "we found your fingerprints."

The room went deadly silent.

Dirk recovered quickly. "How could you know those fingerprints are mine?" he asked with a sneer.

Ozorio pulled out the pewter pitcher and set it on the table.

Dirk looked over at me. "You foul bitch. So this is the sort of shoddy muckraking you really do. Did they pay you a bounty for this? Are you so hard up that betraying your friends is the only way you can finance your debauched life with that hairy Jew?"

I saw Caleb go rigid with the attempt at control.

"No, Dirk," I said sweetly, "I did it all for free; doesn't that make you bust a gut? Unlike moral degenerates like you, I have a sense of decency concerning what I will do to support my lifestyle."

He turned bright red and jumped towards me, but Caleb got there quickly and pushed him back into his seat with a little more force than was necessary.

Dirk shrugged and said, "This is all circumstantial evidence. So you found a green envelope in my garbage—it could have been thrown there by Francisco." Then his eyes lit up. "Perhaps there's your man—Francisco has access to everything in my home."

"Nice try, Dirk," I said. "And you speak of betraying friends? Francisco has been serving you faithfully for twenty years!"

"I'm afraid, Mr. Croft," said Caleb quietly, "they found a large cache of cocaine locked in a cabinet in your bedroom to which no one but you has the key. And yes, I checked, the police had a warrant."

"Where did you get the cocaine from?" asked *el chefe*. "According to Carlos, you got deliveries once a month." He sat with his lips set in a tight line.

Then it hit me. "The monthly wine shipments from London!"

He turned on me in fury. "Too bad you survived Francisco's little operation on your brakes."

"What is that about?" asked *el chefe*.

"What's this about drug shipments from London?" asked Caleb.

"He gets a carton of wine from Shreve and Asbury every month. Francisco picks it up at Faro airport. I'll bet the bottles are neatly cushioned by something far more effective than bubble-pack."

"Shreve and Asbury—that's one of our oldest, most distinguished vintners," said Caleb grimly. "We'll have to check out who packs Mr. Croft's orders."

"Now, Mr. Croft, we get to the small matter of murder," said Ozorio.

"What on earth are you talking about?" asked Dirk. "Next you'll be accusing me of starting World War Two."

"Senhor Chilton Evans. You were the visitor to his room that Senhora Eddington heard."

"Nonsense. I went directly home after the ball—I have witnesses. Julia will tell you—I was with her all evening."

"Not all evening, Dirk," I said. "I was chatting with her and Pamela in the foyer after the ball for at least a half hour. We were gossiping about who wore what and why. I remember Julia mentioning too bad you weren't there with us because it was just the sort of juicy stuff you adore. She didn't know where you were, but as I recall, her answer when I asked was, 'My dear Emma, we may be lovers but we each come and go as we please, which is the lovely thing about not being married.' "

"So I may have gone to the men's room or outside to smoke a cigar. What does that prove?"

"It was the shoes, Dirk."

For the first time, he paled. Some of his assurance ebbed.

"I couldn't understand why Chilton's shoes were not in his room. Then I realized you knew his cleanliness fetish about not permitting anyone to walk on his floors with shoes. So before you entered his room you removed your shoes and left them in front of his door. After you dosed him with cyanide and were ready to leave, you were probably horrified to see that your shoes were gone. You'd forgotten how they take them away for cleaning. So you went back in and put on Chilton's shoes. Which meant you had to go back the next morning and pick up your own shoes. Someone saw you clearly, Dirk. We have a positive identification."

He slumped down in his chair and stared ahead of him for a few moments as we all observed him silently.

"He had the audacity to ask for a partnership in my drug business. Imagine the gall of that little charlatan? Just because we worked together on the Foundation arrangement, which he couldn't have done without me—I brought in all the contributions; I'm the one with all the right connections. The success of the ball wouldn't have happened without the unwitting help of my nephew. We had planned to go to the bank after the checks had cleared and I would get my share before he left town. Then he tossed his little bombshell that he planned to move to Lisbon and work with me on my drug distribution. The fool had delusions of grandeur—he told me he even had plans to expand. Imagine the cheek of the man. When I demurred, he dared to threaten me with an ultimatum: either I cut him in or he would reveal all the details to some nefarious acquaintances of his who are international drug dealers and will move in and take over my little operation, as he put it, and I would be thrown out or worse. I had no choice but to get rid of him."

"How did you do it, Senhor Croft?" asked *el chefe* softly.

Dirk had been talking in almost a trance. Now he snapped out of it and sat up. "Why, just as I exterminate all pests in and around my home—with the cyanide poison I keep in the garden shed."

"But how did you get him to take it?"

He smiled triumphantly. The man's ego was indestructible. "I told him I was ready to agree to his terms and brought a bottle of my finest brandy to toast the new partnership." He shrugged. "I hated to waste that wonderful elixir on such a Philistine, but there was a job to be done. When he went to get a second glass from the bathroom, I poured cyanide in his glass and then topped it with brandy. It was really quite simple." He laughed. "The idiot mentioned that he thought it tasted funny, but I told him he just wasn't used to twenty-five-year-old fine brandy. We drank, and when I saw the poison taking effect, I took my glass and left. I was a bit set back when I saw my shoes gone missing, but fortunately we wear similar sizes so I just put on his."

A policeman entered and stood next to *el chefe*, who rose and went over to help Dirk out of his chair.

"One minute. Before you go, Dirk, what about Peter Belling?"

He looked puzzled. "Who?"

"That young American who was Leida's lover. How did you kill him?"

He looked at me in astonishment. "Are you insane? Why would I have anything to do with that psalm-singing fool?"

My heart sank. "Because he was sniffing around about drug distribution in town and might have uncovered your operation."

He laughed. "Oh, yes, I did hear about his pulpit-pounding efforts to rid the world of evil. But he was an ineffectual, harmless young idiot who I figured would soon go back to America and remember the entire episode as a romantic adventure. I must confess I was surprised he had the courage to kill himself. But small loss, I'd say. I'm sure Leida found an equally qualified bedmate replacement shortly thereafter."

I came closer to punching a man in the jaw than I could remember. Fortunately, Caleb noticed my clenched fists and the fury in my face and hastened to my side. After *el chefe* took Dirk out of the room, Caleb turned to me.

"Would you really have belted the chap?"

"Worse. I would probably have nearly killed him. He's a fragile older guy and I'm an experienced boxer."

He smiled. "Don't tell me. You learned sparring at that same place where you learned to throw a baseball that enabled you to knock out that terrorist in Brussels?"

"That's right. It was an equal rights camp where there was no gender distinction in athletic activities. I won the medal for winning more bouts than any other girl in my group."

He looked at me soberly. "I'd best watch my step with you, my girl. I can see you're no one to trifle with."

I smiled. "Why, Superintendent, was that your intention?"

Chapter Fourteen

"I'LL BE RIGHT over," said Leida with delight.

Caleb was at his hotel making official arrangements with his office and Abba had gone off on a boat with Inga, which left me free to invite Leida for what I termed "lunch and some girl talk."

You could always tell when it was Leida's car pulling up outside your door because she drove it along the narrow dirt roads of Vila do Mar as though it was Le Mans. Inevitably she brought the vehicle to a screeching stop, which was unnerving since you knew she would be unable to pass a breathalyzer test after ten in the morning on any day. She breezed in wearing the kind of gauzy brown shroud-looking garment she favored since someone told her the color was becoming to redheads, which she happened to be this year. We greeted each other with the usual continental two-cheek kiss method and sat outside where Gloria had put out olives and potato crisps with a bottle of chilled *vinho verde*, the fizzy white wine of Portugal which was called "green wine" because it was young.

She eyed my clothes, as she always did. "Where did you get that suit, what's it made of, and how much did it cost?" she asked as she downed a full glass in a single gulp. Obviously the poor girl was thirsty, and of course, a lush.

I didn't know what Swiss ecoles she attended, but she surely didn't major in manners. I understood those finishing schools gave courses on such invaluable skills as how to pour tea and open fairs, but they apparently left her quite unfinished in the ladylike arts of delicacy and diplomacy. Whatever Leida wanted to know, she asked.

"I bought this outfit in New York, it's made of natural linen, and it costs three-hundred-and-eighty dollars," I said.

"You're crazy!" she said. "That's a fortune. I couldn't pay that."

"Of course you could, Leida—and you should. But you just wouldn't."

"Why do you say that?" she asked suspiciously.

"You can well afford it, but it's just not worth it to you," I answered as if to a child.

"What do you mean?" she asked. "I like to look nice."

"And you do. But you're quite content wearing simple, less expensive clothes."

All conversations with Leida had to be held at a basic, childlike level. It was how her mind worked. You could see why she wasn't on anyone's number-one guest list. She was really a royal pain in the ass.

I called to Gloria to bring out lunch. I wanted to get some substantial food into Leida before she got too looped to answer the questions I needed answered. Gloria came out with bowls of gazpacho and a tray of fish salad, tomatoes, and hot rolls and butter.

"Now tell me something about your lover, Leida." I knew this was a topic that would always get her attention.

"Which one?" she asked with a big grin as she spooned soup into her mouth.

"I mean the poor young American who killed himself."

Her face changed suddenly. For a moment, I thought she looked sad. Then I realized—that wasn't sadness, it was fear. It was the same reaction she had the last time I mentioned Peter—when we were at Graham's. But why?

"Yes, it was terrible. They found him on the beach, drowned."

She had gone through her bowl of gazpacho and was buttering a whole roll. I couldn't control myself.

"Leida, honey, it would be easier to eat that large roll if you tore it into smaller pieces and then buttered each piece as you ate it." Adriaan really should have demanded at least a partial refund from those schools.

She did as she was told like an obedient child.

"How did he come to drown, Leida?" I asked.

"They said it was suicide."

"Who said?"

"Everybody—the police."

"Did you love him very much?"

The question puzzled her. Of course, she didn't understand love, except for her father.

"He was mad about me."

"Then what happened?"

She shrugged. "He just didn't understand." And she began to pile fish salad on her plate.

The words in Peter's suicide note: "There is obviously too much that I cannot understand."

"He said he felt bad for me because the father of my child deserted me. I told him he was crazy." She downed a fourth glass of wine and began to slur slightly. I wasn't surprised. If I had consumed what she had, I'd be incoherent if not comatose.

She laughed. "I told him that wasn't true."

"What wasn't true?"

"Why, that Adriana's papa deserted me."

I put down my fork and waited.

"Boy, did he ever get upset when I told him who her father was," she said with a cunning smile.

I was silent. I knew she was waiting for me to ask the name, but knowing that twisted mind of hers, she would very probably look at me with that mean-and-rotten-kid look and say something like, "That's my secret." I told you that acting was one of the tools of my profession, and feigning disinterest at this moment when I was dying for her answer surely qualified me for an Oscar nomination. I just picked at my salad and sipped wine. Finally, she couldn't stand it any longer.

"It's Daddy," she said with a giggle.

I looked at her uncomprehendingly.

"My daddy, silly. Adriana's daddy is my daddy."

I was speechless.

"Boy, did Peter ever go bananas that night I told him."

It was no mean feat to render Emma Rhodes speechless. I could imagine how it hit the young idealistic minister.

"What did he do when he heard?"

"Oh, he just wouldn't leave me alone after that. He was at my house every morning. He even brought me a Bible, for God's sake."

This was just the kind of revelation that must have pushed his missionary mode button into high gear.

"Then he asked me to marry him and go back to America with him."

The image of Leida as a Westchester minister's wife was mindboggling. Her idea of cardinal sin was to run out of vodka. The one role in which she'd shine would be sickroom visitor; her methods of morale-building for bedridden males would surely become the talk of the parish. It would seem that Peter's reformer zeal was clouding his judgment. Either that or he was so besotted with Leida that we were back to the Somerset Maugham syndrome but this time we were into *Of Human Bondage*.

"What did you tell him?" I asked.

She looked astonished. "What do you think? I told him Adriana and I would never leave my—our—father."

What world was this woman living in? There was not a shred of remorse, shame, or any awareness that incest was illegal and an unacceptable social aberration. Did Peter really believe he could reform her or was that the failure he alluded to in his note? Immorality could often be corrected once you convinced the sinner to give up his evil ways, but amorality was impossible since the malefactor could not comprehend what about his ways were evil.

Suddenly, she turned forlorn. "It was too bad. I really liked him a lot. Adriana was crazy about him. I told him to move in with me, why couldn't we just live here? I wouldn't marry him, of course. Daddy wouldn't like that."

"Did Peter ever meet Daddy?"

She looked confused. Then that touch of fear again. "I don't want to talk about him anymore—he's dead." She jumped up from her chair and started to dance around the terrace in her awkward ragdoll style. I knew I had hit the end of the line with Leida and I had best move on to another venue. I called Wolfie and Andries.

Chapter Fifteen

CALEB AND ABBA sat in the kitchen with me that evening and watched me prepare dinner.

"Good lord, she cooks, too," said Caleb as he sipped his vodka and tonic.

"I used to be the takeout queen of Fifth Avenue when I lived in New York," I said. "But when the co-op board warned me that they might have to assess me for a new incinerator for the building since my pizza and Chinese food cartons were filling up the current one, I decided to learn how to use my stove."

"Is that the large metal box in the kitchen where one stores old pots?" asked Caleb as he swirled the limes around in his glass.

I pulled a long rectangular baking pan out of the oven and began to baste the contents.

"Mmm, that smells fantastic, *hamoodie*," said Abba.

"What is that word *hamoodie*? I've heard you call Emma that before, Abba. Is that some sort of password between you?"

Abba laughed. "No, it's an Israeli term of endearment that means 'my love.' We also use *motek*—'my darling,' and *ahuvati*—'sweetheart.'"

"You have many words of warmth and affection in your country."

"We're a very warm and affectionate people," said Abba. "We know we must love each other because sure as hell no one else does."

I lifted out the pan and set it on the tile trivets in the middle of the dining room table. "Dinner's ready, gentlemen. Will someone please bring in the salad from the fridge?"

"This is fantastic, Emma," said Caleb as he spooned a third helping on to his plate. "I'm glad I gave up being a vegetarian, if just to enjoy this."

"You were a vegetarian?" asked Abba. "You don't look like one."

"I never knew they were identifiable, Abba," said Caleb.

"Sure, Caleb," I said. "Can't you just see it on a WANTED poster? 'Six-foot-two-inch vegetarian. Brown eyes, brown hair, last seen munching a stalk of celery.'"

Abba snorted with annoyance. "You people obviously don't understand the finer points of detection. An individual's appearance is not just defined by his physical features but in most cases by his interests, work, and personal philosophies."

"You mean you could pick out a podiatrist in the street?" I asked.

"Listen, smartass," Abba said, "if I was hunting for a mathematician, I wouldn't look at guys with nineteen-inch necks and highly developed pecs and abs. People who become vegetarians take on the commitment for one of two reasons: health or principle. In the first case, they're usually thin and pale—tofu and groats may be nourishing but they don't put roses in your cheeks or a helluva lot of flesh on your bones. In the second case, they're not only thin and pale but they have the special quality of 'cause' people— I can spot it a mile off."

"I can see how you find me visually confusing," said Caleb. "I'm not thin, I have no fanatic gleam in my eye, and you would have a difficult time ascertaining if I'm pale," he said with a smile.

"That's a pretty big heap of generalizations you've just tossed out here, Abba," I said.

Abba shrugged. "I know. Now you're going to tell me the entire Miami Dolphin football team are vegetarians. Generalizations are just that—they have exceptions. But in my business, we need to start somewhere. For instance, I would make the generalization that gorgeous sexy women like you would be total fuckups in the kitchen. Yet look at this marvelous *meichel* you whipped up for us."

And he reached for a fourth helping. "Sweetheart, this chicken is better than my stubborn Aunt Goldie's, whom the family has never forgiven for going to her grave without giving anyone her special recipe. Whose recipe is this?"

"Mine. I made it up."

"You?" they said in stunned unison.

I smiled proudly. "Me. You see, I figured an immediate switch from two-minute take-out warm-up to three-hour Julia Child projects would give me the bends—I needed a decompression technique that would get me through the transition. So I started developing my own recipes that had three requirements. One, all ingredients had to be purchasable in one store. Two, the one dish would be a meal in itself, and three, it had to be cooked and served in one pot. That means no running from store to store to buy esoteric ethnic foods and rare spices, and not having to deal with dozens of serving dishes and pots. In other words, easy to prepare, easy to serve, and easy to clean up."

"If it's that simple, I could make it for the wild bunch who seem to show up in my apartment Saturday nights. So tell me. Unless you're one of those women who don't give out their recipes. Or like my mother used to do with my brother's wife, leave out a critical ingredient so the dish tasted like shit and my sister-in-law looked like a kitchen klutz."

"You want the recipe right now?" I asked.

"Right now." And he took out the notebook and pen he always kept in his pocket.

"Good lord, he's serious," said Caleb.

"Fuckin'-A," said Abba. "I'm always serious when it comes to food."

"Then write legibly please, and in English," said Caleb. "I'd like a Xerox. I must confess I'm getting a bit fed up with takeout curries and fish 'n' chips. Perhaps it's time for me to get married," he said, looking at me.

"I think it would be cheaper to buy a cookbook," said Abba.

"O.K., here goes," I said and he started writing. "Cut chicken into eighths or smaller. Then thinly slice potatoes—you don't even have to peel them; the skin is healthy—carrots, onions, and parsnips. Layer the vegetables in the pan and spread the chicken on top. Salt and pepper everything to taste. I like a lot of kosher salt, freshly ground pepper, and some hot pepper on the chicken. Put it into a three-hundred-seventy-five-degree oven uncovered for about one-and-a-half hours. After about one half hour, pour in a half cup of white wine and half cup of water and swish them around to make sure they mix with the pan juices. Baste every fifteen minutes until chicken is brown and crisp. It's actually better if you let it sit covered for at least a half hour on a hot tray before serving, and longer is even better. It allows all the flavors to blend. But somehow I didn't think you fellows would sit still for that tonight."

"The aroma would've driven me wild and I would've gotten crocked in the interim," said Abba.

"You neglected to mention quantities, Emma," said Caleb.

"That's up to you, your number of guests, and their appetites. I figure a per-person allotment of half a chicken, two carrots, two potatoes, two onions, and two parsnips."

I watched with the great satisfaction every cook derives from seeing her food demolished with relish.

"Another thing that makes the dish such a winner is that it sits right on the table for self-help at will," I added. "For a larger group, I place pots at either end of the table. It's easier for me and less embarrassing for the hearty eaters."

"Like me," said Abba as he carefully scraped crispy potatoes from the sides of the pot. "I don't have to keep noodging you to bring me seconds and thirds."

"Or be hesitant about making repeated trips to the buffet for fear of being publicly branded a glutton," said Caleb.

There was a loud knock on the front door and Mark strode in, his face like thunder. He stopped in front of me.

"Mata Hari, I presume? I've just seen my uncle and he told me all about who and what you really are. How dare you drag an innocent man through the mud of your squalid activities just to make a name for yourself! You spy and lie and use people for money, which as I see it makes you no better than a street whore."

Abba and Caleb were on their feet in seconds. Mark looked at them scornfully. "I suppose you two 'gentlemen' are her cohorts. How egalitarian—a Jew and a black. Do you share the fees or does she just pay you off in sex?"

"I am Detective Superintendent Caleb Franklin of Scotland Yard, and you, I presume, are the not-so-honorable at the moment Mark Croft. I suggest you sit down and calm down before you do or say anything stupider than you already have."

Mark turned red and sat down at the table. I had turned to stone.

"If you are speaking of the arrest of your uncle, thanks to the unpaid efforts of Miss Rhodes, virtually conclusive evidence has been presented that puts him at the head of a drug distribution network that has been functioning in this area for some time. His own confession confirms her accusation of the murder of his colleague Chilton Evans. Of course, all this must be proved in a court of law, but I will tell you that the evidence and witness testimony are dead-on as can be."

I hadn't moved. Abba sat down and I noticed him unclenching his fists.

Mark sat quietly for a few moments. "I seem to have made a perfect ass of myself, haven't I? I just came from the gaol where I was, as you can understand, rather shocked to find my uncle in custody for heinous crimes, which he disclaims and blames all on Emma." He looked straight at me. "He called her a female Judas for betraying and selling out his and my friendship for a handful of silver."

"The fucking nerve of the son of a bitch to compare himself to Jesus, one of the most saintly men in the history of mankind," said Abba.

That snapped me to attention. "Abba, you're Jewish."

He smiled. "So was Jesus. Can't I be proud of one of our own boys who made good?"

I had to laugh, which from his pleased expression, was the main purpose of his statement.

I turned to Mark. "I am a sort of private investigator—it's what I do to make a living. I was working on another case that led me inadvertently to Dirk and his clear identification as the head of an active drug distribution network, which I, of course, had to turn over to the chief of police. This is not a minor just-enough-for-his-own-use affair, which would fit the description of the activities of a good number of my friends, which I would never reveal to the authorities. But your 'innocent' uncle has been maintaining his elegant lifestyle by running an elaborate, extensive drug distribution ring that resulted in the death of at least one boy last week and undoubtedly many more, plus the inevitable destruction of many other young lives. He admits to coldly killing Chilton in a cruel, inhuman way that asphyxiated him slowly and painfully just as, in his own words, he does away with garden pests. I appreciate that you love your uncle but you had better face the fact that he's not the urbane charmer you thought. Those constant witty antipeople barbs we all regarded as entertaining and harmless indicated a virulent cynicism. He felt no compunction about destroying others in order to suit what he saw as his entitlement to good living. I'm sorry that he's your uncle, but I see him as a danger to society and I would turn him in again tomorrow to keep him off the streets."

Then I got up and went into the kitchen to put up coffee. The coffee-bean grinder was making its usual loud noise so that I didn't hear Mark come in until I felt his arms around my waist, which I carefully removed. I turned to face him. He was utterly anguished. I was surprised to notice that his saddened state didn't touch me and I felt completely unmoved by his obvious deep distress.

He looked at me with total misery in his eyes. "I've lost you, haven't I?"

"That certainly would cover the situation—for the moment."

His face brightened when I added the last three words. "You mean there's hope?"

"I don't know. I can only speak for now, and at this time the feeling I had for you has been replaced by a rock. Whether it will go away in time, I don't know."

"Then I'll wait, Emma darling. Lord, how could I have been such a blind idiot? How could I have believed him for a moment? I knew that Uncle had gone through the money he made on that initial offering in which he was involved. In fact, I learned the figure had been grossly overstated—Dirk liked people to think he was wealthy and I saw no harm in allowing him that small conceit. I blame myself and our family. We knew his style of living had to be costly, but foolishly preferred to close our eyes rather than question the source. He never came to us for money and we were content to allow things to go on as they were rather than ask if he needed help." He took my hands. "But you—how could I ever question you? You're the best thing that's ever happened to me. How could I for a moment take the word of someone I deep down know is bent over someone as pure and honorable as you?"

AFTER HE LEFT, the three of us sat on the terrace drinking coffee. I told them what he had said.

"It wasn't what he thought of you that really upset you, was it?" asked Caleb.

"No. After all, he's only known me for a few days and he's known his uncle all his life. I could understand how he would believe his uncle that I had used both of them for my own ends, if you'll pardon the expression."

"It was the other stuff."

I nodded. "I can't forget the disdain and utter disgust on his face."

"You mean because he thought you had sunk to the absolute nadir by fucking a Yid and a Schvartzer?" asked Abba.

"Ah, Abba, I never cease to admire your knack for reaching the heart of a matter with such delicacy of language. But in a word, yes."

"He's an aristocrat," said Caleb, "from a family who for generations has believed that blue blood is truly different from the common red in us lesser mortals. I shouldn't even include myself in the 'mortal' category because I think he regards me as a step down on Darwin's evolutionary scale. It's hard if not impossible to shed beliefs that have been inculcated in you from birth."

"But he's nuts about you, Emma—and he's rich. Maybe he can change."

"I'm not sure it's worth the risk." I yawned. "Hey, guys, it's late—I'm ready for bed." Then I walked over to Caleb and touched his shoulder. "How about you?" His eyes widened and then he smiled.

Abba arose and said, "Goodnight, children. I'll see you both in the morning."

And he did.

Chapter Sixteen

THE NEXT MORNING, I left my guests sleeping, picked up a dozen crusty, hot rolls at the *padaria* and brought my goodies into the little house Wolfie and Andries rented from Adriaan at the end of a small road near Santa Eulalia. I was delighted to see and smell that the coffee was already made and the butter and cheese on the table. The coffee in the Algarve is a strong, full-bodied brew from Angola and the butter is fresh and sweet from local farms. Breakfast was my favorite meal and I was starved. The three of us polished off the dozen rolls and part of the bread and two pots of coffee. What was amazing about this achievement was that we still managed to talk nonstop.

They had heard about Dirk's arrest, of course, and were relentless in their efforts to get all possible details from me. His fall from grace filled them with gloating joy, as it probably did many people in Vila do Mar. Dirk's de facto position as social arbiter of the town had made him extremely unpopular with those he shunned and deemed unworthy of joining his social set. Wolfie and Andries were part of Adriaan's world, which automatically disqualified them from entering Dirk's. Although Adriaan's financial position made him eminently acceptable to Dirk, his lack of discretion, crude behavior, and total disregard for the amenities and graces made him satyr-non-grata in Dirk's social register.

Being barred from the sort of activities Dirk hosted and attended was a great source of bitterness to Wolfie and

Andries since these were just the sort of superficial, glittering, gossip-ridden entertainment they adored.

I could never understand anyone's antagonism to or awkwardness with homosexuals. I was as comfortable in this household as in any heterosexual one; their relationship was typical of all couples who had been together for years, replete with the bickering, nagging, and other signs of marital fondness. What they did in the bedroom to consummate their feelings for each other was not my concern any more than that of straight couples I knew. If I refused to socialize with anyone who went in for unconventional sex practices, my address book would be a single page.

I really enjoyed being with these two. They were smart, witty, and intellectual. One of the handicaps of being very well educated was that you found yourself frequently making allusions to knowledge you assumed was universal or using words you thought were commonplace, only to be brought up short by the blank looks around you. In time, you became accustomed to preevaluating your vocabulary and subject matter before conversing with people. With Wolfie and Andries, I had no such restrictions. They were well read, well informed, and highly intelligent. The only considerations in my exchanges with them was the awareness that any information I divulged would be all around town within twenty-four hours.

When I completed the details on Dirk's downfall, I was wondering how to get to the topic that brought me here without conveying any implications of its seriousness, which might have caused them to hold back. Sometimes, the best tactic was to wait until someone else got close enough to the subject for you to jump in without it looking premeditated.

"So you're writing about suicides," said Andries casually. Once again I was reminded that there was no need for a newspaper in Albufeira as long as we had Wolfie and Andries.

"I hear you want to know about that pathetic creature, Peter. Such a shame; he was such a sweet, pure boy. Once he fell into the clutches of that Dutch man-eater, if you'll pardon the expression, disaster was inevitable."

"The day she got that letter from him, she came tearing in here screaming like a banshee, totally out of control," said Wolfie.

"What letter?" I asked.

"The dumb bitch told him who had sired her cub and that poor innocent wretch went into shock. Obviously ministers are trained to talk about incest, but not prepared to meet it socially."

I regarded them in amazement. "I can't believe it. You mean you both knew Adriaan was the father of Leida's baby and you kept this piece of horrendous depravity to yourselves for two years?"

Andries smiled. "Don't think it didn't kill us. But prudence won out over prurience, and if you'll pardon the vulgarity, we don't shit where we eat. Adriaan has been a most benevolent benefactor . . . we just came back from two weeks at his gorgeous estate in Uruguay that he lets us use free, and the rent he charges us for this charming place is a mere pittance."

"Of course," said Wolfie, "we have our little ways of reciprocation. We take care of entertaining and distracting Leida while he's having one of his kiddy parties. He doesn't mind so much anymore if she pops in, but he's afraid she'll bring Adriana and he doesn't want to do anything that might damage the psyche of the precious poppet. You see, he has high hopes for her as his future heir. He's given up on Leida; he knows she's a stupid cow. But since the child carries a gene-load of seventy-five percent him, he figures she has got to be a genius."

"You mentioned a letter."

"Oh, yes," said Andries. "That Peter chap apparently tried to convince Leida of the error of her ways and she just couldn't see it. So he gave up and sent her a farewell letter."

"Did you see the letter?"

"Of course. She came in here waving it, babbling about how she didn't want him to go."

"Do you remember the wording?"

"Well, the misguided bastard asked *her* for forgiveness . . . can you beat that? It's like the rape victim asking the rapist for absolution. And then something about inability to understand, and some self-flagellation about his failure." Then he looked at me sharply. "Something the matter?"

I had forgotten how acutely sensitive to emotions he was or I would have done a better job of hiding mine.

"I'm wondering why he didn't just go back home after that instead of killing himself here," I said.

He shrugged. "Leida said something about taking him to meet her father so he'd understand. An encounter with Adriaan would be enough to disturb the balance of any starry-eyed child who grew up on *Father Knows Best* and *The Donna Reed Show*." Then he looked at me shrewdly. "But then you would know about the unpredictability of suicides, since you're researching the subject."

I left before Andries decided to delve any deeper into my thinly substantiated project and forced me to talk on a topic about which I knew little, although according to my parents, that never stopped me before.

I walked along the road for about a quarter mile until I came to elaborate iron gates that led to the low, white, sprawling casa that was Graham's house. I found him taking a morning dip in his pool and sat and waited for him to complete his compulsory morning laps.

"What brings you here at this early hour, love?" he asked as he toweled himself off.

"Oh, I just wanted to take a walk with you along the beach."

"Yeah—right. What's up?"

"Please—I'll tell you later."

He dressed and we walked down the stairs. Graham and Adriaan shared a common narrow stone staircase between their two estates that led to the beach where Peter Belling was found. We had left our shoes at the house and the only sounds were the waves of the ocean and the soft tapping of our bare feet on the stones as we descended. We walked single file, and I was ahead. I walked slowly, looking down as I went. Suddenly I stopped.

"Are you okay?" he asked.

I saw a glint of something almost hidden in the brush foliage that bordered the steps. I reached down and picked it up.

"What's that?" Graham asked.

"Peter Belling's eyeglasses, I'd guess."

"You expected to find them here."

"It was a very strong possibility."

"Do you want to go back to the house now?"

"No, let's go down to the beach."

We sat in the sand at the edge of the water, watching the sunlight bouncing off the waves, and I told him the entire story of Peter Belling. He listened silently, and then said in a tight voice, "How can I help?"

I told him.

"I LOVE THESE spur-of-the-moment parties, Graham," said Leida as she draped her arms around his neck. It was the next day and we were sitting around Graham's pool after a languorous lunch of prawn salad sandwiches and white wine. The guest list consisted of Wolfie, Andries, Leida, and me.

"Yes, love, we know how you love to party," said Andries.

"I'm so glad you were available, darling," said Graham.

"In a world of uncertainty, it's nice that one of the things you can depend on is that Leida is always available," said Wolfie with a sweet smile.

Especially to Graham. She had been trying to get into his bed for years but the crude seduction style that worked wonders with the local fishermen amused rather than aroused Graham. Yet the poor girl never stopped trying. The sad fact was that it was really his friendship she desired rather than his body, but her distorted view of male-female relationships led her to believe that sex could be the only basis.

Graham reached into his pocket.

"Does anyone know who belongs to these glasses?" he said. "I found them last night on the beach stairs."

Leida went rigid.

"Good lord, those are Peter Belling's," said Wolfie. "We always used to joke with him that he looked like a German schoolteacher with those little round spectacles. He must've dropped them that night you took him to visit your father, Leida."

"You told me your father had never met Peter, Leida," I said quietly.

She was now white and terrified.

"Look at how thick these lenses are. He obviously couldn't see without them. Why on earth didn't he pick them up?" asked Wolfie.

"Maybe he couldn't," I said deliberately. "What happened that night, Leida?"

She stood up and looked around frantically, as though she wanted to run.

"Where can you go, Leida?" said Graham. "Why don't you sit down and tell us all about it?" he said soothingly, as though talking to an errant child.

She folded up and sank to the ground, sobbing loudly. No one moved to help her. After about a minute, she started speaking slowly and then everything came out in a rush.

"I wanted them to meet. I thought once Peter saw how wonderful and brilliant Daddy is, he would understand everything. And maybe he would change his mind about going away. At first, we sat around having wine, and everything was nice. I showed Daddy Peter's letter and asked him to convince him to stay." She emitted a loud wail. "Why did I ever have to tell Daddy that Peter liked books?"

"Peter didn't just like books," I said. "He collected rare volumes."

"I know," she said. "He was a bible-something."

"Bibliophile," said Graham.

"So is Daddy. He loves to show off his collection. When he heard Peter was a whatever-you-call-it, he went to the storeroom and brought out those two books he's so proud of. Peter opened them, then he suddenly went crazy."

"How do you mean?" I asked.

"He started, to scream at Daddy . . . De Verrader, he called him. 'You're De Verrader . . . you're a murderer. You should be in prison!' Then he started yelling things about Daddy killing Jews. He said those two books belonged to his friend and Daddy stole them and he was going to report Daddy to the Israelis."

"What did Daddy say?" I asked.

"I never saw him so upset. He went all red. I got so frightened, I thought he'd have a stroke or a heart attack or something. Then he hit him."

"Who hit who?" asked Graham.

"Daddy hit Peter on the head with that stone lion he has on the table." She was crying softly now. "Peter fell and didn't get up. I didn't know what to do. Daddy went into the other room and came back with his coke stuff and that needle he always uses when he shoots up. He stuck Peter with it. Then he told me to give him Peter's letter and he went to the desk and got scissors and cut off part of it. Then he told me to help him get Peter down to the beach. We carried him down the steps—I guess that's when his glasses fell off. We took Peter's clothes off and Daddy told me to fold everything and leave it on the rocks and he dragged Peter down to the water. I didn't see what was happening; it was too dark. I waited at the rocks and Daddy came back alone."

"And the letter?" I asked.

"Daddy folded it up and put it in Peter's clothes. I asked him about Peter, and he told me he left him down at the water. And I was never, never to tell anyone what happened or he might be in terrible danger."

"But he didn't leave him at the water, Leida. He put him in the water to drown," I said.

"But why did he do that—why did Peter say that?" she asked amidst her sobbing. "Daddy was a hero—he saved the lives of thousands of Jews during the war—he told me."

"Abba checked with the Yad Va Shem people," I said. "Yes, there is a Van Dolder who has a plaque dedicated to him on the Avenue of the Righteous. But it's not Adriaan; it's his older brother, Piet, who was the heroic burgomeister of Amsterdam. They also told Abba that Piet had a younger brother who was an infamous collaborator, but he escaped."

Everyone sat as though paralyzed. Wolfie and Andries had looks of horrified disbelief, and Graham's face showed deep sadness.

I got up and walked toward the house to call Miguel Garcia Ozorio.

Chapter Seventeen

EL CHEFE LOOKED very pleased with himself. He sat on my terrace having coffee with me, Caleb, and Abba. Gloria kept running in and out with more and more nibbles and goodies she hoped would please the palate of the very important chief of police of Vila do Mar, whom she was obviously very proud to be entertaining.

"The Ministry of Justice has invited me to Lisbon. I am to receive a special commendation," he said in awed disbelief. "They said I am a role model for police chiefs throughout the country."

"Closing three important cases that have international significance in less than a week is certainly some kind of record," said Caleb. "I would say you eminently deserve it."

"Ah, but it was not I who solved them; it was Miss Emma. It is truly she who should receive the medal," said *el chefe*.

"It was a joint effort, *Comandante*," I said emphatically. "I may have called your attention to the details, but it was you who followed through. A lesser man would've ignored the suggestions of a mere woman, but you had the strength and intelligence to recognize their value and pursue them to the finish."

He was mollified and pleased and gave me a nod of acknowledged concurrence.

The last thing I wanted was notoriety. It was all well and good for Sherlock Holmes to have his achievements chronicled by Dr. Watson and spread over the front pages of the dailies. He welcomed people with problems who came trooping up to Baker Street. Not I. I wasn't looking for clients; they always seemed to find me. I certainly didn't want to get buttonholed at parties, like doctors and lawyers, by troubled individuals who wanted free advice. As a doctor friend of mine told one of those annoying freebie-seekers, "Any advice you get for nothing is usually worth just that." Perhaps if I were a William Kunstler or Ralph Nader type who reveled in publicly championing the almost-lost causes involving injustice to those who could not afford to fight it, then I might have enjoyed the publicity. I have a kind heart, but I also have a weakness not shared by the aforementioned men: I love good living and that comes dear, which means the words "pro bono" could just as well be this year's hottest pasta dish. I'm not looking for glory—just cash.

Caleb was looking pretty exhausted. He had flown home to England yesterday to confer with the home office, which was dealing with the ramifications of a British aristocrat committing international skulduggery and murder in another EC country. The Duke of Sandringham was attempting to effect damage control to protect the name of the family. But unfortunately, he didn't have the experience, staff, and vast resources of the Rockefeller clan, who by now would have given Carlos a huge sum that would secure the financial future of his entire family forever, in return for which he would have accepted full responsibility for the drug running. And Chilton's parents would suddenly have moved into a huge, mortgage-free, stately home where they would have held a press conference to announce that their son had a rare allergy to brandy so it wasn't the cyanide that killed him.

Caleb planned to remain in Vila do Mar for a few days more as an amicus curiae to see that Dirk's rights were not being violated. He announced to me that he had asked for a week's leave on top of his official stay and would it be all right for him to stay with me for that time? Silly man.

"Elizabeth!" I said with pleasure as she appeared on the terrace.

"Please don't get up," she said to all the men who were starting to rise. "I can only stay a minute. I came to thank all of you for your help and kindness. I'm returning to my children now."

"Is the purchase of the new property across the road all settled?" I asked.

"Oh, quite," she said with a broad smile. "Mark's family insists on *giving* the land to us. I thought that was absolutely marvelous of them."

Abba snorted. "Seems to me that's the least they can do after one of theirs tried to pin his crime on you."

Elizabeth looked at me with a small smile. "Mark is such a nice man, Emma, but he's so morose these days. Whenever I see him, he asks about you and talks about you. Perhaps whatever has happened between you will lessen in importance in time."

"Perhaps," I said casually.

I saw Caleb stiffen and look at me hard. I gave one of those enigmatic, hard-to-read Mona Lisa smiles. I'd always found it highly effective to keep men in a mild—but not crippling—state of uncertainty. It kept the relationship alive and prevented the emergence of complacency, which inevitably leads to ennui and ultimately death. Besides, Caleb and I have been together for a very short time. He's exciting, stimulating, and a superb and tender lover, but who knows how we'll feel and fare a month from now?

Suddenly, I heard a loud clumping outside.

"What on earth is that?" I asked.

"Oh, that would be my little thank-you gift for you, dear Emma."

Two men came in carrying a piece of furniture, which they set carefully down on the terrace, and turned to Elizabeth for directions. My eyes widened and I was speechless. It was the exquisite seventeenth-century French desk that had belonged to Hugh Eddington. I recognized it from the Sotheby sale a few years ago when my bid for one hundred thousand pounds was passed over.

"Elizabeth!" I managed to gasp out. "You can't do this. I mean, do you realize the value of this desk?"

"Its only value to me," she said simply, "is that it allows me to show my gratitude to a dear friend who has saved my life. Please, take it with my thanks."

Chapter Eighteen

TWO HOURS LATER, the Bellings were sitting in my living room admiring the new furniture, which I had placed in the corner facing the entrance to the room. Gloria brought in a tray of coffee and Bolo Rei candied fruit and nut bread.

"We can't thank you enough, Emma. You're a marvel—you asked for only two weeks and did it in even less," said Martin.

A peace seemed to have come over them. The sadness was still there, as it would be possibly forever, but the fervid anguish was gone.

"What will happen to Leida?" asked Anne after I had told them all the details.

"She's out on bail. They've charged her as an accessory, but she really didn't know what was going on. I think the charges may be dismissed."

"I don't have any real anger towards her," said Martin. "She's just a pathetic victim like Peter. But that her father escaped to Uruguay, that this monster should go unpunished infuriates me," he said bitterly.

"He won't," I said.

They looked at me in astonishment. "But there's no extradition from Uruguay."

"I guess I didn't mention the department that my friend Abba works for in Israel—it's the one that tracks down Nazis. They're the group that brought in Adolph Eichmann." Then I added with a smile, "I gave him Adriaan's address. I got it from Wolfie and Andries."

Martin reached into his pocket and handed me a check. "Thank you. I know we can't bring Peter back but it helps a lot to know that he did not kill himself."

"It clears his name, and it clears our hearts," said Anne with a smile.

I handed them a package.

"What's this?" Anne asked.

"Open it."

They gasped when they saw the two beautiful old volumes.

"I told Leida that these must be returned to their rightful owner. So please give them to Mr. Van Wyk. Tell him it is Peter's farewell gift."

About the author

Cynthia Smith was the author of best-selling non-fiction books until she turned to crime. Her Emma Rhodes mysteries were acclaimed by critics and mystery fans. She has been an Associate Adjunct Professor at New York University where she taught advertising and marketing and also ran her own advertising agency. She lives in Florida overlooking the Gulf of Mexico where she writes when not distracted by the dolphins cavorting under her window.

You can contact Cynthia at cynthiassmith@verizon.net.

Turn the page for an excerpt from the third Emma Rhodes mystery, *MISLEADING LADIES*, available from Busted Flush Press in March 2010...

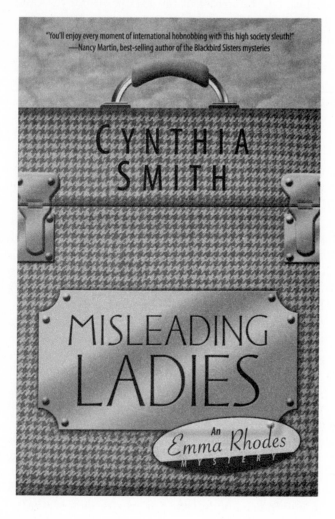

"You'll enjoy every moment of international hobnobbing with this high society sleuth!"
—Nancy Martin, best-selling author of the Blackbird Sisters mysteries

CYNTHIA SMITH

MISLEADING LADIES

An Emma Rhodes MYSTERY

I WAS ON my way to a few days R&R after a rather emotionally draining case that resulted in my voluntarily giving up the chance to be a duchess. Since I was responsible for the arrest of my aristocratic lover's uncle for murder and drug-running, thus causing the venerable family name to be spread across the infamous smut-'n'-scandal British press, I presume I was not regarded as ideal daughter-in-law material by his noble family. That's their side of the story. From my point of view, although my mother would dearly love to punctuate her conversations with references to her daughter the duchess, as you get to know me better, you'll understand how difficult it would be to picture me spending my life pouring tea, opening bazaars, and having my pantyhose peeled off nightly by a lady's maid.

At the moment, I was just looking forward to spending a small part of the $20,000 gratuity gift I had just earned. (I hate to use the crass term of "fee." For one thing, it's undignified. Secondly, the tax people react unpleasantly to the word.) I had booked myself into bed-and-breakfast at Jeake's House on Mermaid Street in the medieval coastal town of Rye and was looking forward to roaming the marshes and walking its ancient cobbled streets.

When I entered the first-class compartment of the Charing Cross-to-Hastings train, a solitary young woman with an old-fashioned, maroon crushed velvet hat over long dark hair and the equine features of the British upper class was in the middle of the going-forward trio of seats. Piled on the window seat next to her were two Harrod's boxes and three Peter Jones' bags. She glanced up through horn-rimmed glasses and with a look of instant dismissal went back to writing furiously on a yellow legal pad. I sighed inwardly. I had carefully chosen a mid-morning train that would be more likely to have an empty window seat so that I could enjoy the sheep-dotted lush green fields of Kent. What I hadn't figured into my equation was that an off-peak hour train would have only two first-class compartments. I had already noted that the other one had a mother and two small children, one of whom was in the process of projectile vomiting. Unfortunately, I cannot ride backwards without getting queasy. So I broke my usually inflexible rule to never engage in conversation with anyone on a public means of transportation. (The only place I lift that proscription is when I fly on the Concorde, where the risk of being trapped by a garrulous chicken parts salesman is minimal.)

"May I help you to move your things to another seat so that I can sit at the window?" I asked.

She regarded me with that frosty unflinching look with which the English upper class usually preface some devastatingly rude remark to their perceived inferiors.

"I will take the window seat," she said in predictably purse-mouthed public school diction and then proceeded to move her belongings and herself. It was just that sort of aristocratic sense of entitlement that had contributed to my rejecting marriage to my handsome future duke.

So much for my careful planning for a pleasant, relaxing trip through the English countryside.

I had spent a good deal extra for a first-class ticket to insure that I could sit back and enjoy the beauty of Sussex. Now here I was stuck for hours in a compartment with a member of the western world's most arrogant, insensitive, and ill-mannered genus, the British Upper Class. I settled back morosely and got a flash of optimism. Maybe she'll be getting off shortly.

"Are you going far?" I asked hopefully.

"Tunbridge Wells," she answered without even looking up.

I didn't have a clue where that was and how long I'd be treated to her prickly presence.

"Well," I said brightly, and rather shrewdly I thought, "that should give you plenty of time to get your work done."

She looked up. "That is only one half hour from here, and I am not doing work." She hesitated for a moment and examined me closely. I felt like a horse at auction. She was apparently deciding whether I was worth conversing with any further. I guess I passed the test.

"I am getting a divorce."

Uh-oh. Here we go again. I sensed another one of those instant confidante situations coming on. People tell me things. I must project some sort of simpatica that makes perfect strangers reveal to me the most intimate details of their lives, often within minutes of our meeting. I have learned that even seemingly tight-lipped, tight-assed types are prone to pour out to me the sort of personal specifics that would make a bartender blush. My first instinct was to step through the private door she had opened. After all, that is how I make my lavish living. The second thought was to ignore the invitation. I really was not ready to become involved again.

"Don't make the mistake of being too soft," I said before I could stop myself. "The worst thing you can do in a divorce is to allow pity or guilt to affect your judgment when you make up your list of entitlements."

Score one point for instinct, curiosity, and my insatiable Ms. Fixit complex.

She rested the pad and pen on her lap and turned full circle to face me, her entire demeanor now warm and friendly.

"That's just what my solicitor keeps saying," she said with a smile. She jumped up and moved to a going-backwards seat. "Please, take the window," she said warmly. "I didn't realize you are probably on holiday and would so enjoy the passing landscape. Kent is actually quite lovely, especially at this time of year."

There are definite perks to becoming personal with people. If you happen to press the right button, you might even turn a potentially disastrous encounter into a rather pleasant one. Even a pit bull becomes friendly if you toss him a sirloin. I settled happily into my coveted seat but felt I owed her a little more conversation for my quid pro quo.

"It sounds like you have a good lawyer," I said. "But aren't there enough excellent matrimonial attorneys in London? Why are you headed for Tunbridge Wells?" I eyed her maroon, big plaid Jaeger suit which made her look like the sofa in a men's club, silk shirt, and handmade boots.

The hat, held in place by two jewel-topped hat pins, looked bizarre but expensive. She was an example of that unfortunately not uncommon combination of poor taste and rich pockets. "You don't strike me as someone who has the need to pinch her pence."

She laughed and her entire face changed. This might end up to be not too bad a trip after all.

"This solicitor handled Daddy's divorces when he was practicing in London. He semiretired to Tunbridge Wells last year, and I felt he was worth the trip."

I wondered who Daddy was. She held out her hand.

"I'm Juliet Bishop—that's my maiden name." She turned sad and hesitated for a moment. "I guess I'll be returning to it after the divorce."

Now I knew Daddy. Even if you weren't interested in the antics of the aristocracy, this duke's messy marital history would be familiar since it had been chronicled constantly in full prudent detail by the English press. He was a flake with a rifle—perfect material for the excessive front pages of the evening papers. Of course, when you're of the nobility, they never call you crazy you're referred to respectfully as "eccentric."

I now regarded my traveling companion with interest. Titles don't impress me but money does. Before you begin to regard me as some superficial twit whose values run to bimbo-basic, let me give you a bit of my history. Like many mothers, mine reared me on the aphorism "It's just as easy to fall in love with someone rich rather than someone poor." My anti-parent rebellion took the form of dating a series of intellectuals and radicals whose I.Q.'s were higher than their weekly incomes. By the time I reached my late twenties, grunge had begun to lose its appeal. I found I didn't mind eating at dreary diners and cheap Chinese restaurants, but only if I wanted to and not because I had to. My epiphany came about when my untenured college instructor lover took me on his idea of a romantic weekend to a rustic cabin he had rented in a state park. He spoke passionately of Thoreau and the glories of back-to-nature simplicity, but the need to nurture my poetic soul was unfortunately outweighed by the discomfort caused by the lack of indoor plumbing and limitless supply of swarms of black flies. So call me shallow—I then and there decided that Mom was right. From then on, I began to look with great favor upon the well-heeled and have managed to make them the basis of my social and business lives. Look into your deepest heart—wouldn't you find it pleasanter to go by limo than by bus? And wouldn't you prefer dinner parties where you're served caviar and duck cassoulet rather than salsa and chicken nuggets? And don't tell me you wouldn't give up a week of heart-shaped tubs in the Poconos for a cruise in the Caribbean. Since my business and personal lives overlap (my clients almost always come from social involvements), I work for only the rich and famous. After all, they're just as needful of my services and they do show their appreciation so much better than those in less fortunate financial positions. I'm not a snob, I'm a realist.

I shook her proffered hand. "I'm Emma Rhodes," I said with an answering smile.

"Have you ever been divorced?" she asked.

"No."

I saw her glance at my ringless left hand, which meant I had to talk fast to head off the personal inquisition. I didn't want to hear the usual "But how come such a pretty, smart, etc. girl like you isn't married?" I'm weary of the assumption that no woman can be single by choice, fired of having to defend my opting for independence and my preference for lovers rather than husbands. My life is my business, but her life was mine. I was in it this far with her, I might as well press for more details.

"Why are you getting this divorce?" I asked. "Obviously it's you who wants it." Implicit in that statement, of course, was the assumption that no man in his right mind would willingly give up such a prize. A bit of flattery always works wonders. Only in this case, it was more than a bit. Which is why I was so startled by her next remark.

"I just cannot stand his insane jealousy a moment longer," she said with trembling lower lip.

"He was after my money," or "He was unfaithful." That's what I expected. But jealousy?

Juliet Bishop had the classic look of the British royals, which means a long face, slightly underslung jaw, and the long thin nose that they consider aquiline and I consider correctable. Juliet's tweedy bottom took up far more of the seat than any woman of her age should. And then there was the brown hair that just hung dead straight. The hat looked like something she had picked up from the Queen Mother's dustbin, and why was she wearing the weird object altogether? Often hopelessly unattractive women accept their limitations and wisely opt for giving themselves style and character. If so, her goal was commendable but her taste was not. She came off as the archetypical 1940s movie heroine who appears dreadfully plain at the beginning of the film and then whips off her glasses in the second reel to emerge as a stunning beauty. Only in Juliet's case, all that would happen if she removed her glasses would be to reveal small, uninteresting blue eyes. I don't believe that physical perfection is the sole requisite for attractiveness, sexual or otherwise. Some of the most charismatic people I know possess none of the elements of conventional good looks. And many of the men and women I have met who were born with perfect physical beauty are crashing bores, perhaps because they felt they didn't have to do anything more than present themselves to get instant admiration and never got around to working on their personae. But Juliet was not appealing, she was not adorable, she was dull.

"Your husband is jealous? That's not surprising," I said with a professional smile. "The assumption that other men find you alluring reinforces his belief in his own excellent judgment in picking you."

Lord, I'm good. She looked pleased. And then a shadow passed over her face.

"But you cannot know how impossible it is to live with. He's accused me of sleeping with my voice teacher—good heavens, the man is sixty-eight years old—and he's *Polish*."

Obviously one of the ethnic groups suitable only for musical interludes.

"And he insists on being there when my fitness instructor comes."

Now that's a little more understandable. Those chaps are heavily into exercise of all kinds.

"It is driving me mad. Even the hostler who takes care of my horses. Why, I've known Redmond since I was a little girl. He taught me to ride. Oh, he's quite attractive, I grant you, in a rather crude rough way. But how could Sidney think I could ever have an affair with a *stableman*?"

She had to be kidding. Half the ladyships I know are boinking their chauffeurs, and the other half are having it on with their gardeners. A touch of dirt under the fingernails titillates rather than turns off. The upper-class women I know look upon their employees as purveyors of services— and that means all kinds. Lady Chatterley may have been a fictional character, but she was based on real people.

"He follows me, he checks up on me. He disbelieves me. It's demeaning and often embarrassing. Now he's gotten it into his head that I'm having an affair with Geoffrey Fraser, a man I was with at university. Just because I went to hear him lecture at the Courtauld on Bloomsbury. Actually Geoffrey's a dreadful bore and I went simply as an obligation. Sidney came with me and was certain Geoffrey was sending me sly, intimate glances. The idiot, Geoffrey cannot see two feet in front of him, he's blind as a bat. But Sidney went into a rage when we got home. Perhaps it's because he is fifteen years older than I, which I keep telling him makes no difference at all to me. I simply cannot bear it a moment longer."

I've seen it many times, where an older man marries a younger woman and spends the rest of his life in delighted wonder that this glorious young thing agreed to have him. Never mind that she's a hopelessly unattractive forty-year-old who regards him as her last desperate hope for marriage in a youth-oriented society where men of her age are trolling for twenty- and thirty-year-olds. He never gets over how her clear eyes and comparatively firm skin are willing to accept his cataracts and love handles.

"What does Sidney do—for a living I mean?"

"He's an actor, and a very fine one," she said proudly.

"What's his name?"

"Sidney Bailey," she answered.

I recalled a sandy-haired man who played supporting roles, the kind of actor who has a familiar face but no name. He must be up in his late fifties now. Come to think of it, I haven't seen him on the screen for some years.

"Didn't I see him in *The Ipcress File* with Michael Caine?" That's one of those good old movies that come up on TV every now and then.

"Yes," she said with shining eyes. "Wasn't he wonderful in that?"

If that was Sidney's last paying job, he wouldn't be jumping handsprings about her wanting out of the marriage.

"I assume he's fighting the divorce."

She shook her head. "No—he told me he only wants me to be happy."

Right.

"How much is he demanding of your community property?"

"Nothing," she answered. "He even insists I keep the house."

"What house?"

"The one he bought for me in Kensington, right off the High Street."

Wait a minute here. I know the area and those places go for from 800,000 to a million pounds.

"*He* bought it? You did say he was an actor."

"Oh, yes, but he also has rather large real estate holdings. He owns buildings all over London."

Going back to my old man-young wife theory, if he's that rich, why did he ever marry *her*?

"He's a brilliant businessman, which his father was not," she said. "He grew up very poor, in the East End. The family business was almost in ruins, and Sidney was forced to leave his acting career and take over. It turned out he had a real genius for real estate, and he has built it into a virtual empire," she said with proprietary wifely pride.

Aha. The mystery is solved. Poor boy meets baronet's daughter. The British reverence for nobility is chronic. Humble Sidney will probably be forever dazzled by the fact that a member of the aristocracy is willing to talk to him, let alone marry him. When he looks at her, he doesn't see the plain exterior he sees the awesome blue blood interior.

"Where did you two meet?"

The likelihood of them running into each other socially seemed remote, since they would hardly move in the same circles. Sidney is not famous enough or rich enough to break through the barriers erected by the English highborn.

"In hospital," she answered. "Sidney was having some minor surgery done at St. Albans." She noticed that I looked puzzled. "I'm an aide there. You see, I adored biology and science in school. But my scores weren't high enough to be accepted by a proper medical school, and Daddy and Mummy wouldn't hear of me becoming a nurse. So I volunteered my services to St. Albans; I've been working there for almost ten years. I'm even allowed to assist one of the neurosurgeons now in the surgical theater," she said proudly.

"So you met over a bedpan," I said.

She laughed. "It was mostly the sponge baths that built the friendship. He was shy at first, most men are. What I tell them at first to put them at their ease is, 'I will wash down as far as possible, then I will wash up as far as possible. You wash possible.' He was my favorite patient. I can't say it was love at first sight for me—he looked god-awful of course—but I grew very fond of him."

I sat back and looked at her. "You're still very much in love with him, aren't you?"

Her eyes filled with tears. "Yes."

"Then why are you divorcing him?"

She looked miserable. "I really have no choice. I've tried everything to convince him that I love him, that I'm not interested in any other men. Believe me, being brought up by parents such as mine, I long ago swore that when I married, I would never be unfaithful. Nor would I ever divorce. Now here I am," and she took out a linen handkerchief to wipe away the now flowing tears.

I really did not want to take on another case at this point, but this one had my name on it. The chance meeting offered the promise of the kind of trouble which I am ideally suited to settle to the pleasure and profit of all those involved, including me. Actually, it was just this sort of encounter that got me started in my unique profession.

I am a P.R.—a Private Resolver. Please don't confuse this occupation with P.I.'s, those heroic seedy loners who spend their lives tracking down malefactors, living in mobile homes with beer-filled fridges and vintage collections of McDonald's and Dunkin' Donuts cartons. I have three homes: an apartment on New York City's Fifth Avenue, a flat in Chelsea in London, and a house in the Portuguese Algarve. Like Kinsey Milhone and V.I. Warshawski, I wear turtlenecks, jeans, and sweats, but the balance of my wardrobe contains gowns by Givenchy, suits by Donna Karan, shoes by Manolo Blahnik, and bags by Prada. Unlike the earnest but underpaid sleuths so beloved of mystery book writers, I never get stiffed by a client, because I deal only with people who can easily afford my high tariff and like my terms, which appeal to the gambler and bargain-hunter traits so prevalent among the rich. I only charge for success. I either settle or solve the situation within two weeks or I'm out of there and no one's out a nickel. No up-front money, no daily rate, no expenses. It's a straight deal—I produce and only then does the client produce $20,000 or the equivalent thereof in any hard currency.

Why do I limit myself to two weeks? That's simple. I have a very low threshold of boredom and a very high I.Q., which means that's all the time I need and if it required more, I'd lose interest. That combination of little patience and big I.Q. used to drive my schoolteachers to distraction. I never saw the point in wasting my time and brain on anything that I considered uninteresting or useless, which resulted in constant admonishment for not working up to my potential. Until finally, to get them off my backs, I announced I was suffering from Minimal Focal Faculty. Everyone being so hot on respecting learning disabilities, and most being too insecure to admit their own ignorance of this diagnostic term (which I made up), they instantly accepted my behavioral aberration and thenceforth gave me compassion instead of censure.

My 100% success rate is based on the fact that I only take cases that interest me and that I believe I can solve quickly. (If that isn't a sign of a high I.Q., then what is?) I got started in my unique profession quite by accident. On a Scandinavian trip I had been sent on by the Wall Street law firm who employed me as an attorney, I met a woman in trouble. During that memorable hydrofoil trip from Copenhagen to Malmö, I heard the sordid details of her life, featuring a potential personal scandal that could have wrecked her and her very wealthy and respected English family. I figured out a solution within ten minutes, which I didn't tell her, of course. People never respect fast answers they're only impressed if they think you've worked on the problem for weeks. I offered to resolve the matter and gave her my terms, which I made up on the spur of the moment. Two weeks later, she was ecstatically grateful and t was $20,000 richer. One of the shining moments of my life was when I handed in my resignation, telling the stunned senior partner that I no longer wished to submit to his law firm's indentured servitude of sixty-five billable hours per week demanded of junior law associates so that he and the eighty-six other partners could spend their days golfing at Winged Foot. I had a new career that not only paid better but gave me the time and freedom to enjoy my earnings.

"Maybe I can help you," I said to Juliet.

"You?" She looked at me with incredulity. "How?"

People always regard me dubiously when I make this offer. You can't blame them. What they see is a 5'6" woman with a size 8 figure, long dark brown hair and huge brown eyes. I've always ignored the fact that I'm beautiful but have to forever deal with the reality that others cannot. It usually takes a bit of talking before they can get past that and realize I have a mind.

I explained what I did for a living and what I could do for her. I could see her eyeing my Burberry raincoat and cashmere scarf and trying to reconcile the image with Columbo.

"You mean you think you could stop my husband from being jealous and paranoid?"

"Not necessarily. But I could find a way that would enable you both to live with it."

She looked hopeful, but doubtful. "You say you've done this sort of thing before? Can you give me some sort of references?"

"I can't give you a list of satisfied clients because one of the things I guarantee, besides success, is total discretion. But I've worked out problems for people whose names you would instantly recognize."

That very satisfied lady from the Malmö boat continues to recommend me enthusiastically to all her friends. It's amazing how much concupiscence, cupidity, and stupidity is rampant among the rich.

"What do you have to lose, Juliet? All you need do is delay your divorce negotiations for two weeks. If at the end of that time I haven't alleviated your problem and you still find marriage untenable, it will have cost you nothing."

"And what will it cost me if you are successful?" she asked, obviously very much intrigued.

"The minimum I expect from my grateful clients is the equivalent of $20,000, in any hard currency, which is about 12,500 pounds."

She didn't blink an eye. I knew she wouldn't. In her circles, that's the monthly American Express bill.

"Minimum? You mean they sometimes give you more?"

I smiled. "Frequently."

She eyed me narrowly. "You mean they're that pleased with your services?"

"I once received a Picasso painting from someone who told me what I had achieved for her family was priceless. Who can you go to to help you through a difficulty like this? A lawyer charges for every hour he expends on you, even if his efforts result in total failure. A shrink charges for every forty-five-minute hour and does nothing except ask how you feel about your problem. I charge only if the goal is achieved."

She looked at me speculatively. "You must be rather certain of your ability to succeed."

I smiled. "I won't take on a case unless I am."

She sat up straight, thought for a few seconds, and then held out her hand with a wide smile. "Done."

For the next half hour, I sat with the legal pad taking notes. She told me that Sidney had moved out of the house but they saw each other constantly. She gave me his current address and phone number plus a list of his friends, many of whom I knew casually or well. She got off at Tunbridge Wells to tell her solicitor to hold off, and we said goodbye with the assurance that I would be in touch with her in two weeks.

"Not before?" she asked in surprise. "You mean I won't know what you're doing until then?"

"No."

I find that little word one of the handiest in the English language, and I marvel at how little advantage is taken of its valuable properties. I could have told her that since she wasn't paying me per diem I owed her squat in the explanation department. And that I regard progress reports a time-wasting nuisance demanded only by deskbound bureaucrats or controlling clients, both of whom I abhor and avoid. Now should I have told her all this? She'd have only gotten pissed and then I'd have had to deal with her annoyance. It's easier to just say, "No."

I cut my planned five-day stay in Rye down to one, which just gave me time to visit Hilder's Cliff, from which you can see fifty-three parishes over Romney Marsh, and take my usual walk through cobbled streets that have not changed appreciably since the fourteenth century. I love peeking in the mullioned windows of the tiny, oak-beamed, crushed together houses that are a delight to look at but must be hell to live in. Whenever I see these types of preserved dwellings I marvel at the British tolerance for abject discomfort. But then, this is a country where you'll see two Bentleys in the driveway of a stately home whose occupants walk around in custom-made clothing over woolen underwear because there's no central heating. In the winter, British upper-class noses run as much indoors as outdoors since both temperatures are the same, and unless you station yourself within three feet of a fireplace, your lips will turn blue (thus the term "stiff upper lip").

I enjoy antiquity but I'm not one of those romantics who sighs longingly for the simplicity and tranquility of "olden days." The frequent sackings and burnings by Danish invaders and the Normans, the bloody battling among various kings and queens for control of this strategically placed town made life in those "olden days" sound no less risky than a midnight walk through Hyde Park. And if you think that living in a quaint seaside village makes you impervious to big city crime, just check the local newspaper for all the ads for home security systems. I guess the answer is that there's just no place to hide from human nature. But I never failed to get a charge out of genteelly sipping tea in the Mermaid Inn, knowing that hundreds of years ago smugglers and highwaymen used to haul their contraband into the cellars and cutthroat buccaneers were carousing right where I was sitting.

However, I did not forget my new case. That evening, after having freshly caught grilled sole with a large mug of cider at a waterside pub, I made a few calls to friends in London. By the time I got back the next day to my flat on the King's Road in Chelsea, I had arranged an encounter with Sidney Bailey.

Read more in MISLEADING LADIES, coming soon from Busted Flush Press.

Back in print, the dazzling high-society *Emma Rhodes* mysteries by *Cynthia Smith!*

Noblesse Oblige
(978-0-9792709-4-9 / $13)

Impolite Society
(978-0-9792709-7-0/ $13)

Misleading Ladies
(978-1-935415-04-6 / $13 / March 2010)

Silver and Guilt
(978-1-935415-05-3 / summer 2010)

Royals and Rogues
(978-1-935415-06-0 / summer 2010)

"You'll enjoy every moment of international hobnobbing with this high society sleuth!"

> —Nancy Martin, best-selling author of the Blackbird Sisters mysteries

"Kiss Miss Marple and Jessica Fletcher good-bye . . . here's a woman sleuth who provides us with vicarious glamour, brains, and beauty on an international scale."

> —Judith Crist, film critic

"Brash, beautiful and smart as hell, Cynthia Smith's heroine will hook you from page one."

> —Leann Sweeney, author of *Pushing Up Bluebonnets*

Busted Flush Press books are available from your favorite independent, chain, or online booksellers.

Visit **www.bustedflushpress.com** and
bustedflushpress.blogspot.com to see what's coming from BFP next.
And while you're there, sign up for BFP's e-mail newsletter.

Don't miss Busted Flush Press's award-winning anthologies...

Damn Near Dead: An Anthology of Geezer Noir
(edited by Duane Swierczynski) Paperback original, $18
(0-9767157-5-9) *Introduction by James Crumley.*

Original stories by **John Harvey, Mark Billingham, Laura Lippman, Colin Cotterill,** and more!

"The best anthology I've read this year."
—Jennifer Jordan, *Crimespree Magazine*

"Some [of the stories] are hilarious; many are sad; all are the kind of stuff that makes Miss Marple look like a Girl Scout."
—Dick Adler, *Chicago Tribune*

> **Includes:** **"Cranked"**, by Bill Crider (*2007 Edgar Award nominee! 2007 Anthony Award nominee! 2007 Derringer Award winner!*) **"Daphne McAndrews & the Smack-Head Junkies"**, by Stuart MacBride (*2007 Derringer Award nominee!*) **"Policy"**, by Megan Abbott (*2007 Anthony Award nominee!*)

A Hell of a Woman: An Anthology of Female Noir
(edited by Megan Abbott)
Hardback, $26 (978-0-9792709-9-4) / Paperback, $18
(978-0-9767157-3-3) *Introduction by Val McDermid.*

Original stories by **Christa Faust, Naomi Hirahara, Annette Meyers, Vin Packer, Sandra Scoppetone, Zoë Sharp,** & more!

"*A Hell of a Woman* not only features original stories... but also includes a 51-page appendix honoring female pioneers of noir fiction and film that is worth the price of the book alone.... *A Hell of a Woman* is not only an exceptionally entertaining anthology, it's an invaluable resource that will be cherished by aficionados of the genre."
—Paul Goat Allen, *Chicago Tribune*

> **Includes: Cornelia Read's "Hungry Enough"** (*2008 Shamus Award winner!*) **Daniel Woodrell's "Uncle"** (*2008 Edgar Award nominee! 2008 Anthony Award nominee!*)

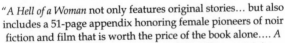